The
TRASH HAULERS

A NOVEL BY
RICHARD HERMAN

FIRST EDITION
2015

This is a work of fiction and all characters, incidents, and dialogues are a product of the author's imagination and are used fictitiously. Any resemblance to actual persons, living or dead, places, or events, is entirely coincidental.

THE TRASH HAULERS. *Copyright © 2015 by Richard Herman. All rights reserved. No part of this book may be reproduced, stored in a retrieval system, or transmitted by any means without the written permission of the author except in the case of brief quotations embodied in critical articles and reviews.*

First published as an original eBook by Endeavour Press Ltd.
2015

www.endeavourpress.com

Also by Richard Herman

The Peacemakers
Caly's Island
(writing as Dick Herman)
A Far Justice
The last Phoenix
The Trojan Sea
Edge of Honor
Against All Enemies
Power Curve
Iron Gate
Dark Wing
Call to Duty
Firebreak
Force of Eagles
The Warbirds

In memoriam

Sheila Kathleen Herman
A Suffolk lass who roamed far from home
and tended her gardens.

The Brief

The Vietnam War that ran from 1955 to 1975 had many names and was a game changer for the United States. The North Vietnamese were fighting to rid themselves of the last vestiges of French colonialism and reunify Vietnam under communist rule. U.S. involvement started with advisors to what was then French Indochina but rapidly escalated after the Gulf of Tonkin incident in 1964. The war became increasingly unpopular stateside, and the turning point for the U.S. was the 1968 Tet Offensive, which was a military disaster for the North Vietnamese but a political victory. The war ended for the U.S. with the withdrawal of its forces in 1973. By the time the war ended in 1975, over three million people, including 58,286 Americans, had been killed.

The war changed the way the U.S. fought and the venerable UH-1 helicopter, the Huey, became the symbol of mobile warfare in Vietnam. However, the underlying reality of all warfare is logistics and the movement of personnel and material is absolutely critical. The North Vietnamese created the Ho Chi Minh trail, a marvel of logistical organization, primitive but effective, while the U.S. relied on airlift and truck convoys. The workhorse of tactical airlift in Vietnam was the C-130 Hercules cargo aircraft. It was an unglamorous job, hauling everything from toilet paper to visiting celebrities, and the aircrews were simply known as trash haulers.

0500 HOURS

Cam Ranh Bay, South Vietnam

"Please sign here," the pretty staff sergeant manning the post office desk said. She shoved the thick registered letter across the counter and gave Captain Mark Warren a studied look. The return address was a lawyer's office in Riverside, California.

"You see a lot of these?" Mark Warren asked. The sergeant nodded in answer and gave her hair a little flip, hoping to catch his attention. She had never considered challenging the Air Force's prohibitions on fraternizing, but she liked the captain's looks, and, well, this was Vietnam. She wanted to stroke his thick dark hair and decided he could stand to gain a few pounds – and she was a good cook. Mark Warren was attractive in an offbeat way. At five foot ten, the twenty-eight-year-old C-130 pilot had a slightly crooked jaw from a high school football injury, a pleasant smile, and friendly blue eyes. Suddenly, she felt sorry for him. Registered letters from lawyers were always bad news.

Warren scribbled his name on the return card acknowledging receipt and shoved it back across the counter. She glanced at a wastebasket and arched an eyebrow. Without a return receipt, there was no proof he had ever been served – just more fallout from the Vietnam War. "Nah," Warren said. "Send it. It was gonna happen. Just a matter of time."

The sergeant nodded. For her, the captain was another casualty of the war, and, even from behind her counter in a remote post office, she had seen it too many times.

Warren shoved the letter into the calf pocket of his flight suit without opening it and headed for the exit. It was still dark and his new navigator, Captain David Santos, was waiting outside. "O Club for breakfast?" Warren asked. Santos nodded and they made the short walk to the officers' mess.

"No rain today," Santos predicted.

"Do you think?" Warren replied. "Wait until next month." The two men grinned. South Vietnam's dry season ran from November to April, but 'dry' was a relative term. Warren broke a slight sweat as they walked but the tall and dark Santos seemed unaffected by the heat and humidity. "Don't you ever sweat" Warren asked.

"It's my Latin blood," Santos said. His mother was from Brazil, and his father, a career diplomat in the State Department, was a seasoned ambassador with White House connections. Santos had grown up in various capitals in South America and spoke Portuguese, Spanish, and a little Italian. Later, he had attended Rice University before joining the Air Force. He had trained as a navigator and that led to an assignment with the 374th Tactical Airlift Wing flying the

The Trash Haulers

C-130 Hercules, the superb cargo airlifter made by Lockheed.

The Wing was based on Okinawa, and Santos had cut a swath through the single schoolteachers on the island. His amorous exploits had reached legendary status in the officers' club stag bar, and, if the rumors had it right, included a few bored wives of his fellow officers. As a result, their squadron commander made sure Santos spent at least twenty-five days of every month off-island and in Vietnam, less than five hours flying time away. Warren was the last in a long list of aircraft commanders who had been charged with keeping the well-connected navigator out of trouble while in-country. The two men stomped their feet to knock the white dust-like sand off their boots before entering the mess. They called Cam Ranh Bay "The Sandbox" for good reason.

"Heads up," Warren warned. "Stanley Super FAC is on duty." He shot a glance at Lieutenant Colonel Stanley Hardy, the C-130 detachment commander from the 374th in Okinawa, who was standing inside the entrance talking to the wing commander. Hardy was the poster boy for a professional military officer, the rugged all-American West Point graduate with a firm jaw, straight teeth, and lopsided smile. In reality, he was a career-driven fast burner who had been promoted early to major and lieutenant colonel. The aircrews believed he was a man who used lower ranking officers for kindling as he slashed and burned his way to higher rank. They scooted by Hardy and worked their way down the cafeteria-style chow line. "Stanley Super FAC just doing his thing," Warren said, "brown nosing the heavies."

Santos grunted in disgust. "Stanley Super FAC, my ass. Hardy Hemorrhoid, if you ask me. You must have loved being his co-pilot flying Blind Bat." Blind Bat was the night flare mission the 374th flew out of Ubon Air Base in Thailand. The C-130s cruised the Ho Chi Minh trail in Laos, kicking out two-million candlepower flares and looking for supply trucks. Once they found a truck, the aircraft commander became a forward air controller, FAC for short, and called in strike aircraft.

Warren was the most experienced Blind Bat pilot in the 374th and had been assigned as Hardy's instructor pilot for ten days to check him out on the flare mission. The ten days had turned into twenty-five days, and Hardy had been rewarded with a Distinguished Flying Cross. Warren and the rest of the crew were each awarded an Air Medal, the lowest flying medal in the Air Force pantheon. The going joke among the aircrews held that an Air Medal and a dime would get you a cup of coffee unless you were on Hardy's crew. Then the coffee cost a dollar.

"He's a damn good pilot," Warren said.

"Pilot, yes," Santos replied, "but aircraft commander?" The aircraft commander was the pilot in command of the aircraft and responsible for the lives of all on board. "I don't think so." They walked in silence for a few moments. "He's out to prove something," Santos allowed. "Your navigator on Blind Bat said you saved their asses more than once."

"He is aggressive," Warren said. Hardy had twice ignored the compass headings their navigator had called for while chasing trucks and flown into flak traps. Both times, the night sky had lit up with heavy anti-aircraft artillery, and Warren had taken control of the C-130 to fly them to safety.

The Trash Haulers

The last time had resulted in an over-*g* that almost ripped the wings off the big cargo aircraft, but they had made it. It came as a complete surprise to Warren, and the crew, when Hardy took full responsibility for the incident. "He did take the heat for the over-*g*," Warren added.

Santos snorted. "It's not like he had a choice, considering your nav had tape recorded both incidents. That really pissed Hardy off, and he wants those tapes. The guy's dangerous. He will blindside you. Count on it." Santos nodded towards the far end of the room. "Boz is sitting in the corner." They stopped at the coffee urns and filled their mugs before joining First Lieutenant Steven "Boz" Bosko, their copilot. Bosko was a cheerful, slightly over-weight, twenty-six-year-old from Florida. He was also a very promising pilot who wanted to jettison the Air Force for a job with the airlines as soon as he could make it happen. They sat down and attacked their food, not sure when they would eat next. "Stanley Super FAC coming our way," Warren said under his breath. The three men stood as Hardy joined them.

"Seats, gentlemen," Hardy said, remaining on his feet. "Gentlemen, you've got to cut me some slack here. I just spent ten minutes apologizing to the wing king for your military appearance, or lack thereof. Colonel Mace is of the opinion you look like ragbags, and guess what? He's right. You all need a haircut, Lieutenant Bosko, trim your mustache or shave it off, and all of you, expose your boots to some polish. Captain Warren, make sure it all happens. Today."

Warren came to his feet. "Yes, sir. If the barbershop is still open when we land."

Hardy's voice grew stern. "I'm not in the mood for excuses. Just make it happen."

"Yes, sir," Warren said. The two men stared at each other – hard. Hardy spun around and stalked off.

Bosko started to sing, loud enough for Hardy to hear, doing a rich imitation of the rubbery, plaintive wail of Eric Burdon's *We Gotta Get Out of This Place.*

Santos joined in with gusto. Hardy paused for a moment, then pressed ahead without turning. He was fully aware of Santos's father and family connections. Hardy made a mental note to mark Santos's personnel file with a PI for political influence.

Warren sipped at his coffee, now lukewarm. Bosko caught the look on his face as he stood. "I'm going for a refill," he said, "need a 'fresher?" Warren handed him his mug and thanked him. Santos stood and said he would meet them at the C-130 operations shack near the flight line. Warren's eyes followed the navigator as he made his way to a table where two Donut Dollies were quietly having breakfast. The Donut Dollies were Red Cross civilian volunteers who brought a tender smile, a listening ear, and an endless supply of silly games to help build morale. Warren arched an eyebrow, fully aware of what Santos had in mind. He stifled a smile at the stricken look on Santos's face. "Shot down in flames," he said to himself, relieved that he would not have to deal with any fallout from that venture. Cam Ranh Bay was a fighter base and fighter jocks are an aggressive breed both in the air and on the ground. Bar fights were common enough, especially when women were involved.

The Trash Haulers

"Looks like Dave struck out," Bosko said, setting a steamy mug of coffee in front of Warren. The lieutenant smiled broadly, enjoying Santos's failure.

A quick survey of the room confirmed that the two pretty girls had raised the morale of every other man with their easy rebuff of Santos's lustful intentions, and Warren's respect for the Donut Dollies went up another notch. Without thinking, Warren pulled the registered letter out of his calf pocket and used a table knife to slit it open. As suspected, his wife had filed for divorce and a separation agreement was attached with a letter from her lawyer, written in nasty legalese, claiming the terms were more than equitable and generous.

Equitable and generous meant she got the house, the car, 500 dollars a month alimony, and half his retirement – if he made the Air Force a career. He got the bills. Losing the house in Riverside California was especially painful. It was his family home where he had grown up, and he had lived in the bachelor flat over the garage when he attended the Riverside campus of the University of California studying electrical engineering. After graduating in 1961, he had joined the Air Force and gone on to pilot training. Later on, it had been his refuge when home on leave, and he had inherited the home when his parents were killed in a car accident. He decided that giving up the old Victorian was a non-starter. Warren groaned when he read the paragraph dictating he pay all legal costs, including the lawyer's fee.

"Been served?" Bosko asked.

"I've been expecting it," Warren replied. He gave himself a mental kick for ever dating Chandra, much less marrying her. She was a beautiful natural blonde with a

7

model-thin figure, and everyone said they were perfectly matched. But the reality was much different and Chandra defined the term 'high maintenance'. "She wants everything. Unfortunately, I am a California resident, which means she will get it."

"No kids, right?"

"Chandra said she wasn't ready." Chandra was one of the first women liberated by 'the pill'.

Bosko thought for a moment. "Mark, she does have a reputation."

Warren felt his face flush. "Santos?"

"No." Bosko shook his head for emphasis. "Dave's got a bum rap. He's never hit on any wife, but he has turned down a few offers. Anyway, that's the word among the wives. The rumor of the day says that Chandra's got the hots for General Clearly's son." Clearly was the senior ranking Army officer on Okinawa, a four-star general, and the military governor of the island. "The kid is a real asshole, a long-haired hippy creep. Big in the anti-war movement with big bucks on his mother's side of the family – soup, ketchup, and mustard. Word has it that Chandra wants to marry him, the sooner the better."

Bosko leaned forward and lowered his voice. "Look, my dad is a lawyer and he can delay a divorce for years under the Soldiers' and Sailors' Relief Act. He can get you registered as a Florida resident in a heartbeat, and if Chandra wants a quickie divorce, she's got to be reasonable and negotiate. Call my dad on MARS." MARS was the Military Auxiliary Radio System that patched telephone calls through amateur radio operators in the States. "I call home all the time and I'll give him a heads up."

The Trash Haulers

Warren nodded. "I'll give him a call." He stood up. "Let's go. We got time to make the Huck and Judy show at wing headquarters." The Huck and Judy show was the morning intelligence briefing by two very talented and intelligent Air Force captains who spoke Vietnamese. They had a better sense of the situation on the ground than anyone at higher headquarters. The tall, and very attractive, Judy, and the diminutive Huck had been assigned to the intelligence section at Military Assistance Command Vietnam headquarters, or MACV for short, in Saigon but were banished to Cam Ranh Bay for not pushing the party line in their briefings to the brass. That, in itself, would have been tolerated except they were seldom wrong – and that was totally unacceptable.

"Best show on base," Bosko said.

The Laotian-South Vietnamese Border

The early-morning dark still held the mountains captive, casting a surreal sense of calm over the rugged landscape. Shadows moved quickly in the night, blending together then moving on as a stream of heavily-burdened men and women moved out of the valley and followed narrow trails up the mountain only to disappear into the numerous caves that pitted the mountainside. Occasionally, the clatter of equipment, the crunch of a footfall, or a softly spoken command broke the silence. Finally, the moving shadows tapered off.

A lone figure emerged from the biggest cave as the first light of the new day broke the horizon and the last of rear guard struggled in, all carrying heavy loads. Colonel Tran Sang Quan looked to the east, certain the bombers would come from that direction. He didn't move until all of his people were safe from harm, hidden deep in the mountain. Tran commanded a Binh Tram, one of the twenty logistical transportation regiments that linked together in a chain to move material and personnel down the Ho Chi Minh trail in Laos and into South Vietnam.

He closed his eyes and gave silent thanks for the Soviet trawlers that had reported the B-52 bombers taking off from Guam, some 2450 miles to the east. The five-hour flying time had given the Viet Cong spies nested in the Quang Tri Province Chief's household time to relay the Province Chief's approval for a strike outside the normal Arc Light areas. The U.S. Air Force's Strategic Air Command had free rein to drop bombs at will, without approval, in Arc Light areas. Tran's transportation regiment straddled the Laotian border with South Vietnam and directly supplied the People's Army of Vietnam units and Viet Cong operating in Quang Tri Province in the northern part of South Vietnam. Tran's area was outside the Arc Light area and there was no doubt in his mind that his regiment would shortly be on the receiving end of a massive carpet-bombing.

Tran had immediately ordered an evacuation and rushed everyone to safety in mountain caves. They carried what equipment and material, mostly medical, they could, but had to leave much behind. Thankfully, the invaluable supply trucks had departed hours earlier for their northbound return run. Tran hoped they could salvage most of what had been abandoned, which would be critical if he was to survive the wrath of his superior, the general commanding Group 559. General Dong Sy Nguyen had a well-deserved reputation for valuing material over personnel.

The Trash Haulers

Tran Sang Quan savored the quiet moment and breathed calmly, gathering strength for what was to come. He stood exactly five-feet six-inches tall and weighed 130 pounds. At thirty-two years old, Tran was the youngest colonel in the People's Army of Vietnam. However, there was no rank or insignia on the green uniform that hung from his wiry frame. That was a violation of army regulations, but the generals who made policy in Hanoi didn't have to live and fight in the jungles of Laos and South Vietnam. Tran's hair was cropped short, and his eyes and facial features revealed a trace of European blood in his heritage, but there was no doubt that he was Annamese. In full light, a doctor might notice the slight trace of yellow in his eyes caused by the yellow fever he had contracted in Central Africa while escaping from Algeria in 1957.

Tran was an eager student in Paris in 1956 where he was seduced by the success and charisma of Ho Chi Minh in his battle to liberate Vietnam from its French masters. A college professor at the Sorbonne, a dedicated communist, had arranged for Tran to travel to Algeria and experience that war firsthand, learning how to defeat the French. It was a rare opportunity and he had spent his twenty-first birthday observing the Battle of Algiers, the most dramatic and bloodstained episode of the Algerian War. It was the last of the old-style "colonial wars" pitting the French army and colonists against the indigenous Arabic tribes. Because of his ethnicity and fluency in both French and Arabic, the young man had moved between both sides, watching and learning. He had seen how the French used brute force and torture to terrorize the population and cut through the FLN, the *Front de Libération Nationale*.

Equally appalling, he photographed the FLN's use of terrorist bombs, killing and maiming innocent children, women, and men. But the most valuable lesson for Tran was the infighting he witnessed that had wracked the leadership of the FLN. Later, both the FLN and the French wanted to capture and interrogate him. Tran ran for his life, escaping southward across the Sahara. He finally boarded a freighter in Durban, South Africa, that carried him to India where he made his way to Hanoi, returning to the city of his birth. It had been a gut-wrenching experience for the young Vietnamese, but he had learned an invaluable lesson – how to defeat a modern, western army.

"Colonel Tran," a woman's voice said, capturing his attention. It was Lieutenant Colonel Du Kim-Ly his second in command and his common-law wife – all in accordance with party doctrine. "The cadre are accounted for. The Regiment is safe."

Tran's face was impassive. "Double-check."

"We have," the lieutenant colonel replied, fully aware of Tran's methods. "But I will check again."

"That is not necessary," Tran said. His concern for his people was unique among the higher ranks of the People's Army of Vietnam, and, as a consequence, he had earned the distrust of his superiors. Valuing personnel over material was considered an American weakness. But the men and women under his command would follow him anywhere, and he did more with fewer resources than any of his fellow commanders, and, more importantly, he had a well-earned reputation for literally delivering the goods.

"Colonel Dinh has not arrived," the woman said.

The Trash Haulers

"The Colonel's guides are not familiar with the area," Tran replied. "They're probably lost." Nothing in his soft tone betrayed the deep contempt he held for Dinh Hung Dung, who was a well-placed member of the Military Affairs Committee that coordinated policy and strategy between Hanoi and the geographic commands in the field. Dinh and three of his braver staff were traveling down the Ho Chi Minh trail on a so-called inspection tour. In reality, it was a political shakedown reminiscent of the infighting Tran had seen in Algeria. Sooner or later, Tran would have to choose sides, a decision he didn't want to make.

"Please ask Captain Lam to find Colonel Dinh and bring him to safety," Tran said. Lam was the commander of the infantry company under Tran's command and would carry out the order, even if it meant carrying the corpulent Dinh up the mountain.

"Yes, Colonel," the woman replied, leaving him alone. Tran sat down on his haunches and slept, his back against the rock face of the cave's low entrance.

Loud voices echoed up the trail and woke Tran long before the missing men arrived at the cave. Captain Lam led the way, setting a brisk pace for the men following him. "Quickly, quickly," he urged in a low voice, motioning the men into the cave. He kept glancing to the east, looking for the bombers he knew were coming. A small soldier carrying the rotund Colonel Dinh staggered out of the thick underbrush. Dinh was straddling a wooden frame strapped to the soldier's back that was normally used for carrying wounded. He complained loudly. The soldier almost

13

collapsed as he sat Dinh on his feet. "Well done," Lam told the young private. "Go inside." Lam turned to Tran. "My apologies, Colonel." Tran motioned Lam into the cave as the last of the rescue party arrived. Like Dinh, all three of his staff were carried on the backs of soldiers.

Dinh was in high dudgeon and turned on Tran. "You exceeded your authority. Members of the Military Affairs Committee are not herded like water buffalo or carried like sacks of rice. And why did your captain apologize to you? I deserve the apology." Dinh waited expectantly. Although he and Tran were equal in rank, in the grand pecking order of the People's Army of Vietnam, Dinh was a celestial being and Tran a mere mortal.

"Captain Lam apologized for the noise," Tran explained. From the look on Dinh's face, the celestial being didn't have a clue. "The Bru have sharp ears and know how to set ambushes."

"The Bru?" Dinh asked.

Tran hid his disgust for the portly Dinh as he explained what the desk-bound colonel should have known. "Bru is the name of the local Montagnard tribe who scout for the Americans." The Montagnards were the indigenous hill people of the Central Highlands and were closely allied with the American special forces operating in the area.

"The Americans are fools," Ding snapped.

"Maybe in Saigon," Tran replied. He had interrogated a downed American pilot before shipping the wounded officer up the Ho Chi Minh trail. The American had described the brass in Saigon as "REMFs", rear echelon motherfuckers. Discretion had kept Tran from sympathizing with him. There was no doubt that Dinh was the Vietnamese version of a

The Trash Haulers

REMF. Again, discretion marked Tran's words. "But the Americans here know how to fight."

Dinh wasn't having any of it. "Perhaps we need regimental commanders who possess the will to fight." The threat was obvious. "For the truly motivated, the Americans are easily defeated."

"Perhaps," Tran said, his voice low and without emotion, "the Colonel can instruct me on how to easily defeat that." He pointed to the east where two B-52s in close formation overflew their initial point and headed for the valley below where Dinh had been minutes before. Two more B-52s rolled out behind the first element, slightly displaced to the south. A third element of two was right behind. The bombs started to stream down, and, thanks to long experience, Tran knew what was coming. "We must go inside," he told Dinh, leading the way into the dark cave. Two soldiers hurried to board up the entrance with heavy planks as the first of the rolling explosions shook the mountain, turning the heavy jungle below into a mass of green pulp.

Tran checked his watch. It was exactly 0600 hours. "Amazing," he whispered. The bombers had flown over 2400 hundred miles and hit their time-on-target almost to the second. Dinh held his hands over his ears, his face contorted in fear. "It is safer down there," Tran said, motioning deeper into the cave. The stench of the packed bodies inside was stifling and overpowering. Dinh bolted in the direction Tran was pointing.

Tran stared at Dinh's back. His second in command, Lieutenant Colonel Du Kim-Ly, stepped out of a small alcove hidden in the shadows. "Why didn't you let him die in the valley?"

15

The memories of Algiers came back. "That would have been counterproductive. We do not fight among ourselves."

"Dinh will have you replaced in disgrace after he sees what we lost from the bombing," she predicted.

"But we will be alive," Tran replied.

"And so will Dinh," Kim-Ly added. "He is a fool."

"Fortunately, he is capable of learning. That is why General Giap sent him here."

Kim-Ly stared at her commander, her lover, her world, wondering how he knew what motivated Giap. There was no doubt in her mind that Tran was the best commander in the People's Army of Vietnam, and she would personally slit Dinh's throat if he was a threat to Tran. She hurried into the cave, calculating how to monitor Dinh's every word and action. She knew just the girl.

0600 HOURS

Cam Ranh Bay, South Vietnam

Most of the officers filing into the main briefing room in wing headquarters for the morning intelligence briefing were from Maintenance or Logistics with a sprinkling of Security Cops and fighter pilots from the 12th Tactical Fighter Wing. Warren and Bosko were among the last to arrive and found places to stand against the back wall. "Like you said," Warren said in a low voice, "the best show on base. I think we're the only trash haulers here."

A major came through the side door at the front, took a deep breath, and bellowed "Room! Ten-hut!" Everyone came to their feet as the wing commander, Colonel Robert L. Mace, and his staff marched into the room and took their seats in the front row. The last man in line was Lieutenant Colonel Stanley Hardy.

"It figures," Warren muttered.

"He's working on the Brown Nose Cluster to the MSM," Bosko replied. Warren chuckled at the copilot's play of words on the MSM, or Meritorious Service Medal. The medal was awarded for outstanding staff work, and an Oak Leaf Cluster indicated it had been awarded a second time. "Hey," Bosko added, "you gotta kiss a lot of ass to get the Brown Nose Cluster."

"Seats, gentlemen," Mace called. The audience shuffled back into their seats. Immediately, the lights dimmed and two captains wearing jungle fatigues stepped to the podiums. The tall and lithe, and very attractive, Judith Slovack took the podium on the right as the short and wiry Ronald Huckabee stepped to the podium on the left. He made a show of climbing on a wooden crate to reach the microphone.

Slovack opened the briefing. "Colonel Mace, gentlemen, good morning. This is your intelligence briefing for Wednesday, January 31, 1968." The screen lit up with a 35mm slide of the logo of the 12th Tactical Fighter Wing superimposed over an outline map of South Vietnam. A big star was superimposed over Cam Ranh Bay, and Colonel Mace's name filled the bottom.

The soft click of the projector echoed over the room, and the screen cycled to a photo of the American embassy in Saigon. "Today is the first day of the Tet Festival celebrating the lunar New Year. It is the most important celebration in the Vietnamese culture. The Viet Cong opened the festivities by attacking the American Embassy at approximately 0300 hours. The VC rapidly breached the walls and ran through the compound. The action is on-going, and at last report, most of the compound has been secured. There was also a wave of similar attacks, mostly in I and II Corps. Headquarters MACV" – she pronounced it MacVee – "is not overly alarmed and is discounting the significance of the attacks."

The Trash Haulers

The image cycled with a soft click and the image of the coastal city of Qui Nhon came into focus, creating a zooming in effect. Huckabee stepped to the side of the screen with a handheld microphone. "On Sunday, January 28, South Korean combat teams from the White Horse Division captured two small groups of VC and took possession of two prerecorded audio tapes, both with the same message." Huckabee pressed a button and a stream of Vietnamese echoed from the loudspeakers. After a few seconds, Huckabee cut it off. "If I may translate, 'loyal comrades are urged to join in the general offensive, which has started in already occupied Saigon, Hue, and Da Nang.' The tone of the words is definitive and positive, announcing an accomplished fact. To make a statement like that and then be proven wrong would be a major loss of face."

Now it was Slovack's turn. The image on the screen cycled to another map of Vietnam, this time with little fires scattered across all four Corps areas of South Vietnam. "As of 0500 hours this morning, attacks have been reported in over one-hundred towns, including thirty-six of the forty-four provincial capitals. The timing and extent of the attacks indicates a well-coordinated plan. We queried MACV by flash message as to the current status but have not received a reply."

Huckabee stepped to the front of the stage. "Colonel Mace, gentlemen, the scale and timing of the attacks is so unique that I'm forced to conclude the Viet Cong and North Vietnamese have mounted a major offensive. Expect a wider outbreak of fighting within the next twenty-four hours." A hard silence came down as Huckabee and Slovack stood together at the front of the stage ready to answer any questions.

Colonel Mace stood. "I've just gotten off the secure line to Headquarters Seventh Air Force in Saigon and they assure me that this activity is little more than the death spasm of a defeated enemy. You Intel pukes need to spend more time reading intelligence summaries than the headlines from the commie sympathizing press in the States." He turned and scanned the room. "Let me remind everyone here that the way home is through Hanoi. We've got more important work to do than listen to defeatism from liberal Intel pukes. Dismissed." He stormed out of the room with his staff in tow.

"Ouch," Bosko said. "Will Mace fire them?"

"Probably," Warren replied.

"Do you think they got it right?"

Warren's lips pulled into a frown. "Oh, yeah."

"Let's go," Bosko urged in a low voice. "Hardy's seen us. Coming our way."

"Crap," Warren muttered. They scooted towards the exit.

"Gentlemen," Hardy called, "hold up." He pushed through the rapidly dwindling crowd. "While I'm glad you made the briefing, your time would have been better spent at the barber shop. Or are you suffering from short-term memory loss?" He fixed them with a hard look. "We take our marching orders from Colonel Mace, and you are not to discuss what you've heard here with anyone. It is defeatism pure and simple that we will not be a party to."

Warren was confused. "How is a warning of an enemy attack in a war zone defeatism?"

The Trash Haulers

Hardy's face turned to granite. "Are you hard of hearing? A defeated enemy does not attack."

"Apparently, the VC haven't got the word," Warren replied.

Hardy's face turned red. "I don't have the time to discuss strategy, much less policy, with a captain. Your orders are simple and I don't like repeating myself. Make sure everyone on your crew gets a haircut today and get some polish on your boots." He turned to Bosko. "And you will trim your mustache. Today. Have I made myself clear?" The two junior officers nodded, anxious to escape. "As always, I expect you to conduct yourselves as members of the world's finest Air Force. That is why I told Colonel Mace you will fly the Air Force Surgeon General's Golden Spirochete to Nakhon Phanom in Thailand today. Needless to say, Colonel Mace wants it off his base ASAP."

"I'm sure he does," Warren conceded. He managed not to smile.

Hardy did a sharp about face and marched for the exit. The two pilots looked at each other and broke out in hoots of laughter. The Golden Spirochete was a purple guidon, or fanion. Guidons are small, swallow-tailed flags with a unit's identification mounted on a six-foot staff and carried on parade. In a very real sense, they represent the unit. This particular guidon was embroidered with a golden spirochete, the spiral-shaped bacteria that caused syphilis. It was awarded each month to the hospital or clinic with the highest venereal disease rate in Southeast Asia, supposedly in an effort to motivate the unit to curb the soaring rates. "Hey," Bosko finally managed, "We can get a Thai haircut while we're there." The Thai barbershop outside the main gate at

21

Nakhon Phanom was famous for the pretty girls who worked there and infamous for offering much more than haircuts.

"All things considered," Warren said, "I don't think that would be a wise idea."

Again, they roared with laughter. Hardy heard them and turned, fixing him with his command look before disappearing through the door. "Yep," Bosko said, "he's definitely oh-six material." O-6 was the alpha-numeric designation for a colonel while O-5, Hardy's current rank, indicated a lieutenant colonel. Warren, a captain, was an O-3 and Bosko, a first lieutenant, an O-2.

"Rank times IQ is a constant," Warren intoned.

Bosko paused as it sank in. "Hey, that's funny." Their laughter echoed over the deserted room. The copilot made a mental note to pass the remark on to Santos.

Phu Bai, South Vietnam

Three hundred miles north of Cam Ranh Bay, and fifty miles below the Demilitarized Zone that separated North and South Vietnam, the sun was breaking the horizon and casting long shadows over the big U.S. Army base outside the town of Phu Bai. Phu Bai had been a sleepy town in Quang Tri, the northern-most province of South Vietnam but the war had changed all that. Now, Quang Tri Province, along with the four northern provinces, made up the military region known as I Corps.

A lone runner circled the parking apron where the helicopters were lined up in precise rows, each parked in its own L-shaped revetment. Each revetment cast a long shadow across the PSP matting, the pierced steel planking that held the mud at bay. The Army had also used the

The Trash Haulers

planking to sandwich sandbags between two walls of PSP, creating the open bunkers the Hueys could easily taxi into for protection.

The runner automatically counted the helicopters. "Twenty-nine," he muttered. The 571st Medical Company Air Ambulance had lost another aircraft, but he fully expected it would be replaced within hours. Dust Offs had that priority. He made a mental note to check on the status of the crew. Unfortunately, he had been in-country eight months and knew the odds. He picked up the pace.

The crew chiefs servicing the helicopters looked up as he pounded past. For the most part, they shook their heads. More than one muttered something about "fuckin' stupid" as no one ran in their Army unless they were ordered to, or they were running away from something, like incoming rockets. WO-1, Warrant Officer-Grade One, Wilson Tanner was a strange sight. He was wearing a tee shirt, running shorts, and combat boots. He would have worn his Smith and Wesson .38 revolver, if he could have found a way to keep the shoulder holster from flopping around. Other than when he was running, the Combat Masterpiece was his constant companion. He kicked into high gear. There was no doubt the wiry twenty-one-year-old could run. At five foot eight inches, he set a blistering pace, his shaved head glistening with sweat.

He circled by the cluster of tents he called home. Most had dirt floors, but he had dickered with the Seabees, Naval Mobile Construction Battalion 58 to be exact, and for two bottles of Jim Beam the Seabees had "diverted" the plywood sheets and 2x4s he needed to cobble together a floor. His fellow tent mates appreciated the effort and concluded, rightly, that Tanner's main concern was to protect his small library. One of his buddies making his way back from the showers yelled at him. "How many more laps, Professor?"

"Done," Tanner shouted back. He headed for the Ops Shack to check the duty roster. He had better be on it.

He never made it. The in-coming shriek of mortars drove him into a heavily sandbagged bunker. He hunkered down and covered his ears as a barrage of mortar rounds walked across the base. A series of secondary explosions was ample proof that they had bracketed in the parked helicopters.

Not sure what was coming next, he crawled to the bunker entrance and chanced a quick look using the smoke and dust as cover. Just as quickly, he pulled back inside as the unmistakable rattle of AK-47s echoed over his head. Without his .38, he felt totally naked. He focused on the gunfire. The attackers were firing in long bursts. "Fuckin' newbies," he grunted. The AK-47 was a highly reliable weapon but had to be fired in short three or four round bursts for any accuracy. The gunfire grew closer. He found a trenching tool, the Army's short-handled folding shovel, and quickly scooped out a deep hole in the back corner of the bunker. Adrenaline did work wonders.

He retreated to the entrance, cocked the shovel like a baseball bat and waited. "Fuck," he muttered, totally out of options.

A hand grenade rolled through the entrance. Tanner used the shovel as a scoop and tossed the grenade into the hole he had just dug. He hunkered against the wall and covered his hears, his mouth open. The grenade exploded, deafening and showering him with dirt. He yawned, trying to clear his ears. Nothing. He shook his tee shirt, adding to the dust cloud inside the bunker. He chanced blinking his eyes. He could see. A shadow filled the entrance and he cocked the shovel, ready to swing.

A young soldier holding an AK-47 edged into the bunker. Tanner swung his shovel in a horizontal arc like an ax, cutting into the soldier's throat. He threw a body block into the attacker as he grabbed the AK-47. They slammed into the far wall and the soldier fell to the ground. Tanner swung the AK-47 like a club, smashing into his attacker's skull. He stood motionless over the body, staring at it. "Sweet Jesus," he groaned. He had just killed a teenage girl. He checked the AK-47 and, holding it at the ready, inched out of the bunker. The gunfire had moved on and was centered on the far side of the base. He made a dash for the ops shack, passing eight burning helicopters.

"Tanner!" a voice called. "Over here." It was Tanner's company commander, a captain and West Point graduate on his second tour. "A mortar got your aircraft and crew chief." He pointed to another helicopter in the end revetment. "Find a peter pilot and get the hell out of Dodge." A peter pilot was a young and inexperienced copilot fresh from training in the States who was always teamed with an older aircraft commander until he could be seasoned enough to stay alive.

Tanner tossed the AK-47 to his company commander and trotted past a smoldering revetment, the Huey a burnt-out hulk. A young pilot who looked all of seventeen was standing upwind of the smoke, a look of total shock on his face. "Perkins!" Tanner bellowed, recognizing the second lieutenant. "Follow me." The baby-faced pilot fell in behind him as they made the long dash to the end revetment. "Not a good day," Tanner said, breathing easily.

"What we gonna do?" Perkins asked. He was on the edge of panic.

"What we always do," Tanner replied. "We're Dust Off." They skidded around the edge of the bunker. Dust Off was the call sign for medevac helicopters named in honor of Major Charles Kelly, a pilot killed early in the war while extracting wounded.

The crew chief and medic assigned to the helicopter were already there and untying the rotor blades. The crew chief looked at them in relief. "Mr. Tanner!" Tanner had a reputation for being a bit weird, but he was acknowledged as the best aircraft commander in the 571st.

"Let's go!" Tanner shouted.

Now routine kicked in as the four men who had never flown together melded into a crew. Tanner climbed into the left seat, the aircraft commander's position on a Dust Off, while Perkins jumped into the right seat. Tanner grabbed his shoulder harness and quickly strapped in, tightening his seat belt. Then he reached for the helmet hanging from a hook above his head. He hoped it would fit. It did. While he was strapping in, Perkins hit the start trigger on the right collective, bringing the single turboshaft engine to life. The crew chief slid the 'chicken plate', the armored plating that protected Tanner's left side from enemy fire, forward and into place. Once Tanner was strapped in and the intercom hot, he calmly said, "I've got the controls." He could have been on a routine training mission and Perkins visibly calmed.

The Trash Haulers

Perkins fell into the routine, now all business. He looked over, confirming that Tanner's hands were on the controls. "You've got the controls." He quickly strapped in as Tanner rolled up the throttle, carefully bringing the engine's 1100 shaft horsepower on line. He had to be careful, making sure the long blades did not build RPM too fast and overpower the tail rotor's effectiveness that kept the airframe from spinning with the blades like a top.

"Incoming mortars from the south," the crew chief called from behind Tanner.

"RPM 324," Tanner replied as the swirling blades reached one hundred percent. "Let's go."

"Clear right," the medic who was strapped in behind Perkins called.

"Clear left," the crew chief said.

For the first time, it was breaking their way. The long wall of the revetment was between them and the incoming mortars, shielding them from the attack coming from the south. The helicopter was pointed to the west, and Tanner backed out of the revetment to the east. Once clear, he eased in right pedal as he increased the collective, lifting the Huey a few feet higher as he turned to the north. Tanner was hunched slightly forward, his concentration absolute as he flew the machine. Although he had never flown with the three men, much less know them, he had to rely on them to do their job. For now, it was a question of Tanner's situational awareness – did his perception of what was going on match reality? If it didn't, they would just be another statistic, casualties of the Vietnam War. "Small arms fired coming from the right," the medic sitting behind Perkins called. Tanner played the controls and jinked left, then up,

27

before jinking left again and then back to the deck, darting between burning revetments, their airspeed touching ninety-five knots.

Clear of the field and the attack, the crew visibly relaxed. Perkins studied Tanner for a moment, taking in his running shorts and combat boots. "Nice fatigues you got there, Mr. Tanner."

Tanner never missed a beat. "Hell of a way to go to war."

0700 HOURS

I Corps, South Vietnam

"What now, Mr. Tanner?" Tony Perkins, the copilot, asked as Tanner circled to the north of the burning base, now well clear of the attack.

"We do our job," Tanner replied. "Contact Company on the VHF." He hoped the Ops Shack was back in business.

Perkins dialed in the frequency. His voice was calm. "Dust Off Ops, Dust Off Two-Seven, holding two miles north of you. Any trade?"

The Company's CO answered. "Roger, Dust Off Two-Seven. We've got a pickup for you." He rattled off an eight-digit code. Without writing it down, Perkins spun the decode wheel and read off the coordinates for the pickup point.

"That's Firebase Lonzo," Tanner said. He turned to the southwest and climbed to two thousand feet. "Ever been there before?" Perkins said he had never been that far into the highlands. "It can get real sporting," Tanner told him. He glanced at the fuel gauge and mentally calculated the flying time to the firebase: just over an hour. "We need to refuel first."

They headed for the nearest fuel dump as Perkins keyed the FM radio, calling for clearance to refuel. "Dust Off Two-Seven, five minutes out."

The voice that answered was hurried, on the edge of panic. "Dust Off Two-Seven, we are taking mortar rounds and are hot."

"Not the best of news," Tanner grumbled. He hit the transmit button. "Say nearest dump." The voice replied with an eight digit code.

This time, Perkins wrote it down. He spun the decode wheel and plotted the coordinates on his chart. He groaned. "It's fifty miles away." He glanced at the fuel gauge. "It's gonna be tight. Isn't there anything closer?"

"There were yesterday," Tanner replied. "But they're smoking holes today."

Cam Ranh Bay, South Vietnam

"The sun's been up forty-five minutes and it's already too damn hot," Steve Bosko moaned, climbing down from the shuttle bus. It was a short ride from wing headquarters to the C-130 operations shack, but the copilot's flight suit was damp and his face flushed.

"And this from a southern boy," Warren said, ragging on him. "It's air conditioned inside." He held the door for Bosko.

Dave Santos, their navigator, was standing at the waist-high scheduling counter collecting the paperwork. The captain standing behind the counter looked up and grinned. "So you get to take the Golden Spirochete to Naked Fanny." Naked Fanny was the nickname for the airbase at Nakhon

Phanom in Thailand. "Hemorrhoid Hardy said to make it happen today. You got a passenger. No cargo."

"Lovely," Warren replied. "Any cargo out of Naked Fanny?"

"Situation normal; unknown. Check with ALCE. Be flexible." ALCE, short for Air Lift Command Element, was the small detachment located at each airbase that managed the movement of logistics and personnel. After landing, pilots checked in for their next assignment while their aircraft was offloaded. Over all, it was a fairly efficient system, but when things went wrong aircraft were scattered haphazardly to hell and back.

"What's our call sign for today?" Warren asked.

The captain opened the small safe behind the desk and pulled out a two-inch thick paperbound book stamped SECRET that listed the call signs for each aircraft. The names changed daily, supposedly to deny the enemy vital intelligence. However, many claimed it only confused the aircrews, especially in the heat of combat. The captain found the right page for their unit, the 374th. "Today, you are Roscoe Two-One."

Santos slapped his forehead. "We get to fly and die as a Roscoe? What comedian came up with that one? This war is so fucked up. Hell, if I had a draft card, I'd burn it."

"You'll have to get in line," the captain muttered. He gave them the tail number of their aircraft. "You've got 56-469 today."

"Shit-oh-dear," Santos moaned. "First, we get the Golden Spirochete, then Roscoed, now sixty-nined. We are totally screwed." The Hercules they were assigned to fly had a bad reputation thanks to a series of minor incidents, none serious.

"Pun intended?" Warren asked. He changed the subject. "We heard the VC are kicking butt and taking names. Any word?"

"Intel is clueless, as usual," the captain replied. "Hardy said not to worry, they've shot their wad and it's business as usual. I don't know why, but he ordered everyone to wear a survival vest today. Covering his ass, I guess." He checked their paperwork. "Okay, you're good to go. It's now 0712 local, call it 0715. See you in twelve." The last was a reminder that they had a strict twelve-hour crew duty day and had to be on the ground when it expired, hopefully at Cam Ranh Bay, so Maintenance could turn the aircraft and launch it on another mission while they went into crew rest. The Air Force had learned through hard experience that fatigue was a killer and flying beyond twelve hours, especially under the stress of multiple takeoffs and landings in a combat zone, was a sure-fire recipe for an accident.

"Would we disappoint you?" the good-natured Bosko joked.

"Right," the captain replied, "and you'll respect me in the morning."

"Make that in twelve hours," Bosko added.

"Have a good one," the captain said, sending them on their way.

Their last stop was at PE, Personal Equipment, where they checked out survival vests. Each green vest carried a small first aid kit, a survival pack, an AN/PR-90 survival radio, and a Smith & Wesson Combat Masterpiece revolver with twelve rounds of ammunition. Although the aircrews

The Trash Haulers

were required to wear the bulky vests, most would shed them after a few hours but keep them close at hand.

Outside, a crew van was waiting to take the three officers to the flight line where six C-130s were parked in revetments. They rode in silence as Santos went through the paperwork, sorting it out. As the navigator, he had to play bookkeeper and fill out the many forms required by the paper-pushers who lurked in the various headquarters around the Air Force. Warren pulled out the letter from the divorce lawyer and reread it. He actually felt relieved. He shoved it back into the calf pocket on his flight suit as the van clanked to a stop beside a waiting C-130A. The three men clambered down the steps. Each carried their flight gear and an AWOL bag with a change of clothes and shaving kit in case they got caught out for a few days, which often happened.

By modern standards the C-130 is a medium-size cargo plane, but up close and personal, it is big. The A model they were flying was ninety-eight feet long with a 132-foot wingspan. Its oversized vertical stabilizer rose fifty-three feet into the air and gave the aircraft outstanding stability and rudder authority. This particular A model had rolled off the Lockheed assembly line in 1956 and grossed out at 124,200 pounds, a lightweight when compared to the newer E models operating at 155,000 pounds.

The loadmaster, Staff Sergeant Glen "Flash" Flanders, was waiting for them. Flanders stood exactly five feet ten inches tall and was built like an oak tree. There was not an ounce of fat on his sturdy frame, and his dark skin glowed with health. The African American could load cargo so quickly and efficiently that he was recognized as the best loadmaster in the 374th.

"She's good to go, gentlemen," Flanders told them. "No cargo, one passenger on the way as we speak. And we got a loadmaster trainee taggin' along, Airman First Class Billy Bob Boyle. It's his last flight before his checkout ride." The training for wannabe loadmasters, normally young airmen from Maintenance, was challenging and difficult. The final step was a checkout flight where a senior loadmaster from the Wing's Standardization and Evaluation section went along on an actual mission and graded their every move and bombarded them with questions. It was a test that few passed the first time.

"And you're gonna fine tune him," Warren said.

Flanders pulled a face. "I'll try. The kid's got an attitude problem."

"What the hell, Flash," Santos said, "we all got an attitude problem."

"Let's get this show on the road," Warren said, throwing his gear and AWOL bag on board. The crew was a fine-tuned team and went to work. Bosko and Santos climbed up the three steps of the crew entrance door on the left side of the aircraft forward of the long, three-bladed props, while Warren pulled out a checklist. He opened the book to the correct page but didn't refer once to it as he walked around the aircraft, giving it one last visual check. His practiced eye looked for leaks, loose panels, cut tires, safety pins not removed. Even though the crew chief and his flight engineer, Technical Sergeant Mike Hale, had gone over the aircraft, he still found a loose screw on an access panel aft of the left wheel well. He buttoned it up and made a mental note to mention it to Hale.

The Trash Haulers

A bus from Passenger Services stopped in front of the revetment and a lone officer climbed off followed by a sergeant with a clipboard. He gave Flanders the passenger list and quickly climbed back aboard to deliver other passengers to waiting C-130s. Warren studied his passenger, a young and attractive woman wearing a new set of jungle fatigues. The black-colored rank on her collars announced she was a captain, and the small caduceus over her left breast pocket identified her as doctor. She was carrying a six-foot pole covered by a blue sheath; a guidon. He suppressed a smile. "The lady with the Golden Spirochete," he murmured. He walked over to introduce himself. He read her nametag – Pender.

Flanders glanced at the manifest and introduced them. "Captain Warren, our passenger, Captain . . ."

"Doctor Livingstone, I presume," Warren said, interrupting the loadmaster. He liked the way she looked at him with bright, inquisitive hazel eyes, taking his measure. She stood five-foot nine-inches tall in her jungle boots, definitely too broad in the hips to be considered stylish, but extremely feminine. Her dark-blonde hair was pulled back in a bun and framed high cheekbones and a perky nose that was just a little too small for her face.

She laughed. "Mr. Stanley, I presume." She extended her right hand.

He was captivated. "Sorry, wrong continent, wrong man, wrong century. I'm Mark Warren, your pilot for this fun-filled flight to Nakhon Phanom."

"Lynne Pender." They shook hands. Her grip was unusually strong for a woman.

"Ever been to Thailand?" Reluctantly, he released her hand.

She shook her head. "I just arrived on base last week. Fresh out of Sheppard." Doctors, dentists, and nurses did their basic training at Sheppard Air Force Base in Wichita Falls, Texas. For most, it was a short prelude to a two-year tour before returning to civilian life.

"I see you get to deliver the Golden Spirochete."

"Do I detect a trace of humor, Captain?"

"I'm trying to hide it," Warren replied.

She forgave him with a smile. "It is funny. But I'm a surgeon and like to think I've better things to do." That explained her firm grip. She didn't mention that she had been assigned the duty after being introduced to Colonel Mace and firmly rejecting an offer to share his bed. Fortunately, her father was a retired Marine colonel, and that specific situation had been covered at Sheppard in an informal training session with a veteran nurse. Her "no" was followed with a reference to the chaplain. The trip to Nakhon Phanom was Mace's revenge, a pathetic attempt to stroke his damaged ego. For the most part, Captain Lynne Pender considered it an adventure but felt better venting her frustration.

The Passenger Service bus was back and slammed to a halt. A different sergeant jumped down, closely followed by the two captains from Intel, Judith Slovack and Ronald Huckabee. The sergeant helped them off load four suitcases and two stuffed B-4 parachute bags with all their personal belongings. Flanders, the loadmaster, quickly signed the manifest and helped the sergeant and two officers lug their bags to the loading ramp at the rear of the aircraft.

The Trash Haulers

"Ladies and gentlemen," Flanders said in a loud voice. "I am Staff Sergeant Glen Flanders, your loadmaster for this first-class flight to Nakhon Phanom. By regulations, I am required to brief you on emergency procedures. In the event of a fire, you will hear me shout 'Follow me!' Please do so in order to avoid becoming a crispy critter. Once we have your bags loaded, follow me aboard and we can finish your passenger brief and we can get this delightful experience on the road."

Warren shook his head at Flanders's very non-standard passenger brief and climbed through the crew entrance. A tall and gangly teenager was waiting just inside. "Airman Boyle?" Warren asked.

"Yessir," the airman answered.

"Welcome . . ."

Boyle cut him of in mid sentence. "Am I the loadmaster here or not?"

Warren took the airman in, not liking what he saw. His flight suit was dirty, his hair too long for a tropical climate, his boots needed cleaning, and his survival vest hung loosely over his shoulders. Warren didn't care about spit and polish, not in a war zone, but he did care about basic hygiene. "Staff Sergeant Glen Flanders is the loadmaster on this aircraft. You can learn a lot from him." He shouldered Boyle aside and climbed the short ladder onto the flight deck.

"But Flanders is a . . ."

Warren turned and stared down at him. "Sergeant Flanders is a what?"

"Nothing, sir."

Warren had caught Boyle's hard twangy southern drawl and chalked his attitude up to racism. He decided to give the

37

teenager a break. "This is the Air Force, Boyle. Get used to it. Now, go give Sergeant Flanders a hand." Fortunately, Boyle read Warren correctly and disappeared down the crew entrance steps without a word.

Warren settled into the left hand pilot's seat and unzipped his survival vest, getting comfortable. Steve Bosko was already in the copilot's seat running the cockpit checklist with the flight engineer. Dave Santos was seated at the navigator's position directly behind Bosko, facing outboard to the right, still sorting out the paperwork. The flight engineer, Technical Sergeant Mike Hale, was sitting behind and between the two pilots. His seat was slightly higher so he could reach the overhead instrument panels. But that was no problem for the skinny six foot four sergeant. He was the tallest man in the squadron and his red hair covered numerous scars from banging into low objects on the aircraft. He had to be especially careful of the sextant, when installed for overwater flights, that hung from the overheard directly behind his seat. A pleasant demeanor, friendly blue eyes, and a mass of freckles concealed a very intelligent and deeply religious man. He was known for 'going by The Book,' and wanted to make chief master sergeant before he retired.

"Time to light the fires," Warren said. "Aux power on." The flight engineer's hands danced over the instrument panel as he fed power from the auxiliary power generator into the electrical bus, bringing the aircraft to life. Bosko turned on the radios and checked in with ground control. Before he could request an engine start, ground control told them to shut down. Another passenger was on his way out.

"Hurry up and wait," Santos moaned.

The Trash Haulers

"Must be a VIP," Bosko decided.

"I think I'll go howdy our passengers," Warren said. He wanted to find out why Colonel Mace had kicked Huckabee and Slovack off his base. And there was the attractive captain.

The Laotian-South Vietnamese Border

"Why are we going this way?" Colonel Dinh moaned, reluctant to leave the safety of the cave so soon after the B-52s had carpet-bombed the valley.

Tran heard the panic in his words and suppressed a smile. "It is the only way to the command post," he replied. "Besides, we must be seen if the cadre is to have confidence in our orders." An explosion echoed over them and Dinh flinched, struggling to remain calm. Both men knew they were being watched and evaluated by every man and woman in the Binh Tram. Reluctantly, Tran decided to run cover for the colonel, allowing him to save face. "Ah, that is our clearance teams at work. They immediately detonate any bomb that has not exploded. Some are duds but the Americans also use delayed-action fuses on bombs they drop. Those are the most dangerous." Another explosion punctuated his sentence.

Dinh flinched again, on the edge of panic. "How many more?"

"We cannot be sure. Intelligence tells us that each B-52 coming from Guam carries sixty-six bombs, and we counted six B-52s." He ran the numbers for Dinh, again disgusted that the colonel didn't know what they dealt with in the forward operating area. "That means the Americans dropped 396 five-hundred pound bombs for a total of 198,000 pounds,

39

almost 90,000 kilos, of explosives. Normally, three percent of the bombs fail to detonate, or twelve bombs." On cue, two more explosions echoed over the valley. "That was number eleven and twelve," explained. "Our teams will continue to search, but we must get back to work, salvage what we can, and prepare for tonight." He fixed Dinh with a steady look. "The war does not stop for B-52s."

Silently, they made their way into the valley, following the small stakes with strips of green cloth wrapped around the top. The carpet-bombing had turned the thick jungle into a massive green trash heap. A nearby explosion deafened them and Dinh fell to the ground, screaming incoherently. He slowly calmed. "You said that was all!"

Tran squatted beside the prostrate colonel. He suppressed a smile. "I said we cannot be sure and our clearance teams are still searching."

Dinh came to his knees and Tran offered him a hand. Dinh shook his head and struggled to his feet unassisted. "I must survey your losses." He pulled himself to his full five-feet two-inches and fixed Tran with a hard look. "There will be consequences for your dereliction."

Tran's face was impassive. "Perhaps the colonel can show us how to avoid the bombs."

"The directives are very clear," Dinh explained, his voice patronizing. "It is called 'dispersal'. Do not concentrate the material in your care. Even a child understands that."

"Ah, yes," Tran replied. "Even a child." He spun around and headed down the marked path, into the devastation. Dinh scrambled to follow. It was the bravest thing the colonel ever did. Tran paused by an old bomb

The Trash Haulers

crater that had been dug out and encircled by a reinforced berm of logs and sandbags. Inside, a stack of crates and sacks of rice were neatly stacked. "Only a direct hit can destroy a cache like this," Tran explained. "The directives only ordered us to disperse our stores and equipment, not how to protect them." They followed the path, assessing the damage. Tran calculated that one out of every six storage areas had taken a direct hit. It could have been worse, much worse. They finally reached the far side of the valley and scrambled up a low ridge and into a large bunker dug into the side of the hill. "Our command post," Tran said.

Kim-Ly was waiting and handed Dinh a folded note. "A confidential message from General Dong." General Dong Sy Nguyen was the commander of Group 559 and responsible for the Ho Chi Minh trail. She waited for Dinh to sign that he had received the message. She handed Tran a clipboard. "The first damage estimate," she said, loud enough for Dinh to hear. "We estimate eighteen percent destroyed or damaged. They missed the petroleum dump."

"Casualties?" Tran asked.

"Two members of the clearance team were killed when a bomb they were defusing detonated prematurely."

"And your operational status?" Dinh demanded.

Kim-Ly thought for a moment. "Our teams need six more hours to fully sweep the area and be fully operational."

"Unacceptable," Dinh growled. He was answered by another explosion.

Tran spoke in a low voice, but loud enough for everyone to hear. "Perhaps the colonel will personally train our clearance teams how to be more efficient?"

41

Every man and woman in the command post caught the insult and Dinh knew it would spread like a wild fire, racing up the trail by word-of-mouth and reaching Hanoi within days. But thanks to the message in his hand, he had another card to play. "Your disrespect is duly noted. But that is not my concern. The message I just received orders me to find out why the necessary logistics are not reaching our gallant soldiers fighting and dying at Khe Sanh – and to correct it." A satisfied look spread across his face. "As this is your area of responsibility, please explain."

Tran sensed the danger. "I am fully aware of the problem." He stepped to the large-scale map on the back wall of the bunker and pointed to a town inside South Vietnam. "As the Colonel knows," he said, using the standard politically correct jargon, "this Binh Tram is the logistical base for our gallant soldiers fighting the Americans at Khe Sanh."

"I'm not a fool." Dinh snapped. He pushed Tran aside and used his fingers to span off the distance from their location to Khe Sanh. "Thirty-five kilometers," he announced. He made no attempt to conceal the contempt in his voice.

"As the bird flies," Tran replied. "However, it is over seventy kilometers by trails that only porters can use. The situation on the ground is much more complicated than on the Truong Son Strategic Supply Route." He used the official North Vietnamese name for the Ho Chi Minh trail. Tran pointed to a spot eight kilometers to the east of their headquarters and well inside South Vietnam. "This is the hamlet of A Xóc."

"And that is your bottleneck?" Dinh said, not really asking a question.

"The hamlet is deserted. Unfortunately, the Americans have turned it into a Special Forces camp that blocks the ford crossing the Se Pang Hieng. The Se Pang Hieng is not a big river, but the crossing is very treacherous and it blocks the way south to Khe Sanh. The Americans know this and have reinforced the camp they call Se Pang with Bru, who pride themselves on killing Vietnamese."

"Attack and destroy it," Dinh said.

"General Dong is aware of the situation."

"And my orders are quite clear. Must I repeat myself?"

"I only have one company of infantry available, less than one hundred men under Captain Lam. They are light infantry and to attack a fortified camp like Se Pang is a sacrifice of good men."

"You have other personnel. Use them."

Tran stared at Dinh, wondering if the man was a complete idiot. "Most of the cadre are drivers, porters, mechanics, guides, engineers, medics, cooks, and specialists. They not trained soldiers."

"You have your orders."

Tran carefully chose his words. "I'm sure the Colonel is aware that General Dong has ordered four attacks on Se Pang. Each time the Americans called in their forward air controllers and attack aircraft. The firepower is devastating."

"I am familiar with their tactics."

But not the destruction and havoc they cause, Tran thought. It was fallback time. "May we step outside for a word?" he asked. Without waiting for a reply, he motioned for Kim-Ly to follow him. Dinh hesitated before following them outside.

Tran walked down a side path until they were well clear of the command post. He scanned the area to be sure no one could overhear them. "Colonel Dinh, you need to hear from my closest advisor." He motioned for Kim-Ly to join them. "My second in command, Lieutenant Colonel Du."

Dinh threw her a contemptuous glance. "Ah, your woman. And is she a lieutenant colonel because she shares your bed?"

Kim-Ly lowered her head in submission and Tran stifled a reply. Dinh should have known that General Giap introduced them when she was a newly-promoted lieutenant colonel. Giap had warned Tran that Kim-Ly was well named. "She is truly a golden lion," Giap had said, giving emphasis to her given name. Both understood that Giap intended for them to serve the communist party as one.

"Colonel Dinh," Kim-Ly said, her voice soft and non-threatening, "I am a mere woman and do not fully understand your responsibilities and cares. Please forgive me for what I am about to say. General Dong has sacrificed over five thousand of our frontline soldiers trying to destroy Se Pang."

Dinh stiffened at the number. He was not a fool and knew what that number meant, even for the People's Army of Vietnam. "Where did you get that number?"

"I counted them," she replied. She let it sink in. "May I offer this? Why doesn't General Dong himself issue the order for another attack? Is it because he knows what the Americans can do, and if the attack again failed would the political costs be too high? Is that why he ordered you to solve the problem?" She fell silent, her eyes fixed on Dinh's face.

A little tick played at the corner of Dinh's right eye. "Are you suggesting that General Dong needs a scapegoat?"

"The Colonel can answer that question much better than me," she answered, throwing it back at Dinh. She had made her point, and the tick at the corner of Dinh's eye grew more pronounced.

Dinh had survived in the cutthroat world of Vietnamese politics by playing one side against the other, but now he was the other side. He ran the options through his mental abacus, subtracting and adding the variables that spelled success or failure. "Today, the first day of Tet, is the day we launch phase two of *Tong Cong Kich – Tong Khoi Ngia*. This is the General Offensive, the general uprising we have been planning for years. We are attacking the American pirates and their worthless allies on hundreds, thousands, of fronts. They are being overwhelmed and will not be able to send their aircraft, or reinforcements of any kind to Se Pang. It is only eight kilometers away, and you will attack at first dark. Victory will be ours!"

I Corps, South Vietnam

Tanner ran the numbers as they headed for the fuel dump, guesstimating distance versus fuel remaining. It was going to be tight and they were pushing the envelope. Flying with a new crew was always dicey at first, even under normal conditions. But this was far from an average day, and he had to find out exactly who he was flying with. He knew Tony Perkins was fresh out of helicopter training at Fort Rucker, Alabama, with barely 200 hundred hours flying time – just enough to get him killed. It was the job of the older heads to teach him how to really fly, and given time, the baby-faced pilot might make it. But the crew chief and medic were totally unknown. "Listen up. With full fuel, we can just make Firebase Lonzo and make it back to a fuel dump. But it will be tight. How's the machine?"

The crew chief answered. "She's good, Mr. Tanner. She flies by the numbers, fuel consumption on the good side."

"Sounds good," Tanner replied. "By the way, what's your handle?" In the rush of launching he had not seen the crew chief's name tag.

"Specialist First Class Rick Myers."

"Been in-country long, Myers?"

"I'm a short timer. Eighteen days and a wake-up, then I'm gone, back to the land of the big PX."

"Medic," Tanner asked, "what about you?"

"Specialist First Class Hal Collins. This is my second in-country." A second time in Vietnam meant that Collins was a volunteer, and probably a "lifer" who planned to make the Army a career. Tanner doubted that either man was over twenty years old, but both were highly experienced. *Where do we find them?* Tanner wondered.

Tanner had a visual on the fuel dump and could make out the black amoeba-like fuel bladder, the pump, and four small PSP landing pads, one in each quadrant. "Okay, let's do this one by the numbers. We need five hundred pounds of fuel. In and out in five minutes. Can you make that happen?"

"Can do," Myers promised.

The Trash Haulers

Tanner headed for the nearest pad and gently set the Huey down. He kept the engine running for a hot refuel. Without a word, Myers pulled the release pin to Tanner's chicken plate and slid it back before following Collins out of the aircraft. Collins closed the right door, exposing the fuel cap, as Myers ran for the pump. Collins quickly connected the grounding lines to the helicopter and refueling hose as Myers hit the pump's start switch, bringing it to life.

You've got the controls," Tanner told Perkins as he unstrapped.

"I've got the controls," Perkins replied.

Tanner was out and running for the empty rocket tubes half-buried upright in the ground that served as relief tubes. He stood there, surprised by his bladder's capacity. Finished, he sprinted for the helicopter and bailed into his seat, quickly strapping in. "I've got the controls." Perkins was already unstrapped and jumped out, his turn to hit the relief tubes. He passed Collins, the medic, who was on the way back after his turn at the tubes. Tanner checked the fuel gauge. "Four hundred pounds," he told the crew chief. They were almost full.

Myers backed off the flow and topped off without spilling a drop. Collins grabbed the nozzle and disconnected the grounding wires as Myers now ran for the relief tubes. Perkins and Collins were strapped in and ready to go when Myers made the dash back to the aircraft. He snapped Tanner's chicken plate into place and bailed into the back. "Less than five minutes, Mr. Tanner," he yelled as the shrill whistle of an incoming mortar echoed over the fuel dump.

Tanner lifted off and spun the helicopter away from the fuel dump, again running for safety. In itself, the refueling

47

was no big thing, but it had told Tanner all he needed to know about the crew of Dust Off 27 – they were a team he could take into hell, which he fully intended to do.

Three motor rounds walked across the fuel dump, sending a huge tower of fire and smoke into the sky. Tanner keyed the intercom. "Off hand, I'd say the shit has definitely hit the fan."

0800 HOURS

I Corps, South Vietnam

Tanner held the Huey a few feet off the ground, running from the explosions walking across the fuel dump where they had been refueling a few seconds ago. "Damn, that was a close one," Perkins said. His youngish face was drained of color and he struggled to match his pilot's cool.

"All in a day's work," Tanner replied. From all outward appearances, it was just another routine mission as he turned to the southwest and climbed into the sky. But they all knew it was anything but. Tanner altered course sixty degrees to the left to check on the refueling dump behind them. A huge black plume of smoke reached into the blue sky and three bright flashes erupted on the ground, mute testimony to the accuracy of the mortar teams attacking the fuel dump. He altered course 120 degrees to the right so Perkins could see. "See if you can raise anyone on the VHF and relay the situation on the ground to Division," he told the copilot.

Perkins fingers danced on the radio, cycling to the new frequency. "Dust Off Two-Seven transmitting in the blind.

Be advise fuel dump Oscar Lima is under mortar attack and unusable at this time." His voice was cool and matter-of-fact as Tanner altered course back to the southwest, heading for Firebase Lonzo for the med evac.

Cam Ranh Bay, South Vietnam

"Sergeant Flanders," Warren called as he climbed down from the C-130's flight deck, "we're on hold. Another passenger is on the way." Warren always called the loadmaster by his proper title and never called him 'Flash' like the rest of the crew.

"I'll wait outside and get him onboard soonest." Flanders had learned from long experience that their passenger had to be a high roller to delay a scheduled takeoff, but his job was to move cargo and passengers regardless of rank. He had earned his nickname for a good reason.

Warren sat down next to the two Intel captains on the red canvas jump seats that folded down from the side of the aircraft. "Welcome aboard," he said. "I'm Mark Warren, the aircraft commander." Ronald Huckabee and Judith Slovack introduced themselves. "I caught your briefing this morning," Warren continued. "You're good, really good, but I take it Colonel Mace didn't like what you told him."

The short and energetic Huckabee bounced to his feet. "It was the last straw in a small hay stack." He paced back and forth. "It goes back to when Mace asked for a briefing on the Ho Chi Minh trail."

"The trail is Huck's area of expertise," Slovack added. "He's actually seen it."

Huckabee gave his partner a stern look. "Can't talk about that . . . need to know . . . all that classified crap."

The Trash Haulers

The young captain had been the interpreter on a Heavy Hook mission inserted on the Ho Chi Minh trail by helicopter. Their objective was to 'collect human intelligence resources,' a euphemism for old-fashioned kidnapping, and Huckabee's job was to conduct the interrogation. The helicopter had launched out of Nakhon Phanom and the team spent four days in southern Laos observing the trail, finally capturing a courier with a pouch full of messages and orders. It was a gold mine of information, revealing more of the logistical structure than they ever suspected. Huckabee understood the value of what they had uncovered, but before they could extract the courier, a North Vietnamese patrol discovered them and they spent the next two days running for their lives.

The North Vietnamese were closing in on them when the courier was wounded. It was a stray shot, but not a fatal one. The team managed to slip away, carrying their prisoner. Huckabee knew it was only a matter of time before they were run down. Desperate, he hatched a plan to let the courier bleed out while he scratched out a note in Vietnamese, indicating the courier was defecting with the pouch to prove his good faith. But they had to leave the pouch behind, strapped to the body, to make it work. Luckily, it did and the patrol broke off, giving the Americans the chance they needed to escape. A helicopter extracted them the next day.

"Please forget what you just heard," Huckabee told Warren.

"Heard what?" Warren said, playing the game.

Slovack gave him a grateful look. "Thank you," she murmured, impressed that he did not carry the over-blown ego of so many pilots. She also noted that he did not wear a

51

wedding ring. "Anyway," she continued, hoping to make a connection, "Colonel Mace was totally bent out of shape by Huck's briefing on the trail." Slovack smiled. "You should have seen his face. He almost had a heart attack when Huck said the Binh Tram structure was a logistics marvel of organization and efficiency."

"After that, it was just a matter of time until he got rid of us," Huckabee added. "The briefing this morning was just the last straw."

"So you're on your way to Nakhon Phanom in Thailand," Warren said. "I hear it's considered a remote tour even for the Thai Air Force."

"When the wing commander there heard Mace had sacked us, he asked for us by name," Slovack explained. Nakhon Phanom was the home of the 56th Air Commando Wing. Special operations squadrons flying WW II-vintage attack aircraft, Sikorsky HH-3 "Jolly Green Giant" rescue helicopters, and light visual reconnaissance aircraft made up the backbone of the wing. The A-1E and A-26K were superb at flying close air support and destroying trucks, and the Jolly Green Giant crews were legendary at rescuing downed airman. One of the more effective units monitoring the Ho Chi Minh trail were the Nail FACs, forward air controllers, who flew O-2s. The O-2 was the military version of the Cessna Skymaster, a twin-engine pusher-puller twin boom observation aircraft.

"The news Mace canned you certainly travelled fast," Warren allowed.

"NCO's do talk," Slovack said. "And some colonels do listen."

The Trash Haulers

"At least those with a clue," Warren said. "Too bad it isn't someone in the Pentagon." The two captains didn't answer. Discretion was part of their job and they knew, by name, exactly who was not listening. "So what exactly are the Gomers up to today?"

Slovack answered. "We think it's the 'General Offensive and Uprising' the North Vietnamese have been planning for years. It's a biggy."

"So they're going to kick ass and take names," Warren muttered.

"They're going to try," Slovack said. She looked at the crew entrance. "I think your passenger is here." Lieutenant Colonel Stanley Hardy stepped through the open hatch, shot Warren a hard look, and motioned him to the flight deck.

"Lovely," Warren grumbled under his breath. "Absolutely lovely. Excuse me." He followed Hardy onto the flight deck, hoping everyone was still wearing their survival vests. Fortunately, they were.

"I've got to get to Ubon ASAP," Hardy explained. "Blind Bat Zero-One was laying flares over the Sepong river ford last night just inside the Laotian border and caught five trucks in the open, all headed for South Vietnam. When they went in for a second run, they caught heavy triple A. The detachment commander, Colonel Robertson, was flying in the left seat and was wounded. I just got the word to assume command and need to get there before they launch tonight."

Four months later, Blind Bat 01 would be shot down over the same area.

Warren had flown more Blind Bat missions than any other pilot in the 374th and knew how important the detachment commander was in coordinating the C-130 flare mission with Specter, the AC-130 gunship that was just coming on line. The Blind Bat pilots also had a wealth of operational knowledge that was proving invaluable for the gunship crews. "Ubon is not that far from NKP," Warren said. "I'll request a diversion when we're airborne. We'll get you there."

"Make it happen," Hardy said. He looked around for a headset. "And I want everyone's survival vests zipped."

Santos had overheard the entire conversation from the navigator's station. "And fuck you very much," he said over the intercom before Hardy could hear him.

Warren felt the navigator's frustration but ignored him as he settled into the aircraft commander's seat. He quickly strapped in and looked out his left forward quarter panel, searching for the loadmaster. Flanders was standing in front of the aircraft, tethered to a long communications cord. He gave Warren the start sign, indicating the props were clear. "Starting three," Warren said.

Mike Hale, the flight engineer, reached for the overhead panel and fed bleed air from the Gas Turbine Compressor, the auxiliary power unit embedded in the left wheel well beneath engine two, into the right inboard right engine on the other side of the aircraft. The big three-bladed prop spun up and the engine came on line with a roar. Flanders pointed to number four and Hale used bleed air from number three to start it. The flight engineer shut down the GTC and Flanders scrambled to button up its intake panel while number four spun up. Number four had barely come on speed when Flanders was back out in front, giving them the signal to crank number two engine.

The Trash Haulers

They were a well-rehearsed team and number one was on line and they were ready to taxi out within minutes. Bosko called ground control for permission to taxi, and Flanders motioned them out of the revetment. Warren taxied the big cargo plane out and turned onto the taxipath. Flanders gave the aircraft one last look, looking for leaks and a cut tire. Satisfied they were good to go, he ran to the rear of the aircraft and scrambled on board.

Hardy had found a headset and was standing behind the copilot, watching the routine. "You're rushing the checklist," he said over the intercom, implying the engine start and taxi out was not safe.

"Strictly by the book," Warren replied. He almost said that they had to be fast when things went critical in forward landing strips but thought better of it. "Please strap in so we can get this show on the road," he said, effectively ordering the lieutenant colonel off the flight deck.

Hardy froze and his eye's narrowed. "I'll play copilot on this one. Lieutenant Bosko, if you'd be so kind to move." As detachment commander, he had the authority to move crewmembers around.

"You're the boss," Warren said. He hit the brakes and stopped on the taxiway until they two men switched places. Bosko gave Warren a warning look and disappeared into the cargo compartment.

Flanders checked in from the cargo compartment. "Lieutenant Bosko is strapped in. We're good to go in the rear." Warren released the brakes and nudged the inboard throttles up, taxiing on two and three. He played with the four throttles, varying the rpm and power as they taxied out. The long-bladed props responded with a definite beat; Dah-da, dah-da-da-da-da-da. The Hercules was humming the Colonel Bogey March.

"Strangle that," Hardy ordered. He was on a roll. "And I was not impressed with Sergeant Flanders's passenger briefing. I seriously doubt that our passengers are fully cognizant of all relevant safety procedures." Hardy prided himself on his clear diction that sounded like a formal report.

"They're ready for the test," Flanders replied over the intercom, adding a belated "sir."

Hale shot Warren a wry grin. They waited while Hardy ran through the checklist. "Before takeoff checklist complete," he finally said.

"Let's go," Warren said. Hardy just looked at him. "Call for takeoff clearance," Warren added.

The tower cleared then to taxi into position on runway 02 Right and to hold. Cam Ranh Bay was located on the northern end of the peninsula that formed the bay and the parallel runways cut across the narrowest part, separating the main base from the mainland. They were taking off to the north, with the bay and the mainland on their left, the base on their right, and the beach and open water straight ahead. Then, "Roscoe Two-One, cleared for takeoff." Warren advanced the throttles and the props dug into the air. Without a cargo, the Hercules accelerated quickly, touching eighty knots just after passing the thousand-foot marker. Warren held it on the ground as the weight came off the nose gear.

"Liftoff," Hardy called.

Warren still held it on the ground, gaining speed before pulling back on the yoke, lifting the nose up sharply. "Gear up," he called. Hardy's left hand reached for the gear handle on the instrument panel and flicked the handle to the up position.

"Small arms fire!" the tower radioed. "Departure end of the runway! Mainland side!" Warren didn't hesitate and he wracked the big bird into a hard right turn, turning away from the mainland and cutting across the main base, heading for open water. He looked across the cockpit and out the windows on Hardy's right side. Certain they were clear of the ground and accelerating, he steepened the bank, dropping the right wing even lower and hardening up the turn, away from the threat.

"Roll out!" Hardy shouted.

Warren held the turn for another three seconds before rolling out, now ninety degrees from the runway heading. He headed for open water and safety. "Flaps up," he called. "Okay troops, check for battle damage." Warren called for the checklist and they cleaned up the airplane, still climbing over open water. Warren ran a controllability check and breathed in relief as the big bird responded normally.

Flanders was back on the intercom, "Okay in the rear."

"All systems good," Hale, the flight engineer, said.

Warren relaxed and turned on course, heading to the north, still over water. "All things considered, let's stay offshore as long as possible."

"Exactly what type of takeoff was that?" Hardy demanded.

"A safe one, Colonel."

"I don't need any smart-ass replies," Hardy shot back.

"We can talk about it on the ground," Warren said. "Navigator, ETA for NKP."

Santos had the numbers. "One-hour fifty-minutes en route time. ETA, 1050 local time." He couldn't help himself. "Hey, the barber shop will be open, and we'll miss the noon-time rush."

Quang Tri Province, South Vietnam

The American crawled through the heavy foliage on the lower slope of the karst that rose two hundred feet above him. He inched his way forward, careful to maintain his camouflage, finding a break where he could see into the valley below him. A long line of porters snaked down the main trail in broad daylight. Most were in pairs with a pole slung between their shoulders, carrying a heavy bundle dangling from the middle of the pole, while the other porters pushed heavily laden bicycles.

He focused his binoculars on the bicycles, trying to identify their cargo. It had to be important if they were moving in broad daylight. Finally, he caught a glimpse of the lettering on a wooded case. Mortars. A squad of ten soldiers moved past, also heavily laden. It had all the earmarks of an attack and there was only one target, the nearby Special Forces camp at Se Pang, less than three kilometers to the east.

He checked his watch. An air strike was scheduled to plaster the valley in forty-two minutes, and he had to rejoin his team hiding on top of the karst before the attack. It was a simple plan that called for a helicopter to dart in under the cover of the airstrike to pick up his six-man team while the North Vietnamese ducked for cover. It was gutsy, but it had worked very well in the past. His team was in position and hunkered down, waiting for the pickup, and, normally, he would have been with them. However, the totally unexpected heavy movement across the border demanded he take a look. He had seen all he needed but he had to rejoin his team. He froze as two North Vietnamese emerged from the underbrush and stopped less than twenty feet away. They had scrambled up the karst to watch the men and women moving along the trail.

Fortunately, their backs were to him and he was deep in the heavy foliage. He recognized the taller of the two, Colonel Tran San Quan, and forced his breathing to slow, worried that any movement, however slight, might give his position away. Tran was a well-known commodity in his life and he had a deep respect for the colonel. He studied the shorter, very corpulent colonel standing next to Tran, wondering who he was.

He strained to listen, hoping for a clue. Again, luck was with him and he had no trouble understanding Tran who spoke with a clear and precise voice, probably the result of his Parisian education. The short colonel was another story and slurred his words with a heavy accent the American had never heard. It was obvious that Tran deferred to the man but had little respect for him, another clue. Then he heard the name – Colonel Dinh. The name surprised the American for Dinh Hung Dung was infamous as a hatchet man for the regime in Hanoi and had no business being in Laos, unless he was going after Tran's scalp.

That didn't make sense as Tran was the best commander the North Vietnamese had in southern Laos. He gave a mental shrug. It was all above his pay grade but the presence of Dinh and the movement of supplies and men forward had to be reported soonest. However, radio silence was critical to his survival and he had to make the rendezvous with the helicopter, which would leave without him. It had happened before and he was perfectly capable of evading capture and walking out on his own. *Move on!* the American mentally urged, not moving.

Dinh rewarded him for his patience. "Will you be in position in time?"

"We will be ready," Tran assured him. "You can see for yourself how the cadre moves forward. They are dedicated and willing to make the sacrifices needed to defeat the Americans."

"Which, I suspect, is why you brought me here," Dinh replied.

"Come, we have more to see," Tran told the older man. He pushed his way back into the undergrowth, hurrying back down the slope. Dinh was right behind him. They broke out onto a narrow footpath that ran parallel to the valley along the base of the karst where two women were waiting for them. Without a word, Tran motioned for a walkie-talkie, a leftover from the French at Dien Ben Phu, and hit the transmit button. "Send Captain Lam and a squad to me. Now." He gave his position and broke the transmission. "We are being watched," he explained. "There is an American above us."

Dinh stared at him. "An American? How do you know?"

"I could smell him," Tran replied. "Since he did not kill us, he is probably only an observer, here to monitor our activity. But he might be what the Americans call a forward air controller, which means we can expect an air attack."

The Trash Haulers

Dinh didn't believe what he was hearing. "And you know all this simply because you smelled him? Ridiculous." Another thought came to him. "And was it a coincidence that we were there at the same time as the American?"

"We were there because that is the best point to observe the valley and the terrain," Tran replied. "Which, I suspect, is why he was there."

"And you deliberately put me in danger?"

"No, of course not." Tran pointed to the west. "Right now, our greatest danger is coming from that direction." He thought for a moment. He closed his eyes, pulling into himself. The decision made, he keyed the walkie-talkie. "Initiate Alarm Red. Expect an air attack shortly."

Dinh was furious. "Alarm Red? Doesn't that mean everyone seeks cover? You have effectively cancelled the attack."

Tran ignored him as Captain Lam and a squad of six men jogged up the path. Tran quickly explained the situation. "Captain Lam, there is an observer spying on us. He was hiding in the bush a hundred meters in that direction." Tran pointed to where they had been. "But he may be moving, probably to the plateau on top of the ridge above us. He is not alone. Also, I expect an air attack shortly. If he is in radio contact, he may direct the bombs on his pursuers. We have seen this before and I expect to hear a helicopter once the attack starts. I want him alive. Be careful." The young army captain acknowledged his orders and quickly led his men into the brush.

Dinh's eyes narrowed as his head tilted slightly to the right. The pleasant scene of Tran shaking violently at the end of a hangman's rope played in his mind's eye.

Richard Herman

* * * *

The American scrambled over the edge of the karst and onto the plateau where his team was hidden. He didn't hesitate and ran for the far side as an F-4 Phantom streaked overhead. He was certain that someone was trailing him and not far behind. He dove into the brush and rolled into a shallow depression where his team was waiting. "Glad you could join us, Captain," one of the men said. The captain's reply was drowned out as four five-hundred pound bombs rippled across the valley below them. A green and brown camouflaged helicopter appeared over the crest of the karst, on the side opposite the attack, and settled onto the clearing in front of the team. It was a Sikorsky HH-53, the fabled Super Jolly Green Giant search and rescue helicopter flown by the 56th Air Commando Wing out of Nakhon Phanom.

The six men broke from cover just as the clatter of AK-47s erupted from the far side of the plateau. The Jolly Green lifted into the air and spun, bringing its heavy machine gun to bear on the attackers while the men ran up the rear ramp. The helicopter backed over the edge of the karst, leaving a heavy trail of smoke in its wake.

0900 HOURS

I Corps, South Vietnam

Tanner squinted, scanning the terrain, trying to find a familiar landmark that pointed the way to Firebase Lonzo. Nothing. He pulled a chart out of the helmet bag, pinpointed the fuel dump and the firebase, glanced at his watch, and checked their compass heading and airspeed. He ran the numbers in his head, doing basic pilotage: fifteen minutes to go.

"Myers, Collins," Tanner said, talking to the crew chief and medic in the back, "ever been to Lonzo?" Both replied in the negative.

"Okay, it's a marine firebase on top of a karst formation." Karsts are limestone mountain formations that rise high into the air with steep sides, numerous caves, sinkholes, and underground streams. "It's about six hundred feet above a river valley that pretty well interdicts the North Vietnamese from moving west in that area. They need to take it out big time. We'll be okay on the ground, but getting in and out might get a little sporting."

"Sporting?" Perkins asked.

"Ground fire," Tanner replied.

"Oh. That kind of sporting," Perkins said. Tanner's confidence in the young pilot went up a notch.

"You've got the controls," Tanner said, telling Perkins to fly the aircraft.

"I've got the controls," Perkins replied.

Tanner twisted around and saw the waypoint he was looking for, a distinctive jagged hook-like peak at the end of a north-south karst formation. They were left of course but on time. "I've got the controls," he told Perkins, again going through the routine. He gently increased the collective, gaining altitude. He checked his watch. "We're seven minutes out, see if we've got radio contact on the FM."

"Firebase Lonzo," Perkins transmitted. "Dust Off Two-Seven, seven minutes out for a pickup. Say numbers."

A scratchy voice answered. "Roger that, Dust Off. LZ is cold. We have one litter and two ambulatory. Be advised, heavy smoke is in the area."

"Will call when we have you in sight," Perkins radioed, breaking the transmission. "Where did the smoke come from?" he wondered.

"Probably the Gomers," Tanner replied. "They like to hide in the smoke, but it should be well below us in the valley."

"Will they be able to see us?" Perkins asked. "Maybe we can sneak in unobserved."

"Don't bet on it. They've got observers hiding above the smoke, probably on the side of a karst."

"Clever devils," Perkins groused. They flew in silence, studying the heavy jungle below them, looking for telltale signs of dust on the top of the canopy that indicated activity below. Nothing. "This is the farthest south I've been," Perkins admitted.

"You definitely don't want to go down around here," Tanner cautioned.

Perkins pulled a face. "I think I knew that."

Tanner was starting to like his copilot. But it was testing time. "We're five out. I'll take this one, you handle the radios."

"Roger," Perkins said. He keyed the FM radio. "Lonzo, Dust Off Two-Seven five minutes out for one litter and two ambulatories. Smoke out."

The same voice was there, this time much stronger. "Smoke is out." Ahead of them, yellow smoke marked the top of a very high karst formation.

"Smoke in sight," Tanner said over the intercom.

"Smoke in sight," Perkins radioed.

"LZ is cold," Lonzo replied, telling the crew that the landing zone was not under attack and they could land.

That was what they wanted to hear and Tanner headed for the smoke that was on their nose. "Hold on," Tanner said as he started to jink the helicopter with small random heading and altitude changes to discourage any gunners on the ground from tracking them. As if on cue, a short burst of tracers missed them wide and to the right.

"Tracers in daytime?" Perkins wondered.

"They're shooting in the blind," Myers, the crew chief, explained. "They use tracers so an observer can correct their aim."

Lonzo was on the radio. "Dust Off Two-Seven, I do not have you in sight."

Tanner slammed the helicopter down just as a line of tracers arced over them. He jinked a few more times before pulling up. A short burst of tracers followed them, again missing.

"I have more yellow smoke at our two o'clock," Perkins said over the intercom, his voice amazingly calm. "On top of a karst, two miles, now at our three o'clock." He keyed the FM radio. "Lonzo, pop more smoke and say color."

Almost immediately, green smoke erupted from the yellow smoke at their three o'clock position. "Green is out," Lonzo replied.

"Got it," Tanner said, as they turned away from the first karst still billowing yellow smoke. Now green smoke mixed in with the yellow, mimicking the real firebase. The North Vietnamese had set a very clever trap to lure a helicopter to the wrong karst and into a flak trap. "Those fuckers are good," Tanner muttered. The top of the karst erupted in explosions as Firebase Lonzo walked an artillery barrage across the flak trap.

"Some one down there is having a very bad day," Perkins said.

"Could have been us," Tanner replied, concentrating on the approach. The marines had built the firebase at the end of a long limestone ridge that jutted into a river valley. Erosion had down cut through the ridge and broken the ridge into a series of peaks resembling jagged teeth, isolating the last peak that overlooked the river valley, which allowed the firebase to bring artillery to bear on any river traffic. It was an interdiction tactic that stretched back to when the ancient Hittites first smote the Egyptians, and only the weapons and logistics had changed.

The Trash Haulers

Tanner slowed the Huey and touched down on the small clearing that served as a helipad for Firebase Lonzo. Helicopters had airlifted a company of marines onto the top of the karst, along with a battery of howitzers and heavy mortars, and kept it resupplied. It was only matter of seconds before they could expect incoming fire from the North Vietnamese in the valley below. Collins and Myers jumped out of the Huey and motioned two waiting Navy corpsmen to onload the litter patient. The two ambulatory wounded were right behind them. While Collins strapped the litter down, Myers and the corpsman helped the wounded marines on board.

Within seconds, they were ready to go and Collins was back on the intercom. "We've got their wounded," he said, echoing the words of Major Charles Kelly, the helicopter pilot who turned the helicopter ambulance service into the aggressive and highly effective Dust Off mission. Kelly was killed in action on July 1, 1964, after being warned off a hot LZ. He disregarded the warning and replied, "When I have your wounded." That had set the standard ever since.

Tanner turned and gave the medic a thumbs up. The triumphant look on Collins's face said it all; the reason they were there was on board. "Where do we find them?" Tanner murmured to himself as he lifted the Huey into the air and spun it around, heading for the edge of the karst. He cleared the rim and headed down, trading altitude for airspeed. Immediately, he jinked to the right, back to the left, then right again as they headed to the northeast.

"Collins, where to? Evans or Phu Bai?" Tanner asked. The Army relied on Battalion Aid Stations for emergency stabilizing surgery and then evacuation to a Mobile Army

Surgical Hospital, or MASH, made famous by the TV series M*A*S*H*. Dust Off aircrews had learned through bitter experience that the first sixty minutes was critical.

"Camp Evans," the medic answered.

"Got it," Tanner replied. With a little luck, they could make Camp Evans fifteen miles north of Hue without refueling and have their charges in good hands within the "Golden Hour." From there, it was a short hop to their base at Phu Bai, twenty-five miles to the southeast.

"Have you ever seen them use fake smoke before?" Perkins asked.

"That's a new one," Tanner conceded. "They lured us right in. Luckily, you saw it. I didn't have a clue. That was good thinking on calling for different colored smoke. It got us going in the right direction and gave Lonzo a target. We need to brief Intel ASAP." *And the CO*, he thought. Perkins had potential.

Over South Vietnam

The drone of the engines filled the flight deck as the Hercules leveled off and headed north, sixteen miles off the coast. Satisfied that all was well, Warren kicked back in his seat and closed his eyes to take a short break or even a quick nap, if he was lucky. It was a habit he had picked up from his first aircraft commander, a grizzled trash hauler with over 10,000 hours flying time, and it helped keep him rested and alert during a long crew duty day.

The VHF radio blared in his headset. "Roscoe Two-One, Qui Nhon ALCE." The Airlift Command Element at Qui Nhon was about half way between Cam Ranh Bay and Da Nang, and Warren figured they were being diverted into

The Trash Haulers

Ubon to drop Hardy off. As the lieutenant colonel was still playing copilot, Warren decided to let him handle the call.

"ALCE," Hardy answered, "Roscoe Two-One. Go ahead."

"Roscoe Two-One, you are diverted to Da Nang. Shut down engines and report into Tactical Operations Center for tasking ASAP."

"Copy all," Hardy replied, not showing his frustration.

Warren gave Hardy good marks for sounding good on the radios. Warren ran his seat forward to take control and adjusted his headset. "That's not the diversion I was expecting," he said over the intercom. "Now it gets interesting."

The flight engineer, Tech Sgt Mike Hale, looked worried. "Problems, sir?"

"I'm guessing the situation has gone critical," Warren answered, taking a verbal jab at Hardy.

"We just do what we're told," Hardy said, salvaging what he could.

Warren ignored him and spoke to the loadmaster in the cargo compartment. "Sergeant Flanders, tell the passengers that we are diverting into Da Nang, and ask Captains Slovack and Huckabee to please come with us to Tac Ops."

"Is that necessary?" Hardy asked.

"Sure is," Warren replied. "Something is going down, and Huck and Judy are the only folks around here who seem to have a clue. I want their input." Hardy stared straight ahead and didn't reply. An inner voice told Warren to force the issue now. "Colonel Hardy, I would appreciate your coming along also."

Hardy stared at him, not believing what he had just heard. "That's not your call, Captain."

"Sir, you're on the passenger manifest, not the crew for this flight." Every member on the crew knew that Warren had thrown the gauntlet, and he had done it in the open. Warren was the aircraft commander and the crew had been ordered to report to Tac Ops, most probably for special tasking, and as long as Warren was the aircraft commander, he, not Hardy, would make any decision regarding his crew and the C-130.

However, as the C-130 detachment commander at Cam Ranh Bay, Hardy could always relieve Warren as aircraft commander, but that meant Hardy would have to take over from a captain who was regarded, with good reason, as the best pilot in the 374th. Further, Hardy was under orders to report to Ubon in Thailand, so he couldn't stay with the aircraft. It would take a day or two to sort out the confusion and get the C-130 back hauling cargo with a new aircraft commander, and that wasn't something Hardy wanted to explain to his wing commander on Okinawa.

"Good point," Hardy replied, conceding the issue. "Time to let Lieutenant Bosko earn his pay," Hardy took off his headset and ran the seat back, finished with playing copilot. The men were silent until the lieutenant colonel had climbed down the ladder and disappeared into the cargo compartment.

"I can hardly wait to see your next OER.," Santos said. An OER, or Officer's Efficiency Report, was the annual evaluation that determined an officer's suitability for promotion. "You're toast."

The Trash Haulers

"What are they gonna do," Warren replied. "Send me to Vietnam?"

Santos cracked a smile. "Da Nang in twenty-two minutes, 0950 local," he said, giving them an ETA.

The VHF radio came alive. "Roscoe Two-One, Da Nang. Cleared for the approach, Runway Three-Five. Hostile fire in local area. Keep feet wet to a right hand base. Avoid all boat traffic."

"Roscoe Two-One copies all," Bosko replied.

"That makes sense," Warren said. Da Nang's tower had told them to stay over water and approach from the west and minimize their time over land before landing. "We'll do it hot." He turned onto the base leg as they descended and pushed up the throttles, touching 160 knots indicated airspeed. He sawed at the control yoke, jinking the big aircraft back and forth to discourage any gunner's aim.

"Roscoe Two-One," Da Nang tower radioed, "Cleared to land. Land long and taxi clear of the runway ASAP."

"Cleared to land," Bosko replied. "Landing long." The two pilots were a well-rehearsed team and they came down final, with the C-130's nose high in the air. Warren slammed the big bird onto the runway, throwing the props into reverse before the nose gear was down. "Shut down one and four," he ordered as they taxied in.

Da Nang Air Base, South Vietnam

"Nice landing," Bosko allowed as the outboard props spun down. "I'm guessing 1400 feet."

"Captain Warren has done it in less than 1200," Hale, the flight engineer said, primarily for Hardy's benefit, who he knew was on headset and monitoring the approach and landing.

Santos stood behind the copilot's seat and looked out the right window. "Sum'bitch! Check out the smoke. They took a few rockets."

"More than a few," Warren replied. They were quickly marshaled to an open revetment where a crew chief was waiting. Warren spun the Hercules around with its tail pointing into the revetment. "Scanner on the ramp," he called. Stuffing the C-130 into a revetment without a tug was a well-practiced drill at Cam Ranh Bay, but this was a first time for Da Nang.

Flanders had already raised the rear door and lowered the loading ramp to the level position, opening up the rear of the cargo deck. "Clear in the rear." Warren threw the inboard props into reverse and backed into the revetment. "Slow, slow, stop," Flanders directed over the intercom.

Warren called for the engine shutdown checklist as a crew van drove up. A sergeant jumped out and waved for them to hurry. "Okay, folks," Warren said. "I believe a sense of urgency is required here. Sergeant Hale, please top off the fuel at 20,000 pounds, and cock the bird for a quick engine start. Let's go." He led Bosko and Santos off the flight deck and out the crew entrance door. Hardy, Huckabee, and Slovack were in close trail. Much to every one's surprise, Lynne Pender was the last one to climb into the waiting crew van. Warren gave the doctor his best grin. "Welcome to the war, Captain. What happened to the Golden Spirochete?"

s"Fuck off," she answered.

"Pun intended?" Santos quipped.

Hardy shot Warren his standard look of disapproval. "Maintaining good order, Captain?"

Quang Tri Province, South Vietnam

Kim-Ly spoke in an unusually loud voice, primarily for Dinh's benefit, without referring to the clipboard she held in the crook of her arm. "Our loses were minimal as most of the cadre had time to respond to the Alarm Red. Unfortunately, six of our gallant comrades were caught in the open by the first attack. The second Air Pirate's bombs fell harmlessly."

"And what was destroyed?" Dinh demanded, more concerned about the loss of material.

Again, Kim-Ly spoke without consulting her notes. "Two-hundred liters of petrol, approximately one-hundred kilos of rations, two bicycles, and three Type 53 mortar tubes with forty-three projectiles." The Chinese Type 53 mortar was based on the excellent Soviet BM-37, 82mm mortar. It was the "infantrymen's artillery" and very effective in the hands of a trained crew. Because of its relatively light weight and portability, it was highly valued by the North Vietnamese. She waited for Dinh's reaction.

Dinh drew himself up to his full five foot two inches. "That is unacceptable. General Dong has issued strict orders that those responsible for the loss of any crew-served weapon will be executed by hanging in front of the assembled comrades."

"That will be difficult," Kim-Ly replied, "but I'm sure we can arrange something."

"And why should that be difficult?" Dinh demanded.

"Because those responsible were the six comrades caught in the open by the Air Pirate's bombs. They were trying to carry the mortars to safety. I'm sure we can find one or two bodies that still have a head attached."

Dinh turned to Tran. "This woman is insubordinate."

"Is the truth insubordinate, Colonel?" Dinh didn't answer. "How many wounded?"

Again," Kim-Ly answered without looking at her notes, "we were fortunate. Twenty-one with minor wounds and burns who can return to work. Only three have major wounds and will not survive."

Tran made the decision he hated. "Hide them."

For once, Dinh's outrage came from his heart. "No! I will not allow that. They should be seen and honored by the comrades for their sacrifice."

Tran spoke in a low voice. "Colonel Dinh, we are on the move, pushing ahead rapidly, and our medical teams are well behind us. We cannot properly treat our badly wounded in the field. It is called triage and we must leave them to die. Please remember my men and women are simple people from the countryside, not the highly motivated principals, such as yourself, of Hanoi. The comrades can deal with the death they see, but it will destroy their morale to see wounded left unattended to die."

"There is dignity in such sacrifice," Dinh said.

"Is there dignity in screaming in pain and begging for your mother?" Tran asked. Dinh fell silent and motioned for his three aides to follow him outside. They needed to talk. Tran waited silently until the sound of the four men blundering down the steep hillside died away. He turned to

The Trash Haulers

Kim-Ly, standing close but not touching. He drew comfort from her musky scent. "Were the six men killed the ones who were carrying mortars?"

"Of course not. fThere will be enough killing today without adding to it."

They heard Dinh struggling up the hillside long before he burst into the command post. "How long has the captain been back?" he demanded.

Tran motioned at Lam. The young captain was bent over a chart with Kim-Ly talking quietly. "Less than five minutes, Colonel. Thank you for coming so quickly." He stood and motioned for Dinh to join him by the chart. "Captain Lam, please give Colonel Dinh your combat report."

The captain spoke quietly. "We tracked the American to this location." He pointed to a small plateau on the top of a nearby karst. "There, he rendezvoused with his team. We were still maneuvering into position when we heard the sound of the attacking jet fighters; two F-4C Phantoms, tail code FY."

"Ah," Tran said. "The 555th Tactical Fighter Squadron."

"Is this detail important?" Dinh snapped. "Get to the cause of your failure."

Tran wished Dinh would shut up and try to learn something. "It is imperative to know the enemy," he intoned, repeating a basic truth of combat. "The 555th is the Triple Nickel, who normally fly combat air patrol seeking out MiGs. The fact that they are flying close air support

75

indicates the Americans are over extended. Captain Lam, please continue."

"It was a coordinated attack to provide protection for the helicopter to extract the Americans. It was the helicopter the Americans call the Jolly Green Giant. I counted six Americans boarding the helicopter."

Dinh was beside himself with righteous anger. "You could not destroy six Americans and a helicopter? Are they supermen? Do they carry magical weapons?"

Without hesitation, the young captain replied, "We opened fire on the helicopter, revealing our position. The helicopter pivoted and brought its .50 caliber machine gun to bear, driving us to cover. However, we continued to return fire. The helicopter escaped over the edge of the plateau. It was trailing smoke."

Dinh was triumphant. "So you did not fail and destroyed it."

"I cannot report it destroyed," Lam replied, "only that it appeared to be hit and was trailing smoke."

"And what can we assume from this?" Dinh demanded.

Tran answered. "As it was a Jolly Green Giant, we can assume that it landed at its base at Nakhon Phanom in Thailand. As the good Colonel knows, Nakhon Phanom is the home of the 56th Air Commando Wing. We can assume they will send aircraft to attack."

The reality of what they were up against finally reached Dinh. He sat down. "So we must take protective cover and postpone the attack on Se Pang."

"Maybe not," Kim-Ly replied. The men looked at her. "May I suggest that our main force take protective cover for now but continue to move our Sergey forward and into

The Trash Haulers

position. The Americans will understand that our objective is to destroy the Special Forces compound and will concentrate their defensive forces there. Our Sergey will be there, waiting for them." The Sergey was a twin-barrel ZSU-23mm anti-aircraft autocannon that was feared by aircrews for good reason. Normally it was towed behind a vehicle, but this particular ZSU-23 was disassembled and carried on the backs of men. They needed time to get it into place and reassembled.

"Make it happen," Tran said.

Reluctantly, Dinh agreed. "Please message General Dong of your decision." Kim-Ly nodded. But she would send two messages.

1000 HOURS

Da Nang Air Base, South Vietnam

The crew van slammed to a halt in front of the sandbag revetment that surrounded the low building that served as tactical operations. The seven officers piled out and ran inside. A harried-looking sergeant rushed them into a mission planning room where an intelligence officer, a lieutenant colonel wearing jungle fatigues, was bent over the flight-planning table. He looked up and grunted in approval when he saw Huckabee and Slovack. "I'll be damned, someone with a clue." He motioned them to gather around the table that was topped with a plexiglass-covered map of Southeast Asia. "We've got a Jolly Green chopper out of Naked Fanny down near Ban Naphilang." He pointed to a village in central Laos. "We need to extract the crew and you're all we've got. I'm talking like immediate extraction fifteen minutes ago." He spread out a much larger-scale chart. "They are on the east end of a dirt landing strip."

Warren and Santos bent over the two charts, studying the location. "The strip has got maybe 2000 feet," Warren said. "That's doable." He looked at his navigator. "Dave?"

"I can find it. Sixty-five nautical miles east-northeast of Savannakhet." Savannakhet was the second largest town in Laos. He ran the numbers. "One hundred forty-five nautical miles from Da Nang, forty minutes flying time."

"You need to get the crew and cargo to Naked Fanny ASAP," the intelligence officer said.

"Fifteen minutes to NKP," Santos said. "Piece of cake."

Hardy shook his head. "Savannahket is on the Mekong and might be in friendly hands, but the Ho Chi Minh trail is in the eastern part of the province." He tapped the chart, his finger striking the village. "And Ban Naphilang is smack-dab in the middle of the trail."

Huckabee stepped up to a big wall chart and found the village. "Negative, Colonel." He used a wooden pointer to trace a mountain ridge that ran from the northwest to the southeast, cutting Laos in half. "This is the *Chaîne Annamitique* mountains. The Ho Chi Minh trail is on the northern side of the mountains and Savannahket Province is to the south." He pointed to a break in the mountain chain. "This is the Ban Nap pass. Ban Naphilang and the landing strip are on the southern side of the pass, more or less in neutral territory."

Hardy wasn't having any of it. "More or less? I'm not about to risk one of my C-130s on a 'more or less' just to salvage some cargo."

"Is the cargo Heavy Hook?" Huckabee asked. The Intel officer answered with a nod.

"What the hell is Heavy Hook?" Hardy demanded.

80

The Trash Haulers

Huckabee considered his answer. "It's an intelligence gathering operation. They must have something." The short and wiry officer stared at the floor, thinking. "Casualties?"

"Ten on board," the Intel officer answered. "Two KIA, eight WIA, two seriously."

"How long ago did they go down?" Warren asked.

"Approximately ninety minutes ago, definitely less than two hours."

"The Gomers will get to them before we do," Hardy snapped.

Huckabee ran the numbers, casting a time and distance problem against the capabilities of the North Vietnamese. "Assuming the Pathet Lao are talking to the North Vietnamese, which is always questionable, I'm guessing we've got an hour." Huckabee looked at Warren, waiting for a decision.

"I can help," Lynne said. Warren started to object, but she wasn't having it. "I'm a trauma surgeon, and you've got a great first aid kit on board. Let me use it."

Hardy was genuinely shocked. "Where did that come from?"

"Sergeant Flanders scrounged it up," Bosko relied. Crew chiefs, flight engineers, and maintenance specialists often rat holed spare parts and critical items for quick fixes to keep their aircraft flying. The joke was that a good 'scrounge' was worth five supply officers, and a scrounge often contained ten to twenty thousand dollars worth of spare parts. While highly illegal, scrounges kept aircraft flying. Staff Sergeant Glen "Flash" Flanders had simply created a loadmaster's version of a scrounge.

81

"In my Air Force a scrounge of any kind means a court martial," Hardy said.

"Sir," Bosko said, "do you have any idea how many wounded we've evacuated?" He was being respectful. "Sergeant Flanders scrounged up a first aid kit worth the name so we could save a few lives. It has made a difference."

Warren made the decision. "If there's wounded, we're going."

"Disapproved," Hardy said.

"Sir," Warren said, "may we speak outside?" Without waiting for an answer, he spun around and walked into the hall.

Hardy followed, closing the door behind them. "Well, Captain?"

"Sir, we don't abandon wounded in the field. As long as I'm the aircraft commander, we're going. Otherwise, relieve me."

Hardy stared at him – hard. He quickly ran two possible scenarios through his mental abacus of command. Both involved him standing in front of their wing commander in Okinawa as he explained what happened. "Okay, you got it, Captain."

Warren pushed at the door, but it was blocked by Santos and Busko who had their ears glued to the other side. "Let's go," Warren called. He made a show of checking his watch. "Gear up on the hour." He spun around and headed for the entrance. Slovack, Bosko, Santos, and Huckabee were right behind him.

Pender brushed past Hardy. "Are you coming?" Hardy shook his head. "Pity," she murmured, her eyes full of contempt. Hardy froze at her look. He was a man who worried about his image, especially to senior officers, and had deliberately flown into danger on Blind Bat night flare missions risking his life and his crew to prove his bravery. Yet, Lynne Pender had taken his measure and found him wanting. It cut deep for she was an outsider. He had to prove her wrong.

"Yeah, I had better go along and keep my troops out of trouble."

"Captain Warren can do that, Colonel."

Suddenly, Hardy hated Warren for the way others trusted and followed him. "I'm not what you think," he said, leading the way outside.

"Yes, you are," the doctor said to his back.

Quang Tri Province, South Vietnam

The radio operator pressed his left hand against his headphone as he jotted down the alpha-numeric message. Finished, he ripped off the sweaty headset, dried his hands, and reached for the decode book. He found the current page, quickly decoded the message, and handed it to Tran.

"Very good, Comrade Nguyen," Tran said. The young soldier beamed at the compliment and made a mental promise to do it quicker, and as correct, next time. Tran read the message twice to be sure he had the right location. He had never heard of it. He stepped to the chart on the map table and handed the message to Kim-Ly. She found the village first.

"Colonel Dinh," Tran called softly. "This is of extreme interest." Dinh joined them at the map table, still holding a cup of tea. Tran pointed at the village Kim-Ly had circled with a pencil. "The Pathet Lao report a Jolly Green Giant helicopter crashed at an airstrip two kilometers north of the village of Ban Naphilang."

For once, Dinh understood what he was seeing. "The Pathet Lao are in marginal control of the area. But is it the same helicopter?"

"The time and place are too coincidental," Tran replied. "I think we can safely assume it is the same helicopter."

"And what do you recommend?" Dinh said, his voice low and toneless.

"We ask our Pathet Lao comrades to destroy the helicopter and proceed with the attack."

"Yes, do that," Dinh said.

"I will send the message," Kim-Ly said.

Dinh studied the chart. "And have you delayed too long to attack when I wanted?"

"We will move forward," Tran promised.

"I will tolerate no more delays," Dinh warned.

Kim-Ly decided she would send a second message as soon as Dinh left the command post.

"Colonel Dinh," Tran said, "we must move forward with our comrades."

Dinh almost ordered his chief-of-staff, Major Cao, to go forward while he returned to the Binh Tram in Laos, but thought better of it. Cao was a very-well connected politburo hack, the scion of a prominent Hanoi family, and Dinh knew he must not appear cowardly. And there was something about the woman that worried him. Better that Cao stay behind and keep an eye on her.

The Trash Haulers

I Corps, South Vietnam

"I can't stop the bleeding," Hal Collins, the medic, shouted over the intercom. "We gotta get on the ground ASAP."

Tanner twisted around in his seat to check on his wounded. Collins was bent over his litter patient, applying pressure to the marine's chest. Tanner quickly checked the fuel gauge and ran the numbers; they had 120 pounds of fuel remaining for thirteen minutes flying time. He glanced at the radio compass and VOR: on course and twenty miles to go to Camp Evans. "Collins, I don't think we can make Evans. We gotta land for fuel."

"I don't think he'll make it if we do, Mr. Tanner."

Perkins tapped Tanner on the shoulder and pointed at his one o'clock position. Two Hueys were taking off from a fuel dump. Automatically, Perkins cycled the FM searching for a clear channel, but every frequency was jammed.

Tanner made the decision. They could always land short of Camp Evans for fuel starvation, but that would be a death sentence for the marine. Better to take a few extra minutes to refuel and chance he could hold on. "We'll take on a partial load, minimum time on the ground." He headed for the fuel dump as another Huey cut in from his left, a quarter mile in front. As they approached, he could see three Hueys on the ground, refueling.

The Huey that had cut in front of them was out of fuel and autogyroed in for a hard landing. There would be no minimum time on the ground. On their nose, a pillar of smoke was rising to the sky. It was Camp Evans. He checked the fuel gauge again and headed for the smoke. "We're outta options and going for it," he told his crew. "It's gonna be close but I think we can make it." He slowed to

85

ninety knots as he slowly descended, going for maximum range. Another glance at the fuel gauge. The needle was bouncing off empty. "Okay, where's the landing pad?" Every eye searched for the red cross.

"Three o'clock," Perkins called.

"Got it," Tanner replied. He slowed to forty knots as they descended through 1500 feet. He lowered the collective and pulled back on the cyclic, balancing the Huey as he made a textbook descent and landing. The fuel gauge needle was dead.

The medics were waiting for them and quickly off loaded the wounded marines. Collins sat in the open door and watched them carry the litter into a nearby tent. "He's still alive," he said. They had done their job.

"Well," Tanner said, "we're not going anywhere until we get a browser here."

"I'll see what I can round up," Myers said.

Perkins snorted. "Given the confusion around here, good luck." The crew chief ran for the tents.

"I need to round up some fatigues," Tanner said, deciding it was time to at least look Army. Flying in shorts and a T-shirt was not recommended if they experienced a fire. He pulled on his fatigue cap and ambled into the tent complex, looking for a Quartermaster sergeant.

"What the hell is that?" Perkins asked when he saw Tanner.

The pilot looked down at the flight suit he was wearing. "Beats me," he said. "The corporal said it was some new material called Nomex, and they got a box of flight suits for

The Trash Haulers

field testing. They have no idea how they wound up here, and they just want to get rid of 'em. Feels kinda funny."

Perkins pinched the material around Tanner's wrist and rubbed it between his thumb and forefinger. "Feels like it's pretty warm. Does it breathe?"

"So far, not bad," Tanner conceded. He glanced at Collins and Myers who were sprawled out in the shade of a nearby tent. "How we doing on fuel?"

"Topped up and good to go," Myers said.

"Let's go," Tanner said. "Time to earn our pay." Collins and Myers jumped up and they were airborne three minutes later, headed for their base at Phu Bai, twenty-five miles to the southeast.

Again, Perkins tried to establish radio contact, but jamming and heavy transmission traffic defeated any chance of getting through. "No joy," Perkins said, conceding defeat. He scanned the horizon in front of them. "Oh, my God," he whispered, barely audible over the intercom. "Is that Hue?" All he could see was heavy smoke and flames rising above the ancient walled capital. "One hell of a fight going on down there."

Tanner diverted to the east, angling towards the South China Sea, eight miles to the east, and staying well clear of Hue. He overflew a convoy of olive-drab deuce-and-a-halfs headed for the beleaguered city before turning back on course. He knew the area like his own backyard. "Home plate on the nose at six miles," he said.

Perkins played with the radio and called their company ops. "Ops Shack, Ops Shack. Dust Off Two-Seven, six miles north. Any trade?"

A familiar voice answered. "Glad you're back, Two-Seven. We have more trade at Lonzo. Can you cover it?"

Perkins glanced at Tanner who gave him a thumbs up. "Two-Seven headed for Firebase Lonzo," Perkins radioed.

1100 HOURS

Over Laos

Santos glanced at his watch and reduced the range to ten nautical miles on the APS-59 radar. The dark shadow of a no-return with a bright leading edge, the classical radar signature of a mountain range, split the top of the scope from left to right with a bright break in the middle. The navigator grunted in satisfaction. The *Chaîne Annamitique* was on their nose and he had found the mountain pass where the Jolly Green had crashed. "Ban Nap Pass on the nose," he announced over the intercom, playing with the receiver gain and tilt controls. Then he got lucky. A narrow, very straight dark line broke out of the bright ground clutter, the unmistakable radar signature of a runway. "The air patch is at your one o'clock, four miles."

Warren and Bosko leaned forward in their seats, looking for the airstrip. "Got it," they chorused in unison.

"Well, done," Warren added. Now he had the helicopter in sight. "The Jolly Green is on the eastern end of the runway. "Boz, see if you can raise them on Guard."

The copilot dialed in 243 Mhz on the UHF radio, the emergency channel. "Jolly Green, Roscoe transmitting in the blind. How copy?"

A scratchy voice came over the radio. "Roscoe, read you three-by. Be advised hostiles are in the area. Sit cold."

Hardy was listening on the intercom. "What does that mean?"

"'Sit cold' means they're not taking fire," Warren explained.

Hardy shook his head, his voice heavy with condescension. "I know a flack trap when I hear it. Captain Bosko, have them authenticate."

One of the documents that Santos signed for was a code wheel used for challenge and response. The navigator spun the code wheel that looked like a small circular slide rule. "Alpha Hotel authenticates as Bravo," he said, reading from the code wheel.

Bosko hit the transmit button. "Jolly Green, authenticate Alpha Hotel."

The radio blared at them. "The fuckin' authenticator is on the fuckin' helicopter, asshole!"

"Sounds like a good authentication to me," Santos said.

Warren took over and radioed, "Jolly Green, pop smoke if area clear." On cue, green smoke drifted over the downed helicopter. Warren made the decision. "Okay, folks, we're going in hot on this one and landing to the west, right over the Jolly Green. Sergeant Flanders, raise the cargo door now. When the nose gear is planted on the runway, lower the ramp to the trail position and scan the rear. We're backing up big time and I want everyone lying flat on the deck and not making like a target in a shooting gallery. Get us as close to the Jolly Green as you can." He had to rely on Flanders to keep a safe distance if the helicopter exploded. "I want everyone in the rear to help get the wounded on board ASAP. Airman Boyle, you on headset?"

"Yeah, I hear you," Boyle answered.

"Do a running count so you know who is on and off the aircraft," Warren ordered. "When everyone is back on board, sweep the area and do a final head count. Sergeant Flanders will do the same and we don't go until you both agree. There's five of you back there and we're picking up eight wounded and two KIA. So make sure there are fifteen bodies on board."

"Make that sixteen," Hardy said. "I'm helping."

"Make it seventeen," Santos added. He left it to Warren to tell him not to.

"Okay," Warren said. "Let's do it." He turned onto a base leg with the short dirt runway at his ten o'clock position. The thin plume of green smoke from the downed helicopter still drifted lazily on the air, indicating the wind was calm. "Flaps twenty percent," he called, slowing the aircraft to 120 knots. A lone figure emerged from the brush on the edge of the runway and popped another flare.

"Green smoke," Bosko said. The figure disappeared back into the brush, taking cover.

"Gear down," Warren called. Bosko reached for the gear handle with his left hand as Warren jinked the aircraft back and forth. The unmistakable whine of the main gear lowering echoed from the cargo deck. Now, the rumble of the nose gear added to the noise as it clunked into the down position.

"Three in the green," Bosko called.

"Flaps fifty percent," Warren said, his voice calm. They could have been on a routine landing into Okinawa. Again, Bosko lowered the big flaps.

"Turning final," Warren said. "Flaps one-hundred percent." The flaps were acting like a barn door, extending two-thirds of the length of the wing and hanging almost straight down. He played the throttles, slowing the Hercules and coming down final on a steep glide path with the nose high in the air. It was a masterful display of airmanship as he carried power down final, hanging the big aircraft on its props, slowing to a near power-on stall.

Bosko called the airspeed. "Ninety-five knots, ninety, eighty-five, eighty . . . " The main gear slammed down just before the aircraft stalled. Warren raked the throttles aft and lifted them over the detent, throwing the props in reverse. The nose gear slammed down. "Practicing for a carrier landing, Captain?" Bosko asked, mostly for Hardy's benefit, but there was admiration in his voice.

Ban Nap, Laos

"Ramp in the trail position," Flanders said over the intercom. "Everyone is down on the deck. Clear in the rear." The veteran loadmaster could have been at the bar with a beer in his hand and discussing the weather. They backed up, leaving a cloud of dust behind them.

"Anyone in sight?" Warren asked.

"Negative," Flanders answered. "Getting a lot of smoke and flames from the Jolly Green. I can't see a thing now. Stop. " The nose came up as Warren applied a little too much pressure to the top of the rudder pedals, dragging the Hercules to a stop. The nose slammed back down and

The Trash Haulers

Warren lifted the throttles into the flight idle position, ready for a quick run up and takeoff.

"Ramp is down," Flanders called as he lowered the ramp to the ground for a quick exit.

"We're taking gunfire!" Boyle yelled over the intercom.

"Negative on the gunfire," Flanders shouted. "It's ammo on the Jolly Green cooking off. Two rounds – small caliber. Too much smoke. We need visibility."

Warren cracked the two outboard throttles, creating a wind and blowing the smoke away. "Got 'em!" Flanders shouted. "Someone is waving at us from the brush."

"Go get 'em," Warren ordered, his voice amazingly calm. He prayed that no more ammunition would ignite on the helicopter.

Hardy shouted, "Go! Go! Go!" Pender led the way down the ramp, surprising them by her quick reaction and burst of speed. The doctor could run. Huckabee and Slovack followed her into the brush.

Boyle didn't move and just stood on the ramp, staring at the burning helicopter.

Flanders took three quick steps and closed on Boyle. He ripped off the airman's headset as he hit the off-switch on his, going cold mike. He gave the tall and gangly nineteen-year-old a hard jab in his left shoulder. "Do your job," he growled, "or I'll jam your head up your fuckin' ass." Flanders ran down the ramp and followed Hardy and Santos.

Pender was back, staggering under the weight of a wounded soldier. Flanders helped her carry him up the ramp. Huckabee and Slovack were right behind, working as a team and carrying a badly wounded para-rescue crewman. Hardy emerged out of the brush with a huge man across his back in a fireman's carry. He ran up the ramp and gently lowered the soldier to the floor. Without a word, he ran back, passing Santos who was helping the limping flight engineer from the Jolly Green. "I need a tourniquet," the navigator shouted. Another small-caliber round from the Jolly Green cooked off but only Boyle dove for cover.

Flanders opened the foot locker holding his first aid and looked at Pender. "I need big compresses," she shouted. Flanders threw her a packet with two of the big wrap-around bandages. Hardy lumbered up the ramp, carrying another soldier.

"That's five," Flanders shouted. He found a tourniquet and tossed it towards Santos. But the navigator was already gone, running for all he was worth down the ramp. Flanders didn't hesitate and moved over to the wounded man, deftly applying the tourniquet to his left leg, stopping the flow of blood gushing from a jagged cut.

Huckabee and Slovack, still working as a team, carried an unconscious pilot up the ramp. "That's six," Flanders called. He looked for Boyle but couldn't find him. Hardy came up the ramp carrying the second pilot in his arms like a baby. "That's seven," Flanders called.

"Make it eight," Santos yelled. Blood cascaded down the front of his flight suit as he gently lowered a soldier to the deck. He looked at Pender. "Captain, he's conscious but pretty bad."

"We got 'em all!" Boyle shouted over the noise and confusion. He was crouched down under the flight deck beside the radio rack that held three black boxes. Huckabee and Slovack ignored him and ran back to the helicopter. Hardy followed them.

The Trash Haulers

Pender bent over the last man Santos had carried on board. The lower part of his back was a gaping hole and part of his spine was missing. Without a fully equipped operating room, he would bleed out in less than ten minutes and be in great pain. Her face hardened as she made the decision. She pulled a small plastic tube out of her blouse jacket and uncapped a morphine injection. She jabbed it into his left bicep. "Stay with him," she told Santos. "Call me if he regains consciousness." She turned to the pilot Hardy had brought on board.

Huckabee and Slovack, both breathing hard, stumbled up the ramp carrying the remains of a soldier. A single bullet had blown away half his face. "Over there," Flanders called, pointing to the forward bulkhead that formed the aft of the flight deck, two feet away from the crouching Boyle. Hardy was the last to board, again carrying a man like a baby. But this one had no legs. Flanders motioned him forward to the other KIA. Hardy gently lowered the body and stood, his face a mask.

"Boyle!" Flanders bellowed at the top of his lungs. "Head count!"

"We got 'em all!" the airman answered.

"What's the fuckin' number!" No answer. "Count 'em!" Boyle stood up but didn't move.

Hardy walked to the rear of the aircraft, pointing as he counted. "Sergeant Flanders, I count seventeen souls on board."

The loadmaster spoke into his boom mike. "I count seventeen. We're good to go. Ramp coming up." He raised the ramp as Warren ran the engines up. "Grab someone and hang on!" Flanders shouted as the aircraft started to move.

95

Only Boyle made an attempt to strap into one of the canvas jump seats that lined the side of the cargo compartment. The others followed Flanders lead and grabbed the uniform of one of the wounded with one hand while holding on to anything they could find with the other. Santos threw his body over a pilot, pinning him to the floor. He grabbed a D-ring embedded in the deck and held on as Warren released the brakes.

The Hercules leaped forward as its props cut into the air. Warren held it on the ground until the last moment and pulled back on the yoke. The nose gear came up and they climbed steeply into the sky. A single 9mm round penetrated the ramp and rolled harmlessly on the deck, coming to rest against one of the bodies. They would never know where it came from. "Heading three-zero-two," Santos bellowed, still the navigator. Flanders relayed the compass heading to the flight deck over the intercom and gave the navigator a thumbs up. Warren eased the yoke forward, decreasing the steep climb-out angle as the gear and flaps came up. Pender immediately went to work on one of the wounded.

Hardy knelt in front of her. "We'll radio ahead and have the crash wagons waiting." She gave him a brief nod and never looked up as she clamped a set of forceps over a gaping wound, stopping the flow of blood. Hardy made his away forward as Santos rose up on all fours, the front of his flight suit and survival vest were soaked with blood. Judy Slovack bandaged the head on of one of the soldiers while Huckabee spoke to the huge American Hardy had carried on board. The intelligence officer pulled a small spiral notebook out of his chest pocket and made notes as they talked.

The Trash Haulers

Boyle sat on a jump seat and stared at his boots, not moving.

Flanders pressed his headset to his head, listening to the radio traffic. "We'll be on the ground in fifteen minutes," he called. He handed Santos a towel and bent over the soldier the navigator was sitting with. Flanders stared at the lifeless soldier and shook his head. "I'll take it from here, Captain." Santos staggered to his feet and shed his survival vest that was still dripping with blood. He headed for the flight deck, forever a changed man. Huckabee followed him up the ladder.

"Captain Warren," Huckabee said. "I debriefed the team leader and need to get to Intel ASAP when we're on the ground. And I do mean ASAP."

Warren understood and keyed the radio, calling Nakhon Phanom. "Invert, Roscoe Two-One. Have transport waiting when we land."

"Roscoe Two-One, we're very busy here. Expect a delay." The implication was clear; trash haulers had low priority.

Hardy was on the navigator's headset. "Let me handle this one." He hit the radio transmit button. "Invert, be advised Roscoe Two-One has a code three on board with critical business. I'll let you explain why he was delayed. Please log this request with your initials."

The radio crackled. "Transport will be waiting, sir."

Warren and Bosko stared at Hardy, not believing what they had heard. A code three was the VIP designation of a very high-ranking passenger in the military pantheon that ranked just below the trinity of President, Vice President, and cabinet secretary. "Colonel," Warren protested, "they'll think

97

we have a four-star on board, which we ain't got. The wing commander at Naked Fanny is probably wetting his pants as we speak. He is gonna be one pissed-off colonel."

"And he's gonna be pissed-off at us," Bosko added. "Not you." He shot Warren a worried look. There was no doubt in his mind that Hardy was going for payback.

"We've got the best intelligence team in Southeast Asia on board," Hardy replied, totally surprising everyone, "and they've got something important. What, I haven't a clue, but it's going up-channel ASAP. And I'll take the heat for this one. But I think the wing king will be okay with it." He paused, considering his next words. "What are you going to do about Boyle?"

"Do about what?" Warren replied.

"He's a fuckin' coward," Santos said. "We all saw it."

"Oh, shit," Warren moaned.

"Welcome to the wonderful world of command," Hardy said.

I Corps, South Vietnam

Tanner and Perkins saw the distinctive jagged, hook-like peak at the same time. They were seven minutes out. "Lonzo on the nose," Tanner said. Perkins dialed in the radio frequency for the firebase, but there was nothing, no jamming, no chatter, just silence. Straight ahead, dark smoke rolled off the top the karst and drifted down into the river valley below. "What the fuck?" Tanner muttered.

"Lonzo in sight," Perkins said.

"I got it," Tanner said. He banked away from the smoke and circled to his right, coming around for another look but staying well away.

The Trash Haulers

"I got the binocs on it," Myers said from the rear. "No movement, a couple of bunkers on fire."

Tanner's inner Klaxon went off at full alarm. He rolled out and dropped them like a rock, and banked sharply back to the left, running for cover.

"I saw a couple of muzzle flashes," Perkins said, amazingly cool. "Someone down there has a definite hard on." They knew Lonzo had been overrun.

"Time to RTB," Tanner said. He continued circling to the left and headed for the coast.

"I got a bright flash on the ground," Perkins called. "Four o'clock. I think some one is sending an SOS." Tanner banked sharply to the right and rolled out, heading back to the firebase. Again, a bright light flashed at them. "I'm reading and S and an *O*," Perkins said. "Looks just like the signaling mirrors we used in the Boy Scouts. I didn't know anyone still carried those puppies."

"The Navy does," Tanner said, "and there are marines down there. Let's go take a look. Heads up, just in case the Gomers are trying to sucker us in."

"Tallyho the grunt," Perkins said. "I got one waving at us from the edge of that large clearing at your two o'clock."

"In sight," Tanner said. He skidded the Huey to the right for Myers to focus his binoculars out his side of the cabin.

"I got two grunts waving at us," the crew chief said. "One's way too tall to be a Gomer."

That was enough confirmation for Tanner and he headed for the clearing. "All clear," Perkins called from the left seat as Tanner flew a short approach into the clearing. "Wind's right to left," Perkins said, confirming Tanner's reading. He turned into the wind to kill their forward airspeed and flared

99

hard, banging the tall grass down. The two marines broke from cover. The lead man carried a body across his shoulders. He gently passed his buddy to Collins who pulled him into the cabin. The two marines scrambled aboard.

"Clear!" Collins shouted. He held onto the wounded marine as Tanner lifted off and spun the Huey around. They were clear. He quickly checked the Marine's pulse and gently removed his equipment belt. There was nothing he could do and he looked up at the two other Marines and shook his head.

They nodded in answer. "No way we were going to leave him behind," the taller one said.

Collins spoke into his mike. "Mr. Tanner, we have a casualty." He didn't say wounded.

"Copy," Tanner replied. "What happened at Lonzo?"

"I'll put the corporal on headset," Collins said. He passed a headset to the Marine, and repeated the question.

"We were overrun," the Marine said. "They kept coming up the south side. It was a turkey shoot, but they just kept coming. Like lemmings. Couldn't even touch our barrels they got so hot. We were getting low on ammo when they overran the communications bunker. That's when the captain ordered a fallback to the northern side. He ordered us three to make a break for it. We went down the side." He looked at his fallen comrade. "Jake took a hit."

"Were they VC or PAVN?" Tanner asked. PAVN was the abbreviation for People's Army of North Vietnam, the American name for the North Vietnamese army.

"PAVN all the way. But we made 'em pay for it."

Tanner's jaw hardened. *But at what cost?* "We need to get you to your unit. Where to?"

"Chu Lai."

1200 HOURS

Nakhon Phanom, Thailand

Two staff cars coasted to a stop on the parking ramp as Roscoe Two-One taxied into the chocks. The airman driving the lead car jumped out and snapped the passenger door open. Colonel Bill Sloan, the wing commander, unfolded from the back seat. He was not wearing a Class A blue uniform as protocol dictated for meeting a code three, but a set of jungle fatigues. He stood beside the car, his arms folded across his chest. The deep frown on his face was ample indication this was a distraction he did not need. His eyes followed the four ambulances that drove up to the rear of the aircraft, and he came to attention when the C-130's crew entrance door flopped down.

Sloan's frown turned to granite when Hardy emerged through the hatch and he saw the silver oak leaf on Hardy's flight cap. A lieutenant colonel was far removed from any code three. Warren and Pender, who was carrying the furled guidon, deplaned next. Huckabee and Slovack were the last off.

Hardy took one look at the waiting colonel and went into damage control. He stopped Pender and pointed her in the direction of Base Operations and Passenger Services, directing her as far away from the wing commander's wrath as possible. The colonel's eyes narrowed as he watched Pender walk away with the guidon. He knew what it was and why she was on his base. He spoke to his airman driver and gestured in Pender's direction. The airman jerked his head in understanding and ran after Pender. Hardy marched up and threw a sharp salute.

"My apologies, sir, but I had to get your attention and transportation."

The colonel studied Hardy's nametag before returning the salute. "Lieutenant Colonel Hardy, do you have any idea what's going down around here? I don't have time for dumb-ass games, and this certainly qualifies."

"Sir, may I introduce Captains Slovack and Huckabee?"

"I know who they are," Sloan growled.

Hardy explained. "They debriefed the Heavy Hook team who were on board your Jolly Green that went down at Ban Nap. They need to get to Intel soonest. We called for transportation when we were inbound but only got the run around, which is typical for trash haulers. But this is critical and I had to get someone's attention. And, sir, you really need to hear what they've got."

"Then let Intel get it directly from the Heavy Hook team," the colonel growled. "Not second hand."

"The team are all wounded, sir, and need immediate medical attention." He gestured at the last ambulance as it pulled away.

The Trash Haulers

Sloan had not become the wing commander of the 56th Air Commando Wing by being slow or stupid. In fact, his IQ hovered around 135 and he had an exceptional sense of situational awareness. "This had better be good, Hardy, or I'm putting your ass through the meat grinder." He motioned Hardy, Huckabee, and Slovack into the second staff car and sent them on their way. He looked at Warren, reading his name tag. "You the aircraft commander?"

"Yes, sir," Warren replied.

"Get your ass in the car," the wing commander growled, folding his lanky frame behind the steering wheel.

Warren hesitated before climbing into the front passenger's seat. "Sergeant Hale," he called, "turn the bird and slap a patch on that bullet hole in the ramp." The flight engineer didn't need to be told what to do and Warren had said it for the colonel, hoping he understood battle damage. Warren crawled into the car and squeezed against the door, anxious to get as much space between himself and the colonel as possible.

Sloan grabbed the radio mike and keyed the transmit button, calling his command post. "Invert, send the Roach Coach out to Roscoe ASAP and get the crew fed." The Roach Coach was a well-stocked mobile lunch van that prowled the flight line and Maintenance twenty-four hours a day, and there had better be no misunderstanding what he wanted.

"Roach Coach on the way," Invert replied.

Sloan mashed the accelerator. "Okay, Warren, you got my attention. So who made the decision to take your C-130 into Ban Nap?"

105

Warren did a quick re-evaluation of the colonel. He obviously knew what was going down in his area of operations, which meant his staff was doing its job, and he was not a man to trifle with. "I did, sir."

"Who called the code three inbound?"

"Colonel Hardy."

"Why?"

"Because Captains Huckabee and Slovack need to get to Intel ASAP. I called for transportation to meet us at the chocks when we were inbound, and all I got was the runaround. That's when Colonel Hardy jumped in. Given the confusion that's going down everywhere, we needed to get someone's attention."

The colonel humphed. "Roger on the confusion. Any clues on what Huck and Judy have?" Like most commanders, Sloan did not like being surprised.

Warren caught the "Huck and Judy" and his estimation of the man went up another notch. "No idea, sir. But based on what I've seen in the last eight hours, they're the only ones with a clue."

"Tell me," Sloan replied. He fell silent as they made the mile drive to the Tactical Units Operations Center, better know as TUOC, where Intel was located.

The staff car slammed to a halt in front of the sign announcing "TUOC – Where the Action Starts." Sloan jumped out of the car and strode into the building, a bundle of controlled energy. Warren was right behind him as the colonel led the way into the main briefing room. The chief of Intel, a lieutenant colonel, held the door open and followed them in. Huckabee was already at work in front of a

The Trash Haulers

Plexiglass-covered wall chart. He used a grease pencil to mark in a series of circles and arrows.

The wing commander found a seat next to Hardy and lit a cigarette. "Captain Huckabee, I'm Colonel Bill Sloan and in charge of the organized chaos around here. Glad to have you aboard. What have you got that has me playing chauffeur when I've better things to do?" The colonel was still playing the hard ass, but his words were laced with a sardonic humor.

Huckabee tapped the last circle he had drawn on the wall chart. "Colonel Sloan, your Jolly Green took battle damage when it extracted a Heavy Hook team, less than six kilometers west of the Special Forces compound at the Se Pang River ford." He didn't have to explain that whoever controlled the ford controlled the movement of material and personnel out of North Vietnam into western Quang Tri Provence and Khe Sanh. Huckabee spoke quietly. "The Heavy Hook team had monitored battalion-sized movement in broad daylight moving across the border into Quang Tri Provence."

Again, he did not have to explain the significance of troops moving during the day, but he did. "Expect a major attack on the Special Forces compound at the Se Pang River ford within the next twelve hours, probably after sunset, which is 1745 hours local." With deliberate slowness, he circled the Special Forces compound in red.

"Has this been up channeled?" Sloan asked.

The chief of Intel answered. "It's on the wires but message traffic is backed up. Even FLASH – URGENT message traffic is taking two hours to get through. I've got

107

two troops working the secure telephones trying to get the word to Headquarters Seventh Air Force. No joy so far."

"Keep trying," Sloan ordered. He pulled into himself, analyzing the threat with his own special abacus. "How certain are you, Captain?"

"It will happen tonight, sir," Huckabee replied.

"Okay." Sloan turned to the chief of Intel. "Get the mission planning pukes in here." The lieutenant colonel hurried out to find the three officers who planned special missions.

Sloan had already made the decision to throw whatever he could at the threat. "So who am I up against?" Hard experience had taught him that his opposite number was a critical factor and leadership made all the difference. "I need a face."

Huckabee was expecting the question but didn't have the full answer – yet. "Sir, we've intercepted wire traffic tracking a Colonel Dinh working his way south on the trail. Dinh is the daddy rabbit of the Military Affairs Committee in Hanoi and Giap's hitman. He's one bad actor. He has a history of showing up whenever Hanoi launches a major offensive." He relaxed when Judy Slovack slipped into the room and stood quietly against the back wall. She was holding a thin folder and gave Huckabee a thumbs up. She had found what she wanted in a top secret safe.

Sloan snorted. "Dinh is a political hack and Giap's far too smart to put him in command of even a latrine. So who's the real talent that I'm taking on?" For Sloan, combat was a very personal thing, even at the command level.

Slovack stepped forward. "Colonel Sloan, if I may." She handed him the folder she was holding. "Meet Colonel

The Trash Haulers

Tran Sang Quan, the commander of the logistical transportation regiment in Laos opposite Se Pang."

Sloan opened the folder and read. Slovack watched his eyes move down the pages, fully aware that he could read far faster than she could talk. She waited as he scanned the folder. The three captains who made up the mission planning cell filed in and stood against the rear wall. They all wore flight suits and were highly experienced pilots who had flown countless missions over the Hi Chi Minh trail, engaging the North Vietnamese. They knew the area, the enemy, and the defenses they were going to take on. The three officers were not the rear echelon, deskbound officers at higher headquarters who thought they were fighting a war. They were the foot that knew how to step on the enemy and kill him. Sloan's eyes narrowed as he digested the contents of the folder and passed each page along to Hardy, who, in turn, passed it on to Warren.

Thanks to the French SDECE, *Service de Documentation Extérieure et de Contre-Espionnage*, they had a detailed dossier on Tran, and there was no doubt the French wanted him dead. The colonel studied Tran's photo, fixing the enemy in his mind, and then passed the photo to Hardy and Warren. "This guy is bad news," he said. "I wish he were on our side."

Slovack stood quietly, taking the measure of her new commander. She noted, with interest, that he was not wearing a wedding ring. "Can we answer any questions, sir?"

"Why Se Pang?" Sloan asked, more for the benefit of the three pilots and to reinforce the importance of what they were doing.

Huckabee had been expecting that question. "By capturing Se Pang and controlling the river ford, the PAVN can make an end run around the DMZ. It opens up a short and direct supply route into South Vietnam, and gives the PAVN an invasion corridor into I Corps and Quang Tri Province." He traced the twisted route that led southward from Se Pang and ended at the small town of Khe Sanh.

"Why Khe Sanh?"

Again, Huckabee was ready. "Taking Khe Sanh accomplishes a number of objectives. First, from Khe Sanh the NVA can launch a major attack towards the coast, peeling away the northern most layer of South Vietnam. We have no option and must honor the threat. Second, it will be a major effort on our part, draining both men and material from other areas further to the south. Third, it will distract our attention away from other lucrative PAVN objectives."

Sloan was not a happy camper, but he was a realist. "So, they get us looking where they want us to look."

"Yes, sir," Huckabee replied.

"But what if it fails?" Sloan asked. "Won't that be a major setback?"

"Only in manpower," Huckabee answered. "From PAVN's perspective, it could prove to be a Verdun for the U.S., bleeding us dry."

Sloan nodded, understanding the analogy with the bloody WW I battle of Verdun where the Germans systematically butchered the French army in a vain attempt to bleed it dry. "The political fallout in the U.S. would be devastating."

"Exactly," Huckabee said. "A no-lose situation for them."

The Trash Haulers

The airman that Sloan had sent running after Lynne Pender burst into the room carrying a flight suit. Sloan stood and peeled off his fatigues to change into his working uniform. "Captain Slovack, eyes front."

"Damn," Judy Slovack muttered under her breath. She did like the colonel's tall and rangy looks.

"Well, Captain Huckabee," Sloan said, "let's make it a lose-lose situation for those fuckers. How do we make it happen?"

"Classic interdiction," Huckabee replied. He stepped to a second, much larger scale map of the river valley that led from Se Pang into Laos. He circled an area just inside Laos with a grease pencil. Now he was briefing everyone in the room, even though it meant repeating what Sloan already knew. But it was critical in getting everyone on the same page. "This is the closest Binh Tram, which is commanded by Colonel Tran Sang Quan who is, without doubt, the best commander the PAVN have in the field. We need to target him, and I think we know where he will be headquartered when he moves into South Vietnam." He drew another circle on the chart less than two kilometers from Se Pang. "There's a well-developed cave complex just above the river."

Sloan stood. He had heard enough. "Colonel Hardy, you were right. I needed to hear this. Thank you. It's my understanding you need to get to Ubon and take over the Blind Bat operation. Captain Warren, get him there ASAP. Now get going, we've got work to do here." Warren headed for the door with Hardy in close trail. "Captain Warren," Sloan called. "Give my thanks to your crew. Well done. And pick up that captain of yours. She should be at wing headquarters with my Exec. I'm letting him deal with the

111

Spirochete." A wicked look flashed across his face. "Colonel Hardy, I'm not happy with that. What would you do about it?"

"I'm not sure, sir," Hardy replied.

"I know what I'd do," Warren said.

Sloan actually cracked a smile. "And exactly what is that, Captain?"

"Post it at the guard shack at the main gate with a box of condoms. Make that a crate of condoms. Any swingin' dick headed for town has to salute it and take a pack of condoms."

"The chaplains are going to love that one," Sloan muttered. "Now get your ass outta here and in the air."

"Yes, sir," Warren replied. He followed Hardy outside.

"Captain Warren," Hardy said, "you have just met the best commander in the entire Air Force. I would follow that man anywhere. I hope you learned something."

"Oh, yeah," Warren replied.

I Corps, South Vietnam

"Good visibility," Perkins said from the right seat. He relaxed as he flew the Huey and scanned the horizon. The bright blue of the South China Sea stretched across the horizon in front of them. "This is a beautiful place," he allowed, "and I'm gonna come back some day and see it right when no one is trying to shoot your ass off."

"Roger on getting your ass shot off," Myers said from the rear. "I've counted eleven firefights out my side alone." A bright flash on the ground mushroomed into a cloud of smoke and flames. "Make that twelve," he said.

"I've counted six on the right," Collins added.

The Trash Haulers

Tanner checked his chart and fixed their position. "Chu Lai on the nose," he announced. "Tell the gyrenes we'll be on the ground in less than five."

"They're both asleep," Collins answered.

"Let 'em sleep. You know where the morgue is?"

"The medics can handle it," Collins said.

"Lots of apron on the north side between the runways," Perkins said. "I see a red cross."

"Good as any place," Tanner replied. "You want the landing?"

"Got it." Perkins took control and headed for the big parking ramp.

"Stay north of the river valley," Tanner advised. A shallow river valley opened onto the coastal flood plain where Chu Lai was located. It ran westward into the highlands and offered good concealment and a way to approach the big base.

"River Valley on my right," Perkins said. "We're a mile north." He turned sto the left, banking sharply away from the river valley. Before he could roll out, the Huey rocked violently to a loud bang. "What the fuck!" The young pilot quickly regained control. "We took a hit."

Tanner let Perkins fly the helicopter as his eyes scanned the instrument panel. All okay. He twisted around to check on the cabin and check for battle damage. The marines were wide awake, their eyes darting back and forth. He didn't see smoke or smell anything burning. "We're okay in the rear, Mr. Tanner," Collins said.

"Controllability normal," Perkins added. The XMSN OIL HOT warning light flashed on the Caution Lights Panel on the pedestal between the pilots. The transmission oil

113

temperature was above 110 degrees Centigrade. Tanner checked the transmission oil pressure indicator. The needle was at thirty PSI and falling. They had taken a hit to the transmission located forward of the rotor mast and on top of the fuselage, just above their heads, when they were turning away from the river valley.

"Get'er on the ground ASAP," Tanner said. If the transmission failed, they would have to autorotate in. While always dicey, Perkins should be able to handle an autorotation.

He didn't have to and touched down on the edge of the parking ramp just as the transmission failed. "How about that?" Perkins breathed.

The two pilots shut down the engine as the marines, Collins, and Myers piled out. The rotor was still spinning down when Perkins and Tanner joined them a safe distance away. Myers scratched the side of his neck as he surveyed the damage. He walked closer to get a better look at the transmission case. The forward part of the transmission fairing had been blown away and oil was seeping out of the side of the transmission case. "We got lucky on that one," the crew chief said. "Looks like a single round barely grazed us and ricocheted off."

"The golden B-B," Tanner allowed. "Talk about the luck of the Irish. Look at the way that groove is angled. The shell came up from the left and glanced off to our twelve o'clock. An inch farther forward and it would have gone straight and hit the rotors."

"Here comes the line chief," Myers said.

A Marine gunny sergeant drove up in an M151 MUTT, the latest variant of the venerable Jeep. The white U.S.

The Trash Haulers

Army stars and numbers had been hastily hand-painted over with a yellow USMC. The gunny crawled out and joined the two Marines. The corporal pulled himself to attention. "We got a casualty, Gunny." He motioned at Tanner. "They came and got us."

"Appreciate that," the gunny said. He cocked his head, surveying the damage to the transmission. He could repay the favor. "We got one of those. I'll get maintenance on it. Should have you out of here in three or four hours."

"Much obliged," Tanner said.

The gunny's eyes narrowed as he studied the transmission. "Where did you take the hit?"

"About a half a mile west of the runway," Tanner answered.

"That's our area. Looks like a fifty caliber."

"Friendly fire?" Tanner asked.

"It happens a lot these days," the gunny replied.

Nakhon Phanom, Thailand

The crew were sitting on the Hercules' ramp still eating lunch when Warren, Hardy, and Pender stepped through the crew entrance. The cargo deck had been made shipshape and hosed out. Santos' survival vest was hanging from a hook, scrubbed clean of blood, and drying along with his flight suit. The aircraft smelled clean. Hardy looked around approvingly. "You've got a good crew," he conceded. He pointed at the wet survival vest. "Where's the weapon?" Control and accountability of firearms is critical in the Air Force scheme of things.

"Knowing Sergeant Flanders," Warren answered, "he has the revolver or locked it up." He gestured to a padlocked

115

footlocker tucked under the flight deck next to the radio rack. "Ask him."

"No need," Hardy said.

Flanders ambled up, carrying three brown paper sacks. "Lunch," the loadmaster announced, passing them out. "Courtesy of the Roach Coach."

"And Colonel Sloan," Warren added. "Time to kick the tires and light the fires." He climbed onto the flight deck, suddenly very hungry. "Hey, Boz, you want the left seat for this one?"

Bosko grinned. "Thought you would never ask." The two pilots switched seats so Warren could play copilot.

1300 HOURS

Over Eastern Thailand

The woman's voice crackled with authority. "Roscoe Two-One, go around." Bosko didn't hesitate and firewalled the throttles as Warren acknowledged the control tower.

"Ubon Tower, Roscoe Two-One on the go," Warren radioed.

"Report initial, runway Two-Three," the controller radioed, kicking them out of the landing pattern and telling them to get back in line for landing. Then she relented, explaining the situation. "Inbound emergency, expect a delay."

Bosko circled to the left and rolled out, heading 030 degrees, leveled off, and pulled the throttles back. The airbase at Ubon, Thailand, was spread out to his left and he could see the fighters returning from a strike mission taxiing back into their open bunkers. "I thought they had all recovered," he said.

"That was one hell of a show," Warren admitted. The four trash haulers had watched as eighteen F-4 Phantoms recovered from a mission over North Vietnam, coming down final in formations of two or four to land in a classical circling approach. The jets leveled off at 1200 feet above the ground before peeling off to the left one by one as they passed over the approach end of the runway. They circled to land, lowering their flaps and gear as they descended, and touched down at 2000 foot intervals. It was quick, efficient, and magnificent to watch. "Inbound traffic in sight," Bosko said, "twelve o'clock."

"Got 'em," Warren said. Ahead, he could see the smoke trails of the two Phantoms on the approach. One of the smoke trails was normal, but the other jet was laying down heavy black smoke. Neither pilot said a word, fully understanding the Phantom had taken battle damage. The other jet was escorting him down, watching for flames or other problems. They watched as the Phantom lowered its tail hook to take the approach end barrier cable for a carrier-type arrestment. "Hydraulics probably out," Warren allowed.

Hardy climbed onto the flight deck and stood behind Warren's seat. The flight engineer automatically handed him a spare headset, which Hardy quickly jammed over his close-cropped hair. "Thanks, Sergeant Hale," Hardy said, taking in the situation. Then, "I hope he doesn't close the runway." The Phantom flying on the wing of the battle-damaged jet pulled up and away as the damaged jet touched down. It rolled about three hundred feet before its tail hook caught the cable at 150 knots, slamming it to an abrupt halt. Two fire trucks converged on the Phantom as the two canopies popped open and the pilot and backseater scampered to safety.

"I think the runway is closed," Bosko said, circling back to the right to keep watching the action on the runway. They rolled out on their original heading in time to see the escorting Phantom come down final at 380 knots. The F-4 pilot leveled off at two thousand feet and snapped a barrel roll as he flew past the tower, "Someone got a MiG," Warren said.

"The wing commander will not be a happy camper," Hardy said. Victory rolls were forbidden in case the returning jet had taken battle damage the pilot was not aware of.

"A kill is a kill," Bosko said, deeply envious of the pilots flying the Phantoms.

"Roger, that," Hardy said, totally surprising them. "Now check that out, the runway is open." The crash crews had pulled the damaged F-4 off the runway and a team was resetting the cable.

"Roscoe Two-One," the tower controller radioed, "report initial." She had just reminded them the show was over and it was time to get back to business.

"Let's get this puppy on the ground," Bosko said.

Ubon Air Base, Thailand

A crew van was waiting when the Herk shut down engines on the parking ramp. A sergeant from ALCE clambered onto the flight deck and told them they had a load. "Not much, twenty Mark-24 flares for Cam Ranh." The Mark-24 was the two million candle-power flare the C-130s flying Blind Bat missions dropped to light up the Ho Chi Minh trail at night. A flare was thirty-six inches long and weighed twenty-seven pounds, and, in the world of trash haulers, the twenty flares were a nothing load. "The flares are hazardous

119

cargo," the sergeant said. "We have to bump your passenger."

"The captain won't like that," Santos said. "She needs to get back to Cam Ranh." Warren nodded, not saying anything. As soon as Hardy departed, he would file a flight plan and list her as a crewmember.

"Why in hell are we shipping flares to Cam Ranh Bay?" Hardy wondered. "We need them here." He thought for a moment. "I need to check it out. And for Christ's sake, everyone get a haircut." He looked embarrassed. "Look, it's the only way I can get Colonel Mace off our back. He confuses haircuts and shoe polish with leadership." Hardy had crossed the line criticizing Cam Ranh Bay's wing commander. "Ah, fuck it. Relax and I'll put Captain Pender on the crew list." He spun around and climbed down the ladder to leave. He stopped and looked back. "Mark, you and your crew did good," he said. "Real good." Then he was gone.

"Well, if that don't beat all," Bosko said.

"Who would have thought," Santos added. "He's not brain dead after all."

"I'm gonna get a haircut," Warren said.

Bosko laughed. "Right behind you, boss."

"Hold on," the navigator called, looking out over the ramp. "We got company, ALCE mobile." A pickup with a heavy array of antennas slammed to a stop and Hardy jumped out, running for the C-130. Warren met him at the crew entrance.

"We got an emergency airlift out of Chu Lai for Se Pang," Hardy said. "A platoon of marines plus equipment. Go."

The Trash Haulers

"What about the flares?" Warren asked.

"Get 'em to Cam Ranh Bay as soon as you can. They're flying a Blind Bat mission out of Cam Ranh tonight and need more flares. The situation has really gone critical." Hardy paused for a moment. "Huck and Judy had it absolutely right. Take care." He spun around and ran for the pickup.

Warren shook his head in wonder, not really understanding the lieutenant colonel. "Who would have thought," he muttered. Then, "Sergeant Flanders, you good to go in the rear?"

"Cargo secure," the loadmaster replied.

"Let's crank 'em," Warren ordered. He turned to Pender who was standing behind Flanders. "Chu Lai is a marine base on the coast near Da Nang. Just under an hour's flying time from here. We're picking up about fifty grunts to reinforce Se Pang before heading for the barn at Cam Ranh. The situation is deep serious and it's gonna get interesting. You can come along or catch a hop out of here. Your call."

"Wouldn't miss it for the world," Pender said.

"Hey, Boz," Warren said, "you want the left seat for this one?"

Bosko grinned. "Thought you would never ask."

Bosko rushed the checklist and called for a midfield takeoff. They were airborne four minutes later. "Sixteen minutes on the ground," Santos said over the intercom as he brought the paperwork up to date. "Are we going for a new Guinness Book of Records?"

121

1400 HOURS

Over South Vietnam

The four big props beat at the air slightly out of phase and filled the flight deck with a pulsating echo. Warren played with the syncophase control knob on the right-side console in a vain attempt to synchronize the props and smooth out the sound but with no success. "It's okay, Captain," the flight engineer, said. "They should reset on engine start."

"Chu Lai on the nose at 130 miles," Santos said. He ran the distance against their groundspeed and added five minutes for approach and landing. "On the ground in thirty minutes."

"Roger that," Bosko said, anxious to end the endless beat. He pushed the throttles up and nosed the Hercules over, trading altitude for airspeed. "In a hurry to get on the ground?" Santos asked. Bosko gave a little nod. At best, they would land five minutes early. But based on what he had heard at Nakhon Phanom, it could be a critical five minutes.

"What do you make of Hardy?" Santos asked, changing the subject.

Warren thought for a moment. "Beats me. One thing's for sure, he's a good pilot and can fly the Herk."

"And he's got balls," Santos added. "You should have seen him at Ban Nap."

"The man is a study in contradictions," Bosko said.

"My dad saw it all the time in the diplomatic corps," Santos said. "You get promoted by playing the game. He had to butter up ambassadors, mostly political appointees, who didn't have a clue but made large campaign contributions. We're talking a total lack of situational awareness and incompetence that bordered on the dangerous. He had to play one game with them, and then protect the staff so they could do the real work. Hardy might be playing the same game, keeping the colonels happy and then making sure we can do our job. It's a balancing act."

"Sounds like a double standard to me," Hale said.

Santos laughed. "My dad used to say that if there wasn't a double standard, there wouldn't be any standards." Warren humphed, not sure if it was total nonsense or if he had just heard a basic truth about the Air Force. "Which gets us to Billy Bob Boyle," Santos said.

Warren made a cutting motion across his throat, silencing the navigator. "Sergeant Flanders, is Boyle on headset?"

"Negative," the loadmaster replied. "Sound asleep."

"Hardy did mention court-martial," Santos said. "For the record, the bastard totally freaked out."

"He's just a nineteen year-old kid," Warren said, willing to cut him a break.

"Kid or not," Flanders said, "we're talking one big yellow streak."

"I didn't see it," Warren said, not sure what to do, but anxious to drop the subject. He made a mental note to talk to his commander on Okinawa. But he sensed Hardy would have to press charges as he was the senior officer who witnessed it. "Time to get this puppy on the ground."

"Before descent checklist," Bosko said.

Warren read off each item as the crew configured the C-130. The descent went smoothly and Bosko leveled off over the South China Sea. Warren called the tower as Bosko turned inbound to the Marine base. "Roscoe Two-One," the tower radioed, "cleared for the approach to Runway Three-One Right."

"Son of a bitch," Bosko moaned. "That's the old PSP runway next to the beach. All we need is a cut tire." The pierced steel planking matting left over from World War Two was infamous for cutting tires on landing and takeoff. The copilot flew a right hand pattern to stay over water as long as possible before turning onto the base leg. "There's the problem," Bosko said. "Looks like they're working on the main runway."

Santos stood behind Warren and scanned the concrete runway with a pair of expensive binoculars he kept in his navigation bag. "They're filling in craters. Small stuff. I'm guessing mortar attack."

"Roger on the mortars," Bosko said. "Before landing checklist." He turned short final and lined up slightly right of centerline in an attempt to keep the landing gear off the most worn parts of the PSP where a break in the metal might cut a tire.

Richard Herman

Chu Lai, Vietnam

"Nice landing, Lieutenant," Santos said as they taxied onto the small parking ramp. Bosko stopped parallel to the runway with the beach and clear blue water on their left. "Nice beach," Santos said. "Do we have time for a skinny dip?"

"Not with a female on board," Warren told the navigator.

"I don't think you have anything I haven't seen before," Lynne Pender said over the intercom.

Warren blushed. "You might have warned us you were on headset." He wondered if she had overheard them discussing Boyle. "Okay, cock this puppy for a quick engine start." Bosko read the engine quick-start checklist, positioning switches for fast start, and keeping the Gas Turbine Compressor, the auxiliary power unit located in the left gear well, on line. "I'm getting bad vibes," Warren warned. "Everybody hang tight. Where the hell are the marines?" His inner Klaxon was starting to chime. He didn't know why he was feeling antsy, but long experience had taught him to honor the warning. "If anyone needs to hit the latrine, there's a slit trench over by the beach." He pointed to a low structure built around a few boards over a trench. A five-foot high vee-shaped wall provided a modicum of modesty for any beach goers.

"Captain Pender needs to use it first," the loadmaster said over the intercom.

"Keep tabs on anyone deplaning in case we need to beat feet and get the hell out of Dodge," Warren said. His inner Klaxon kept building, pounding at him with the same pulsating rhythm of the out of phase props. "Come on." He

The Trash Haulers

hated the waiting, but that was part of a trash hauler's existence.

Bosko keyed the radio and called the tower. "Chu Lai, Roscoe Two-One. Any word on our passengers?"

"Negative, Roscoe."

"Lovely," Warren muttered. He leaned forward in his seat and surveyed the area in front of the aircraft, but the rear hemisphere was a huge blind spot that bothered him. Again, he didn't know why, but he didn't question it. "Scanner in the top hatch," he ordered. The forward escape hatch was located in the overhead at the back of the flight deck with a ladder bolted to the aft bulkhead.

Santos grabbed his binoculars, quickly climbed the ladder, and swept the area in time to see a puff of smoke billow up on the far side of the concrete runway, well over a mile away. The dull boom of a mortar round echoed over him. Two more puffs of smoke erupted, this time on the near side of the runway, marching towards them. "Incoming!" he shouted. "Coming our way!"

"Starting three," Warren shouted, ordering an engine start. A fourth explosion echoed over them, much closer. Warren knew they didn't have enough time to bring at least one engine on line and move out of the way, much less start all four and takeoff. There was no doubt in his mind that the big Hercules was the target. "Shut 'em down. Evacuate! Evacuate!" He ripped the number three throttle full aft as Hale's hands flew over the overhead instrument panel, cutting all power on the aircraft. Santos swung down from the top hatch and jumped off the flight deck, bolting through the crew entrance. Bosko was right behind him. Hale was next off the flight deck, and Warren was the last off. He paused before exiting the aircraft and scanned the big cargo compartment. It was empty. He ducked out the crew entrance and sprinted for the sand dunes next to the beach, thirty yards away. Two more mortars exploded behind him.

1500 HOURS

Chu Lai, Vietnam

Warren leaped over a low dune and sprawled into a shallow depression, landing on top of Pender. He let out an oomph as he rolled off. "Sorry," he muttered. Much to his surprise, she rolled on top of him and pressed her hand against his right shoulder blade. "What the hell!"

"You're wounded," she said.

"I'm not hurt," he protested.

"You're bleeding. Not bad. Just a bad scratch."

Three more mortar rounds walked across the beach, sending geysers of sand into the air and showering them with debris. The last round landed in the water and an eerie silence came down. Warren lifted his head to peer over the edge of the sand dune. Much to his surprise, the C-130 was undamaged. "Now look at that," he said.

"Sergeant Flanders," Pender shouted at the top of her lungs, "I need the first aid kit!"

"Roger that!" Flanders shouted as he sprinted for the aircraft.

Warren tried to stand but the doctor pushed him back down. "Don't move," she ordered, gently pulling back the rip in his flight suit and probing the wound. "It's a bit deeper than I thought."

"How in hell?" Warren wondered. He could not remember feeling anything. Flanders was back with a first aid kit. He ripped it open and handed Pender a small bottle of antiseptic. "How did that happen?" Warren wondered.

Flanders grunted as he watched Pender clean and tape the wound. "You were grazed by a bullet," the sergeant said. "Probably a sniper. Luckily, the bastard couldn't shoot." A burst of small caliber gunfire echoed over them and Flanders dropped to the ground. He bobbed his head up and quickly pulled back down. "Looks like the marines are sweeping the dunes at the far end of the beach." A prolonged burst of gunfire split the air followed by a long silence. Flanders stood to get a better view. "Yep, they got someone. I'm guessing that was your sniper."

"My very own sniper," Warren muttered. "Lucky me."

"You're fine," Pender said. "You don't need stitches, but check with the flight surgeon at Cam Ranh." She rolled to a sitting position, kneeling on the back of her calves.

Warren came to his feet and looked around. "Round everyone up and check the Herk for damage." Again, he swept the area, doing a head count. "Son of bitch, where's Boyle?"

"The last I saw," Pender said, "he was headed for the latrine." She pointed in the general direction of the makeshift outhouse she had used earlier. But it was gone.

"Oh, shit," Warren groaned, coming to his feet.

The Trash Haulers

Pender couldn't help herself. "Pun intended?" But Warren didn't hear her and was running for the latrine. She scrambled to her feet and ran after him.

They reached the latrine at the same time and skidded to a stop. A mortar blast had blown the vee-shaped structure in on itself, and they heard a low groaning coming from underneath the wreckage. Together, they pulled at the splintered boards, clearing the debris away. "Boyle," Warren shouted, "are you okay?"

"Help me! Sweet mother of God! Help me! Help me!" Boyle's shrieks crescendoed into a high- pitched scream. Now they could see his hands, reaching up from underneath and clasping the edges of the floorboards.

"How did he get down there?" Warren wondered, pulling more floorboards free. Now they could see Boyle's head barely above the dark muck floating in the trench. "Oh, no," Warren groaned.

Pender didn't hesitate and plunged her left hand into the filth, grabbing Boyle's collar. "We gotta get him out." Warren didn't move. She tried to pull Boyle free but failed. "I can't do it alone," she snapped. Warren quickly shed his survival vest and braced his right hand on the nearest board. He plunged his left hand down into the excrement, grabbing Boyle's flight suit. Together, they pulled the screaming Boyle free and onto the sand. His arms and legs jerked violently as he twisted and turned, flailing in the sand.

"Drag him into the water," Pender ordered, coming to her feet. It took both working as a team to pull the hysterical Boyle over the sand, finally reaching the surf. Pender released the airman and quickly stripped down to her bra and cotton briefs. "You too," she ordered. "Bath time." Warren

131

rpulled at the quick release zippers on the tongues of his boots and stepped out of them as he unzipped the long front zipper on his flight suit. He shed it in one easy motion. Together, they dragged the screaming and twisting airman into surf. The doctor grabbed Boyle's hair with one hand as she splashed water over his head and scrubbed his face. Warren pulled off Boyle's boots and then jerked at the front zipper on the airman's flight suit, finally pulling it off. "Get his underwear," Pender said.

Totally naked, they sat him up in the surf and used sand scrapped from the bottom to scrub him clean. Slowly, Boyle calmed and started to cough. "Scrub your genitals," she said. Boyle spread his legs and piled wet sand over his groin. He rubbed his hands back and forth in a violent sawing motion. "That's enough," she said. "Okay, time to stand up." The two officers each held an arm and lifted Boyle to his feet.

Loud cheers and shouts from the parking ramp rained down on them. Four trucks, the venerable M35 cargo truck better known as the Deuce-and-a-Half, loaded with fifty marines and their gear had finally arrived. The young marines had been willing spectators to Boyle's rescue and were showing their appreciation. "Lovely," Warren muttered, looking for their clothes. He released his grip on Boyle's arm.

Boyle let out another scream and twisted violently, breaking free. Pender lost her balance and fell back into the surf as Boyle ran back into the water, desperate to escape the unwanted attention. He stumbled and struggled back to his feet, still headed out to sea. "He's totally freaked out," Pender said, coming to her feet. Her cotton briefs were thoroughly soaked and Warren had a vision of Venus emerging from the sea. From the loud cheers coming from the beach, he was certain the marines were thinking along similar lines.

"Totally freaked out?" the pilot said, watching Boyle flail at water. "Is that a medical term?"

"Damn right," she replied. "He needs to be restrained." Boyle had reached deep water and was swimming out to sea. She ran after the airman, plowing through the shallow water.

"Crap," Warren muttered, following her. Pender started to swim, rapidly closing on Boyle. Warren started to swim, but couldn't catch her. He was still thirty feet away when she caught the struggling Boyle. Her left hand flashed out and grabbed his left shoulder from behind. With one easy motion, she rose up and slammed her right hand down on the top of his head, driving his head and shoulder underwater. She quickly released him and let him bob back up, coughing and spitting. Still behind him, she grabbed his chin with her left hand and threw her hip into his back, lifting him to the surface. She swam for the shore with a strong overhand stroke. "Life guard?" Warren asked. She ignored him as she dragged Boyle toward the shore. The marines were still yelling and shouting, urging her on.

Boyle started to struggle, still desperate to escape. Pender released his chin and grabbed his hair as she twisted around. Again, she held his head under water and quickly released him. "Calm down," she ordered, "or I will drown your sorry ass." Boyle believed her and went limp. Again, she grabbed his chin and swam a few strokes into shallow water where she could stand. She threw her right arm around Boyle's waist and held his left arm around her neck, her left hand firmly clamped to his wrist. "Walk," she commanded, bringing him safely to shore. Warren followed in amazement.

Flanders was waiting, holding their clothes and Warren's survival vest. "I don't think you want to put these on," he said. The filth from Boyle's flight suit had rubbed off on their uniforms. "You need to wash them out."

Warren grabbed the naked Boyle by the right arm and shoved him towards Flanders, relieving them of their burden. More shouts from the marines carried down the beach as the two officers rinsed their uniforms in the shallow water. "Bosko has a spare flight suit that will probably fit you," Warren said, thankful they had brought their AWOL bags. She ignored him as she knelt and rinsed her fatigues in the surf. She wrung the top out and pulled it on, quickly buttoning up. She stood and picked up her pants, wringing them out.

The marines were still in full flow, shouting and laughing. "Hey," one yelled, "I'd sure like some of that!"

Pender turned and fixed the heckler with a hard look. She threw her pants and boots at Warren. "Take care of these," she ordered as she strode through the surf, heading for the marines. The fatigue's shirt reached to mid thigh and offered a modicum of decency as her bare legs flashed in the sun. The marines fell silent as she crossed the sand with a measured stride. Only the soft crunch of her bare feet in the sand could be heard. She didn't hesitate and marched straight for the heckler, stopping less than a foot in front of him, standing nose to chest. She read his nametag then pointed to hers as she looked up at the tall marine. "Private Denlow, in case you can't read, you can call me by my

The Trash Haulers

nickname, Captain Pender." She tapped the captain's bars on her lapels. "Where's your lieutenant?"

"He's gone ahead with the advance party," Denlow said, a slight smirk on his face. That was a mistake.

"Denlow, I think your sergeant needs to explain the difference between a captain and a private. Can you point the Gunny out?" She suspected the sergeant was watching, deferring to her rank, and waiting to see how she handled it.

Denlow gulped. "Please, ma'am, don't do that. The Gunny will . . . will . . ." The though of what the veteran sergeant would do to him was too painful to think about. "I'm really sorry and promise to keep my big mouth shut." He was pleading. "I'm sorry, ma'am."

A hard silence came down as the marines stared at her. She let them dangle for a moment, staring back. "Apology accepted, Private." She shouldered past him and padded barefoot up the ramp and into the aircraft. As one, the marines stood at attention and didn't move until she disappeared into the aircraft.

"That's one tough lady," a marine whispered.

"No shit," Denlow breathed.

"Gather 'round " Flanders ordered, holding the marines outside while Pender changed into Bosko's extra flight suit. "I am Staff Sergeant Glen Flanders, your loadmaster for this first-class flight to Se Pang. By regulations, I am required to brief you on . . ." The marines nodded in unison as the loadmaster went through his passenger brief.

On the flight deck, Hale was filling out the maintenance forms. "I found six small punctures," he told Warren, "five in the right main gear door and one in the vertical stabilizer. No other damage. I'm guessing shrapnel from the mortars. I

135

used duct tape to patch the five in the gear door, but couldn't reach the one on the stabilizer. It looks more like a puncture and is small. I don't think any of 'em will be a problem. I'll keep an eye on 'em, but we need to start engines and do a systems and controllability check."

"I couldn't find anything else," Bosko said. "And I went over her with a fine tooth comb." The copilot had gone through the interior of the Hercules checking for battle damage while the flight engineer had checked the exterior.

"So she's good to go?" Warren asked the two men. Because of the battle damage, he could have cancelled the mission and headed for Cam Ranh Bay.

"Yes, sir," Hale said, "she's good to go. But Maintenance really needs to go over the bird, pull panels, and crawl under the belly."

"Sergeant Flanders," Warren said over the intercom, "hold the marines while we start engines and do a systems check." He called for the start engines checklist and the crew brought all four engines on line. They were a well-rehearsed team as they checked out the Hercules, making sure all systems were a go. They finished with a controllability check, and, satisfied the C-130 was fully functional, Warren told Flanders to load the marines.

"Dave, you ever been to Se Pang?" Warren asked.

"Negative," Santos answered. "After takeoff, fly three-zero-zero degrees for 136 nautical miles to Khe Sanh." They had been to Khe Sanh many times and could easily find it. "From Khe Sanh, fly three-three-zero for four minutes. Se Pang should be on the nose." Santos was relying on classic dead reckoning to find the Special Forces camp.

The Trash Haulers

"Got it," Warren said. "Okay folks, keep an eye on everything, and we'll head for the barn after dropping off the marines – if this puppy can hold together that long."

"She's a tough old gal," Hale assured him. "And we've had enough excitement for one day."

"Roger on the excitement," Santos said. "We really need to . . . " His voice trailed off as Pender climbed onto the flight deck wearing Bosko's flight suit. She had cinched in the waist and rolled up the sleeves. Pender was not a small woman and she filled it out.

Warren sucked in his breath.

"Lieutenant Bosko," she said, "thank you. It fits perfectly. Bosko could only nod in agreement.

"Welcome to the wonderful world of tactical airlift," Warren said, kicking himself for not coming up with something better. "Time to get this show on the road. Before taxi checklist."

Chu Lai, South Vietnam

Perkins stood in the shade of the Huey and took a long drink from a canteen. His stomach was still churning from the recent attack that had sent them scrambling for cover. He watched as a C-130 taxied out and took the active runway to takeoff to the north. Tanner joined him, also drinking from a canteen. "Talk about rocket city," Perkins grumbled.

"Mortars, not rockets, " Tanner corrected. He gestured at the C-130 as it lifted off. "I think that was the target. Poor bastards."

"I wonder where it's headed?" the copilot asked.

137

Tanner's face twisted into a little grimace, half serious. "Who knows? Some place with a bar, air conditioned quarters, hot and cold running hootchgirls."

"Mr. Tanner," Myers called. "We should do an ops check." The crew needed to start the engine and check out the repairs to the transmission.

"Can do," Tanner replied, crawling into the left seat.

1600 HOURS

Chu Lai, South Vietnam

Tanner shut the engine down, listening for any unusual sounds. All was normal. "Refuel and we're good to go," he told Myers.

The crew chief waved a fuel browser down and motioned it over for fuel. Tanner and Perkins stood back while they went through the routine. Perkins lit up a cigarette and took a deep drag. "Filthy habit," he said. "These damn things will probably kill me."

"Only if you get lucky," Tanner joked. "Prefer cigars myself."

"I didn't know you smoked."

"When I can get Havanas." The line chief drove up in his MUTT. "Gunny," Tanner said, "your troops did good. Thanks."

"My pleasure. We've salvaged a few Hueys and had the parts. Besides, you fix one helicopter, you've fixed 'em all." While not exactly true, there was enough commonality that a good mechanic could figure out how to repair another air frame. "We got wounded at Se Pang, Mr. Tanner. They're calling for air evac."

"Never heard of the place," Tanner replied. "Any idea where it is?"

"About twenty miles northwest of Khe Sanh," the gunny replied.

"Been to Khe Sanh a couple of times. We'll need to refuel coming out but we can cover it."

He turned and headed for the waiting Huey. "Okay, troops, time to get back to business and earn our pay."

Over South Vietnam

Santos played with the receiver gain on his radar and raised the antenna tilt a degree, finally breaking out the Y in the river where a tributary, with an unpronounceable name for an American, split off from the Se Pang river and flowed south. "Se Pang on the nose, seven nautical miles," he announced. He took a mental snapshot of the radar display and quickly shaded in the ridge on his chart, capturing the return. He could find it again using radar, if they approached from the southeast.

Warren leaned forward in his seat, finding the Y in the river. Although he couldn't see it, he suspected the landing strip was on the far side, aligned along the river valley, and the Special Forces compound was on the eastern end, the side closest to the Y in the river. "Tallyho the fox," Warren said, finally acquiring the short landing strip. "Got the camp." He had guessed right about its location. "Well done, Dave."

"Got lucky this time," Santos replied, downplaying the compliment. Still, he did appreciate it. It was one of Warren's traits he admired and had written home about his new pilot, telling his father that Warren was a natural leader. Santos had lamented that it was a rare quality in the Air Force that was becoming more rare with each passing month, and mentioned that Warren was thinking of separating from the Air Force. His father had written back asking that Warren contact him when he was out.

"Air patch in sight," Bosko said from the right seat, confirming they had found the landing strip. Aircrews had mistakenly landed on roads or even open fields, often with disastrous results.

"I'm painting the runway on the radar," Santos said. "You got about 2000 feet, more or less." He played with the radar gain and tilt, refining the image.

"This is gonna get sporting," Warren said. "Sergeant Flanders, get everyone strapped in. I'm gonna plant this one."

"Roger on the Navy landing," Flanders replied.

"Before descent checklist," Warren said, starting the landing routine. They were nine hours into their crew duty day, fatigue was taking a toll, and long experience had proven that checklists were critical to safe operations. It wasn't glamorous or macho, but it worked. Although his shoulder still ached from the gunshot wound, Warren flew a perfect approach into the special forces compound, landing to the west.

Se Pang, South Vietnam

If a high-speed camera had recorded the landing from the edge of the runway, it would have documented how the main gear actually sank six to eight inches into the hard laterite surface on touchdown, only to pop back to the surface, leaving a slight depression in the landing wake. Warren reversed the props as he stomped on the brakes, stopping with 500 feet to spare. "Remind me to never do this at night," he told Bosko.

"How about never again," Bosko replied. "Jesus H. Christ, Boss, it doesn't get much narrower – and it's downhill!"

"Scanner in the rear," Warren said, before backing up. He released the brakes and the big aircraft taxied slowly in reverse. An Army captain wearing the distinctive Special Forces green beret was waiting for them when they stopped. He ran up the ramp and hurried forward to the flight deck as the marines rapidly deplaned.

"I'm Wes Banks, the social director of this fun-filled resort," he told Warren. "The Bru, the local Montagnards, say we're about to take a pounding, that's with a capital 'P' in the next few hours. It won't be pretty if we get overrun, and the NVA will slaughter the Bru. We need to get their families out."

Warren never hesitated. "How many you got?"

"A total of 182. Mostly women and kids, a few old folks. Eighty-five adults and ninety-seven kids."

"Not good," Bosko moaned, reaching for the flight manual to determine their takeoff distance based on weight, field elevation, and air temperature. The C-130 was a great tactical airlifter, able to operate out of short strips like Se Pang but weight was critical. "How much runway you got?"

"Just over 1600 feet," Banks told him.

Warren flipped over his flight data card and jotted down some numbers, working the problem with his copilot. "How we doing on fuel?" he asked Hale.

The Trash Haulers

"11,500 pounds," the flight engineer answered. That translated into 1770 gallons, or three and a half hours flying time.

Bosko rapidly calculated their total allowable takeoff weight for 1600 feet of runway. "82,000 pounds max," he announced. We can on-load 9,500 pounds. The manual says 180 pounds per passenger, so we can take fifty-three adults, or two kids for every adult and be legal."

Warren worked the problem. "Captain Banks, the Bru aren't very big, are they?"

Banks knew where Warren was going. "Not big at all, maybe 130 pounds for the adults, and forty pounds for the kids.

Warren scratched more numbers, rounding off. "Figure 4000 pounds for all the kids, which means we can take forty-five adults." But he was tired and needed a double check. "Sergeant Flanders, what do you come up with?"

The loadmaster had been expecting the question. "I figure all the kids and forty adults. Captain, I'm looking at 'em right now, and they look skinny as hell. I think we can take fifty, maybe fifty-five adults."

Warren stared straight ahead, looking down the runway. "It is downhill," he said. "What's the gradient?"

"No idea," Banks replied. "It's pretty steep. C-123s get off pretty fast." The C-123 was a high wing, twin-engine Air Force cargo plane vaguely similar to the C-130 but much smaller.

Warren pulled into himself, bringing four years of experience and over 2000 hours of flying the Hercules to bear on the problem. How much could he safely load? He knew what the manual called for, and the Monday-morning quarterbacks at headquarters would crucify him for taking off over-gross on a short dirt runway – if they found out. But there was another intangible; how well was the Herk performing? For reasons he could not quantify, he had a great deal of confidence in this particular aircraft. He turned and looked at the flight engineer. "Sergeant Hale, how's she performing?"

"469 is a good bird," Hale answered. "Accelerates better than the average bear."

Warren made the decision. "Load all the kids and fifty adults. No baggage. We'll come back for the others."

"Will do," Flanders replied. The loadmaster was famous for his causal, laid-back attitude, but he was a hard-nosed professional when it came to loading the Hercules and making sure the weight and balance was correct. "According to the book, we'll be a thousand pounds overweight," he announced.

"The tables have a built-in fudge factor," Bosko said. "I'm guessing ten percent. I think we're good to go."

"Anyone have a problem with that?" Warren asked. He was greeted with silence.

Banks stared at the aircraft commander, fully knowing it could be a death sentence for those left behind. But he was military to the core and accepted it. "See you when you get back." He spun around and swung down from the flight deck.

Moments later, they felt the Bru piling on board. Warren leaned back in his seat, trying to relax and gain a few moments rest. A strong whiff of unwashed humanity drifted up from the cargo deck, capturing his attention. It was sour, heavy with sweat, dirt, and urine. And it was life. He almost ordered Flanders to load another ten passengers. But he was responsible for all their lives, and Lynne Pender certainly qualified as a high-value passenger. Was he risking too much? Was he making a bad decision because of fatigue and the wound? "Damn," he moaned to himself.

"Good to go," Flanders called from the rear, sounding very confident.

Warren looked at Bosko. "Hey," the copilot answered, "this is what we get paid for."

"Let's do it," Warren said. "I'm gonna back up as far as we can, main gear on the hard pack. Sergeant Flanders, keep the tail clear and tell me when to stop." He nudged the throttles and backed up another sixty feet before the loadmaster told him to stop. "Before takeoff checklist," he said. The crew rapidly went through the routine. "Here we go." Warren firewalled the throttles as he and Bosko held the brakes. The props dug in as the Hercules strained to be free, shaking violently. Then, "Go!" The two pilots released the brakes simultaneously and the Hercules started to roll, slowly at first, but then with increasing momentum.

At what he judged the halfway mark on the runway, Bosko called the airspeed. "Forty knots. It's gonna be close." They still had enough runway left to abort the takeoff, but Warren held the yoke forward with his right hand, keeping the nose gear on the ground, and his left hand on the nose gear steering wheel. "Boss . . ." Bosko warned. Warren felt the big vertical stabilizer exert its authority and steered with the rudder peals. He grabbed the yoke with both hands, still holding the yoke forward as Bosko called the airspeed. "Eighty, eighty-five, ninety . . ."

At exactly ninety-three knots, Warren pulled back on the yoke, lifting them smartly into the air, well before the main gear crossed the end of the runway. "Gear up." Bosko's left hand shot forward and he snapped the gear handle to the retract position. The two pilots inched the flaps up as they gained airspeed and climbed, clearing the ridge in front of them.

"Nice one," Bosko said. There was admiration in his voice. "Room to spare."

"We could've taken ten more bodies," Warren said, his voice edged with frustration.

"We were pushing it," Santos said. "After taking battle damage at Chu Lai, the freakin' REMFs are gonna go over everything with a fine tooth comb. Why give them more ammo?"

There was no doubt in Warren's mind that he would hear from the colonels. *So what are they going to do?* he thought, *Send me to Vietnam?* One of the realities of the war was that many field grade officers worked hard to minimize their exposure to actual combat by keeping junior officers in country. Warren grinned at the sergeant. "Gotta give the heavies something to keep them busy," he said. Then, seriously, "I think we could've loaded more."

Bosko nodded in agreement. "Taking off downhill made the difference."

"So where do we take them?" Santos asked.

"Beats the hell out of me," Warren answered. "Boz, see if you can raise an ALCE." Bosko worked the radios while Warren checked on their passengers. "Sergeant Flanders, how are you folks doing back there?"

The Trash Haulers

A deep chuckle on the intercom answered. "Got 'em packed in like sardines. Stinks like hell and most of the kids are screaming like hyenas. Captain Pender is examining a few of the babies. She's asking for water."

"Give 'em what we got," Warren said.

"I raised the ALCE at Da Nang," Bosko said. He snorted in contempt. "I got the standard answer – standby."

"Lovely," Warren muttered.

The TACAN, or the tactical air navigation system, finally locked on, giving them the bearing and distance in nautical miles to Da Nang. "About time," Warren said. Inertial navigation systems were just coming on line in the more advanced fighters and bombers, the Global Positioning System was decades away, and trash haulers had to rely on dead reckoning, map reading, limited radar, VOR, and TACAN for navigation in-country.

Santos spun his circular slide rule, the so-called Air Navigation Computer. "ETA Dan Nang 1711 hours local. Man, I could use a good meal." It was his way of urging Warren to call it quits for the day.

A frustrated voice came over the UHF radio. "Roscoe Two-One, Da Nang ALCE. Say number of passengers."

"Da Nang ALCE," Warren answered. "We have 147 souls on board." They waited for the reply.

Another voice came over the UHF. "Roscoe Two-One, be advised we will need to see your passenger manifest and authorization for a pickup for over ninety-two passengers."

"Some REMF playing cover-your-ass," Bosko said.

Warren thought for a moment. He knew how to play the "be advised" game. He keyed the radio. "ALCE, Roscoe Two-One copies all. Be advised we have priority through

147

cargo for Cam Ranh and are running short on crew duty time. Tell passenger service to meet us with transportation for 147 Bru. For the record, Bru are Montagnards and a translator is required."

"Roscoe Two-One, standby."

Bosko snorted. "Handling that many Bru will ruin their day."

"Roscoe Two-One, ALCE. Say Special Forces detachment the Bru are from."

"The great shuffle begins," Warren muttered to himself. "Anyone know what Special Forces Det we're dealing with here?"

Flanders had the answer. "Special Forces Detachment A-101."

Warren relayed the information to ALCE over the UHF. Within moments, the ALCE controller was back. "Roscoe Two-One, you are cleared to Phu Bai to off load passengers. From Phu Bai, proceed directly to home plate with priority cargo. Do not exceed crew duty time."

"Roscoe Two-One copies all," Warren replied. Then, over the intercom, "Boz, Dave, make a log entry that we were directed to Phu Bai just in case some REMF gets a hard-on." Warren gave a silent thanks there was no ALCE detachment at Phu Bai, and they were, more or less, on their own.

"Hell of a way to fight a war," Santos grumbled. "Heading zero-nine-zero." He checked his watch. "Phu Bai on the hour." He reached for the journal in his navigation bag to record the incident in detail.

"Still going to write the great American novel about the war?" Warren asked.

148

The Trash Haulers

"That's the plan," Santos replied, putting the journal safely away. *I will write it,* the navigator promised himself. *Someday.*

Se Pang River Valley, South Vietnam

Tran squatted on his haunches beside the freshly dug bunker and surveyed the river valley below him. Like a good commander, he studied the topography of the battlefield below. The valley was oriented east to west, and framed by ridgelines on the north and south sides. The northern ridgeline was the highest and the terrain on that side of the river all but impenetrable.

He was on the southern side of the river looking north, across the river. He was approximately a hundred meters above the valley floor, and at the top of a slope that led up to the sharp face of a karst formation towering another hundred meters above his head. Hopefully, spotters would be on top and string a land line for communications by sunset. Below him, the river flowed west to east down the valley and appeared to be at a low stage. But could his men ford it?

He had an excellent view of the airstrip and Special Forces camp on the other side of the river, approximately two kilometers to the east. He could still see a few flames and smoke from an earlier mortar attack. The Type 53, 82mm, mortars had given a good accounting for themselves. Now the mortar crews had to move to safety before nightfall.

The open area on his side of the river worried him, for his men would have to cross it to reach the river. The more he studied the lay of the land, the less he liked it. Loud breathing captured his attention, and he looked down the trail leading up from the valley. He waited, his face impassive.

149

Much to his surprise, Dinh huffed his way up the last few meters, leading two of his staff officers. The corpulent colonel collapsed to the ground beside Tran. "I couldn't catch you," he admitted. They had travelled five kilometers in five hours, which, on the trail, was good time.

Tran handed him a flask of water. "Drink slowly," he cautioned. Dinh ignored him and emptied the flask. "What happened to Major Cao?" Tran asked. He suspected that Dinh's chief-of-staff was there to keep an eye on Dinh and report back to Hanoi.

"I sent him back to coordinate with General Dong at the 559th Group. The General must be apprised of our situation." It was a lie. Dinh's inner alarms had finally overwhelmed him, and he had ordered Major Cao to keep an eye on Kim-Ly. For some reason he could not bring into sharp focus, he distrusted her. Long experience had taught him not to ignore his misgivings. He changed the subject. "And did I see a plane takeoff earlier?"

"You did. It was a C-130. It took off at 16:49 hours."

Dinh looked up at the two camouflaged cannon barrels sticking out of the bunker. "Is that the 'Sergey' you spoke of?" He had never seen a ZSU-23 up close before and was surprised at the length of its twin barrels. "And is it fully operational?" Tran nodded in answer, letting the colonel from Hanoi absorb the reality of the weapon. It had taken an herculean effort for the gun crew to carry it forward and quickly reassemble it. Dinh checked his watch. "And was it fully operational ten minutes ago when the C-130 took off?"

"Yes," Tran answered simply.

"And why didn't you shoot it down?"

The Trash Haulers

"We watched the C-130 load women and children," Tran explained. From the expression in Dinh's eyes, it was obvious that he didn't care about violating the Geneva Conventions. "And it would have revealed our position."

Dinh studied the camouflage spread over the gun emplacement, not convinced. He pointed at the runway. "You will destroy any aircraft landing there."

Tran sensed there was nothing he could say to change Dinh's mind until he had experienced actual combat. "Be careful of what you order, sir. You may bring down the wrath of God on our heads."

Binh humphed. "There is no God."

1700 HOURS

Se Pang River Valley, South Vietnam

Reluctantly, Dinh joined Tran and three officers under the hastily rigged canvas canopy that served as a make-shift command post for their second meal of the day. They sat in a circle as the cook passed out bowls of rice. Because Dinh was sharing their meal, the cook had added vegetables and served him first. Dinh looked at the bowl and started to say something but thought better of it. The regiment only ate twice a day and the lack of variety and small quantity was a problem. Tran gave the colonel good marks for his silence and sharing the meal with the cadre.

The telephone operator sitting at the nearby portable switchboard handed Tran a note. The observers at the top of the karst formation a hundred meters above their heads had spotted an inbound helicopter to the east. At the same time, the ZSU, which was twenty-five meters away from the command post but still in sight, traversed in that direction as the twin barrels elevated to forty-five degrees.

"What's happening?" Dinh demanded.

"Our observers report an inbound helicopter," Tran replied. He stood and a woman handed him a pair of high-powered binoculars. He joined the gun captain who was scanning he eastern horizon with a matching set of binoculars. They pivoted as one, trying to visually acquire the helicopter. "There," Tran said, pointing to a spot on the horizon.

"I see it," the gun captain said. He spoke into the intercom dangling from his neck and the barrels of the ZSU traversed ten degrees to the left and lowered.

The telephone operator spoke quietly, her soft voice barely audible. "A red cross is reported on the helicopter."

"Stand down," Tran ordered. "It is a Dust Off."

"What is a Dust Off?" Dinh demanded.

"An unarmed medical air ambulance," Tran explained.

"Destroy it," Dinh said.

"Is the colonel aware a medical air ambulance transports wounded and is protected by the Geneva Conventions?"

"And is it carrying wounded now?" Dinh asked, his voice low and hard.

"It is most likely coming in to pick up wounded from our mortar attack."

"Then it is not protected by the Geneva Conventions until the wounded are on board. You will engage and destroy it." He pointed at the gun captain. "Do as you are ordered."

The gun captain shot Tran a worried look, not knowing what to do. Tran nodded, in effect giving the order. The gun captain spoke into his mike as everyone but Dinh turned their backs on the cannon and covered their ears. Dinh did the same, confused by the silence. They waited.

The Trash Haulers

The ZSU's twin barrels roared with thunder, splitting the air with the sound of death as each barrel emptied a twenty round clip in less than two seconds. Dinh fell to his knees, stunned by the violence of the fusillade.

Se Pang, South Vietnam
Tanner had the landing wired. There was no wind and he came in from the east, paralleling the river. They were decelerating, passing through twenty knots and less than fifty above the ground when the explosion tore the controls out of his hands. The Huey corkscrewed to the left before hitting the ground and rolling across the runway.

Tanner was vaguely aware of coming to a stop. The Huey was on its left side and his shoulder was against the ground. Something heavy was laying across his face and he couldn't see. He tried to push it away but it was too heavy. Frustrated, he reached for the engine control panel on the center pedestal to shut off the fuel. He couldn't reach it. He pushed again at the weight laying on him. It was Perkins. He twisted his head, trying to see, as he pushed at the dead weight.

He caught a glimpse of two men reaching for him as a sheet of flame washed over him. His right leg exploded in pain. His last conscious thought was of darkness and searing agony.

Se Pang River Valley, South Vietnam
Dinh staggered to his feet and looked to the east in time to see the helicopter spinning into the ground, leaving a corkscrew of dark smoke in its wake. He watched in fascination as it bounced and rolled across the eastern end of

155

the runway. He shouted in jubilation and turned, waiving his arms like a conductor. "Victory is ours!"

He stared, not understanding what was happening. Everyone was rapidly packing up, taking the command post apart. The gun crew was disassembling the ZSU and loading four men with parts of the heavy mount. Four other porters were already moving out, carrying the barrels. "What are you doing? Where are we going?'

Tran stopped long enough to get him moving and motioned to the east, closer to the airfield but up a higher slope. "To our next prepared position. We must hide before the Americans return."

"And why should we hide?" Dinh demanded.

Tran swung his heavy pack into Dinh's chest. "Carry this." He pushed the colonel, moving him after the porters. "When we shot at the helicopter, we revealed our position to the Americans."

"So what? And if they return, I will also destroy them, just like the helicopter."

Tran tried to explain as they moved into the underbrush. "It is one thing to destroy a slow moving, unarmed helicopter, but an entirely different thing to engage one of their jet fighter bombers."

"And why must I repeat myself? I will order the Sergey to destroy them just like I destroyed the helicopter."

Exasperated with Dinh's outsized ego, Tran worked to control his anger. "You see our cannon as a threat to the Americans. They see it as a target and are aggressive to a fault when they attack. Now we must hurry. Movement is life."

Dinh recalled hearing that "movement is life" before but couldn't remember when, where, or who had said it.

Phu Bai, South Vietnam

Smoke drifted across the runway, partially obscuring their approach as the C-130 came down final, landing to the west on Runway 27. Warren touched down long and threw the props into reverse, sending a wall of smoke out in front. He dragged the big bird to a stop near midfield and turned right onto the main Army parking ramp, opposite the forlorn civilian terminal on the other side of the runway. An Army private guided them into a parking spot and Warren kept the engines running.

"Dear Lord," Hale breathed, taking in the damage around them. "They really took a shellacking."

"Looks quiet now," Bosko said.

"Yeah, but for how long?" Santos asked.

Warren checked his watch. "Okay, troops, listen up. We've got two hours crew duty time left. I figure we've got enough fuel and time to go back and get the rest of the Bru before sunset, drop them off here, and hotfoot it for Cam Ranh." He was asking for a double check.

Santos was already there. "Figure twenty minutes each way to Se Pang, an hour and ten to Cam Ranh. Add another fifteen minutes for approach and landing, plus ten percent reserve fuel, and we need 8,500 pounds of go-faster juice." The standing warning among trash haulers held that not even Christ could get out of an accident from fuel starvation, which Warren agreed with. They fell silent as the ramp came down and Flanders off loaded the passengers, handing

157

them over to a very confused Army private. "We're pushing crew duty," Santos warned.

"Hey, isn't there a war on?" Bosko asked. "It sure looks like it to me."

"Say fuel," Warren said.

"We got 10,000 pounds," Hale answered. They had 1540 gallons of JP-4, on board.

Again, Warren ran the numbers. They had 1500 pounds, or 230 gallons, of extra fuel. It was enough, and if they did run into a problem, they could always divert into a field along the way. "Loadmaster, say when ready to taxi."

"Standby," Flanders replied. "Okay, cargo compartment swept and negative on mementos. Ramp coming up." The mementos he was concerned with were grenades, unexploded ordnance, body parts, or even babies left behind. It had happened before. They taxied onto the runway for a rolling takeoff at midfield.

"Seven minutes on the ground," Santos said. "That's a record."

"We're definitely safer airborne," Bosko said.

"I hope so," Warren replied.

"ETA Se Pang, 1730 local," Santos said. "Fifteen minutes of daylight remaining."

"Let's make it a quick one," Warren said.

Lynne Pender climbed onto the flight deck, her face etched with fatigue. "I lost a baby, barely a week old."

Warren turned in his seat and reached out to touch her hand. The unknown infant was not the first death he had experienced while in command of a C-130, but he prayed it would be the last. "We lost a baby."

The Trash Haulers

Over South Vietnam

Santos was standing behind the copilot when they crested the last ridge and descended into the Se Pang river valley. Warren called for the before landing checks as he flew a curvilinear approach to a short final. He dropped the gear and called for full flaps as he inched up the power, holding a steady eighty-three knots, five knots above a power-on stall. Two explosions flashed on the hillside approximately a mile in front of them. "What the hell!" Bosko shouted.

A marine A-4 fighter pulled off a bombing run and circled above them. "I got two A-4s working." Santos said. Two more explosions lit the hillside as a puff of green smoke drifted across the approach end of the runway. They were cleared to land. "I have green smoke," Santos called, confirming the smoke. The navigator quickly strapped into his seat.

Se Pang, South Vietnam

Smoke from the burning wreckage of the helicopter drifted across the approach end of the runway, partially obscuring Warren's view. He slammed the Hercules down and reversed the props, landing in a shorter distance than before. "You're getting the hang of it, sir," Hale said, his voice full of admiration, breaking the mounting tension.

"Scanner in the rear," Warren called as they backed up.

"Not much left of that Huey," Bosko said as they passed the burnt-out helicopter. They caught the smell of burning flesh. "Poor bastards," Santos muttered. Tech Sergeant Mike Hale's lips moved in a silent prayer.

"Come slightly to your left," Flanders said, guiding them into the deepening shadows. "Stop!" The ramp was already coming down. The plane shook as the remaining Bru rushed on board.

Captain Wes Banks climbed onto the flight deck, this time wearing a helmet and not a green beret. Lynne Pender was right behind him. "Perfect timing," Banks told them. "We took some deep serious mortar rounds, but close air is suppressing it for now. It's going to get interesting after sunset unless we can get a flare ship to light things up. Our aid station took a direct hit, a marine and two navy corpsmen KIA. All told, we have a dozen or so wounded marines and a Dust Off pilot with a mangled leg and burns."

"We can take 'em," Warren said.

Banks shook his head. "You need to launch soonest, while it's still light. Besides, a Dust Off is inbound, five minutes out."

"A Dust Off can't take that many," Pender said. "So who's taking care of your wounded?"

"My sergeant and the Bru."

"Your aid station?"

Banks' jaw hardened. "Destroyed in the mortar attack."

Pender's eyes narrowed. "So you don't have any medical personnel or supplies, and no idea when you'll get more air evac." Banks nodded. She hesitated for a moment, making a decision. "I'm staying. I'll come out on the last Dust Off."

"I can't let you do that," Warren told her.

"Really? Oh, I'll need your first aid kit." She was gone.

"Are you going to stop her?" Bosko asked.

Warren was coming to terms with the new role of women and wasn't sure if he liked it. "Short of handcuffing her, I don't think I can." *Like we really got a choice when there's wounded.* Then, over the intercom, "Sergeant Flanders, off load our first aid kit for Captain Pender and button up. We need to get the hell out of Dodge."

"The Triple A that got the Dust Off is a mile away, off the west end of the runway, " Banks told them. He pointed in the direction where the A-4s had been working. "It's about one-third the way up the slope. Close air probably got 'em, but can't be sure."

"Got it," Warren said. "We'll keep it tight in and circle out to the south." He reached out and shook Banks' hand.

"God bless," Banks said. Then he was gone.

"Good to go in the rear," Flanders said. "That Captain Pender is one tough lady." There was admiration in his voice.

Warren ran the engines up and released the brakes. With fewer passengers and less fuel, the Herk leaped forward.

Se Pang River Valley, South Vietnam

The gun crew collapsed around the ZSU-23, exhausted from their ordeal. Two women quickly covered it with a canvas tarp and spread freshly cut brush on top. "We are ready," the gun captain told Tran, pride in his voice.

"Well done," Tran told the men. "Because of your effort, we will fight another day." They had moved the anti-aircraft cannon a half-kilometer and reassembled it in less than an hour, record time. The terrain had helped. A clear and easy path had led around a sharp bend in the hillside, and a spinney ridge jutting out from the karst provided the protection and concealment they needed. Smoke from the bombs still drifted over them, but they were safe.

Dinh stood beside the rock outcropping and scanned the airfield, now a little closer. "The American air pirates are taking off!" he shouted, gesturing wildly at the C-130 rolling down the runway.

"Our observers report it is carrying women and a few old men," Tran said. He pointed to the top of the karst and the observation team.

"Destroy it!"

Tran hesitated, not wanting to reveal their position and move again. "We will have better targets."

"And must I repeat myself? Do as you are ordered."

Again, Tran nodded slightly at the gun captain, giving the order to engage. The twin barrels traversed towards the aircraft that was turning in front of them. "Wait, wait," he cautioned.

Over Se Pang, South Vietnam

The gear was still coming up as Warren banked to the left, the wingtip barely clearing the ground. The C-130 climbed like a homesick angel. A solid line of red tracers reached out from the hillside, passing below Roscoe 21. "Triple A!" Flanders shouted from the rear. Warren jinked – rolled out, turned sharply to the left, rolled out, then down, quickly up, and then back to the left as he nosed over. As expected, the tracers drifted off to their right and above them as the gunner tried to anticipate Warren's next move. Warren leveled off and then up as the tracers wavered, passing far behind. Well clear of the threat, Warren turned out to the east.

The Trash Haulers

Over South Vietnam

"Jesus H. Christ," Bosko breathed. "That was a ZSU." The antiaircraft cannon was rightly feared by aircrews. "Thank God there was only one."

"Probably a two-barrel," Warren said. The four-barrel version, a ZSU-23-4, was radar aimed and much more lethal. "Check for battle damage." The crew went through the checks.

"Captain Warren," Flanders said. "I did a visual on the main gear. The left aft wheel is flat and looks shredded. Probably took a round." The Hercules had a tandem landing gear on each side, with one wheel behind the other. They were lucky and had only been hit by a fragment of a single high-explosive round from the ZSU-23.

"Roger," Warren replied. Landing with a flat tire, especially the aft one, on a paved runway when they were relatively light was worrisome but easily handled. They had done it twice before. "Boz, contact Da Nang ALCE and tell them we're landing at Phu Bai to offload our passengers, and to send a repair team with a new tire. We're pushing crew duty and will go into crew rest. Also, relay that Captain Pender is at Se Pang treating the wounded."

"They're going to love that one," Bosko predicted. He dialed in the radio frequency and relayed the message.

As expected, they were told to "Standby." Another voice came over the radio. "Roscoe Two-One, proceed to Phu Bai to off load and await a repair team. Once you are OR, you are cleared for a one-time flight direct Cam Ranh." OR meant operationally ready. "Crew rest is waived for a one-time flight to home plate."

"Roscoe Two-One copies all," Bosko replied.

163

"The feces must have really hit the fan to clear us for a one-time flight out of crew duty," Santos said.

"They need the airframe," Warren allowed.

ALCE was back on the radio. "Roscoe Two-One, confirm you left a manifested passenger on the ground at Se Pang."

Warren answered. "ALCE, that's affirmative. Captain Pender was on crew orders and not a passenger."

The reply was a short "ALCE copies all."

"What was that all about?" Bosko wondered.

"You don't leave anyone behind without a damn good reason," Santos replied. "Some 0-6 is shitting a brick."

"And we know which way that flows," Bosko added.

Exactly six minutes later, the radio squawked and the same voice was back. "Roscoe, Two-One, ALCE. On landing at home plate, you will be met by Security Police and the OSI. Until then, do not discuss the incident at Se Pang among yourselves." The OSI was the office of Special Investigations that handled criminal investigations.

"Copy all," Warren replied.

"The shit has definitely hit the fan," Santos said. "Like big time."

"Oh, yeah," Warren said. He called for the before landing checklist.

1800 HOURS

Se Pang, South Vietnam

"Mr. Tanner, I'm Doctor Lynne Pender." She cut his flight suit away, not liking what she saw.

He looked at the voice. A very pretty woman wearing a flight suit was bent over his legs. "Where am I?"

She talked as she worked. "You're in a bunker at Se Pang."

"My crew?"

Pender lied. "Sorry, I don't know. They just brought you in." She finished cutting his flight suit away. "Well, first things first."

"Lay it out, Doc. What are you looking at?"

An inner voice told her that the truth was the best approach with this man. Besides, she had lied enough about his crew. "You were caught in a fire and have first and second degree burns on the right side of your face. You were lucky."

Tanner closed his eyes and breathed heavily. "My peter pilot protected me. What else?"

"Well, your flight suit was fire retardant and protected your body, but you will have an interesting burn scar down the center of your chest and stomach that looks just like a zipper." She made a mental note to send that up channel and recommend they design an inner protective flap to shield the skin from the front zipper.

"What about my leg? I can't feel it."

Pender examined the lower part of his leg. His right foot was twisted at an odd angle, still attached by a splintered bone, tendon and skin. Part of the lower tibia jutted out of his boot. She released the tourniquet around his thigh. Blood gushed from a severed artery that she quickly sutured, sealing it off. "Can you feel this?" she asked.

"Negative." He raise his head and saw his boot dangling over the edge of the table. His foot was still in it. "That's not good, Doc."

"I'm afraid the lower part of your right leg will have to be removed."

"Did they miss my pecker?"

"You're intact."

"Are you sure? We'll need to do an ops check."

"Mr. Tanner, are you trying to make a date?"

He grinned wickedly. "You bet."

"I will hold you to it," she promised. She reached up and touched his cheek. "Mr. Tanner, I have to operate. I gave you our last shot of morphine and I'm not sure if it is enough. This will hurt. But you will survive." She placed a tightly rolled bandage in his mouth. "Bite on this." She motioned for the four Bru and the sergeant who had pulled him from the burning wreckage to hold him down. She bent over and whispered in his ear. "By the way, I'm very good in the sack."

"Go for it, Doc."

Se Pang River Valley, South Vietnam

"Quickly, quickly," Tran said, urging everyone into the nearby caves. The sound of jet engines echoed over the valley, still faint but growing louder by the second. Luckily, they were able to pull the ZSU into a cave without disassembling it and handling the still hot barrels. He double-checked to be sure the mouth of the cave sheltering the command post was barricaded and sealed. Baring a direct hit, they could quickly clear the entrance. *How much longer do we have?* He gave a silent thanks the sun was down and it would soon be dark. But the setting moon was still casting enough light for the jet fighters to attack, and they knew where the gun emplacement was located.

Again, he looked around. Everyone was safely in the caves and he was alone. He studied the empty gun emplacement, sorry they had to abandon it. It wasn't often a site was so well situated. But movement was life. *What do the Americans call it? Shoot and scoot?* Another thought came to him. *Give them what they want.*

"Bring the big canvas tarpaulin," he called, "and four cans of petrol." In less than a minute, the big tarp was spread out over the empty gun emplacement. Two men rushed out of the far cave carrying four twenty-liter cans of the precious gasoline used to power the communications generators. Tran rolled a small boulder into the center of the tarp, depressing it into the shape of a giant saucer. Overhead, the sound of jet fighters grew louder.

"Pour the petrol on the tarpaulin," he ordered. Rapidly running out of time, he told the men to open the jerry cans and let them drain into the makeshift canvas bowl. He rushed them all to safety inside a cave as the first jet screamed down on a bomb run. It was an F-4 Phantom.

It missed by over a kilometer.

Tran uttered a curse in Vietnamese about pilots being born from dogs. The second F-4 rolled in but pickled off its load early and pulled off high. Tran's luck held and four explosions walked down the valley, the last one detonating 400 meters from the empty gun emplacement. Shrapnel from the five-hundred pound Mark-82 rattled against the karst cliff face above the cave. Desperate, Tran called for a hand grenade. One was quickly passed forward and he ran from the cave, pulling the pin. He threw the grenade into the gun emplacement, hoping the petrol had not leaked out of the canvas. He darted back into the cave as the grenade detonated. A flaming cloud erupted from the emplacement and rose into the dark sky.

Tran breathed in relief. He had created the illusion of a secondary explosion, the sign that a bomb had destroyed a target of value. Now it was time to move again while the moon was still up and they had enough light to see. For a brief moment, he considered leaving Dinh sealed inside the cave. But he needed the communications gear and the six comrades still inside. He gave a mental sigh and gave the order to clear the cave entrance.

The Trash Haulers

Phu Bai, South Vietnam

"It sure gets dark quick after the sun goes down," Bosko said. The worry in the copilot's voice was palpable as an eerie silence settled over the Army base. Fortunately, the setting moon was still casting enough light for them to see on the darkened flight deck. "The VC do their best work at night."

Warren looked out the pilot's side window. The burnt out wreckage of three helicopters and six trucks were grim reminders of recent attacks, and he shared his copilot's concern. "I wonder when the repair team will get here?" he wondered. "We need to get the hell out of here." It was the age-old military tradition of hurry up and wait. Now they were waiting.

"I'm not so sure they'll rig lights to work at night," Hale said. The tech sergeant had changed many wheels and knew what was involved.

The rumble of an outgoing artillery barrage echoed over them. "Damn, that's close," Santos said. Warren agreed with him.

The loadmaster's head appeared at the edge of the flight deck's entrance. "Chow anyone? I heated up some C-Rats." The C-Rats, or C-Rations, were the latest version of the infamous K-Rations of World War II vintage. The individual packets held a complete meal that ranged from ham and eggs to chicken and vegetables. The beans and franks were the favorite, but all provided an edible meal, especially when heated. While they were still airborne, Flanders had opened six packs and heated the cans with the main entrees on the radio rack underneath the flight deck.

169

"Sounds great," Warren called, remembering how Colonel Sloan had made sure they were all fed while at Nakhon Phanom. *What had Hardy said about the colonel? The best commander we've got.* Always pay attention to the basics, he thought. He was still learning. Flanders passed the heated C-Rations up and the men tore into them, indulging in the traditional military pastime of 'bitching and moaning' as they chowed down. "Where is that damn repair team" Bosko moaned.

"At Happy Hour with the Donut Dollies," Santos quipped.

"Where else," Warren said.

"Give me a wheel," Hale said, "and I can change it."

Warren looked a him. "You can do that?"

"Sure can," the flight engineer replied. "Just dig a hole around the wheel."

"No shit?" Bosko said.

"Piece of cake," Hale explained, "as long as it's the aft wheel. Won't work on the forward main. Helps to have a shovel or two."

"Too bad we don't have a wheel," Warren said. They fell silent as they finished eating. Soon, only Warren was still awake as the others dozed off. Bosko had run the copilot's seat full aft and was gently snoring. Santos and Hale had stretched out in back along with Flanders on the canvas jump seats in the cargo compartment.

"Now look at that," Warren said over the intercom, waking Bosko and Flanders. A C-123 was taxing in and headed straight for them. "I think we got our wheel. Not bad. We've only been on the ground an hour." It always amazed him when the system worked with any efficiency.

The Trash Haulers

Maybe there's a Sloan kicking ass and taking names in the world of tactical airlift. Then it came to him; Sloan never had to kick any one's ass. It was all about leadership. "Okay, let's make it happen and get the hell out of Dodge ASAP."

"Captain Warren," Flanders said. "Boyle's disappeared."

Warren muttered an obscenity under his breath. "Maybe he's gone to the latrine."

"His AWOL bag is gone too," Flanders said.

"If he's not back when we're good to go," Warren growled, "we'll be gone too."

1900 HOURS

Se Pang River Valley, South Vietnam

Three figures moved along the hillside trail, still able to make their way in the rapidly fading moonlight. The setting moon was above the horizon but a deep blackness had captured the valley floor. The lead figure stopped on a ledge and pointed to the valley floor. They could barely see the dark mass of the special forces camp. A dim light cracked the darkness as another figure held back the canvas that covered a cave entrance. The three figures moved inside and the canvas dropped back in place, leaving only darkness behind.

Kim-Ly dropped her heavy pack and handed her AK-47 to a woman. She looked around the dimly lit cave, getting her bearings. Sleeping figures rested against the walls, exhausted from moving the ZSU-23 a second time. "Major Cao," Kim-Ly said, "please stay here and rest. We will bring you water."

The major collapsed against the wall without removing his pack. Nothing in his experience had prepared him for the ordeal of the last few hours. They had darted forward, synchronizing their movements to the timing of falling bombs, moving fast but always finding safe refuge at the last moment. He wanted to return to the safety of the Binh Tram in Laos, but Kim-Ly had pressed ahead. Begrudgingly, he gave her high marks for courage.

Kim-Ly thanked their guide and followed her escort deeper into the cave and to the regiment's latest command post. She was careful to step over the telephone lines stretched across the ground. Tran looked up from the table where he was sitting. His face softened and, for a few moments, an inner calm captured him and the sacrifice and pain gave way to the reward of reuniting with his wife. They stood close, not talking or touching. "Someday," he finally whispered, "we will have a son and daughter." She shushed him. "Why did you come?" he asked.

"Major Cao received a message from General Dong to rejoin Colonel Dinh. He is not to be left alone. I think they fear for his life." The implication was clear. In wartime, and away from the highly controlled and protected surroundings of Hanoi, a rear echelon apparatchik like Dinh often led a brief but very exciting life. They always returned home as a fallen hero.

"Dinh is a survivor," Tran said. He shot a look at the sleeping colonel. Dinh was sitting in one of the command post's six folding chairs, his chin slumped on his chest, breathing in honks and gasps.

Major Cao limped into the light. "I must see Colonel Dinh," he said. Tran pointed at the sleeping colonel. Cao moved forward and stumbled over a telephone line on the ground. He fell into Dinh, knocking him over. Dinh came awake, confused at first, not sure where he was. "My apologies, Colonel," Cao said, his voice cringing with the appropriate servility.

"You stupid fool," Dinh growled. If it had been anyone other than Cao, he would have slapped him. "Why are you here?"

"General Dong requests your status," Cao replied, phrasing the general's demands as tactfully as he could. "The attack must proceed on schedule."

"What? I sent a message as to our status after I destroyed the helicopter and the C-130."

Tran joined them. "We are out of contact with the Group, Colonel. No message has gone out."

"Make it happen," Dinh ordered.

"As soon as we can," Tran replied. "May I suggest you only claim the helicopter destroyed. Our observers only reported a probable hit on the C-130 and no smoke or damage was seen."

"Do not tell me what I saw with my own eyes," Dinh said. "Because we engaged the air pirates, we have moved forward. We will attack at the first opportunity."

Tran chose his words carefully, mostly for Cao's benefit. "We have moved our command post and the Sergey forward twice, perhaps a total of a kilometer. However, many of our men are still moving into position and not ready to attack yet As the moon is down, may I suggest we attack at first light?"

"You may not suggest," Dinh said. "And why should I wait once my forces are in place and ready?"

"May I suggest the colonel step outside and see for himself how dark it is? Also, the Bru own the night and they will set traps for the unwary."

"And why do the Bru own the night?" Dinh demanded.

175

Kim-Ly answered. "We only know they are ghosts at night. I suspect they have excellent night vision, probably a genetic mutation. Also, this is their land and they know it like a blind person knows his home."

"Utter nonsense," Dinh said. "Keep moving into position. We will attack when I give the order."

Phu Bai, South Vietnam

The six-man repair team on the C-123 had changed C-130 wheels countless times and went through a well-practiced drill. The setting moon still gave off enough light for the team to insert heavy jacks underneath the fuselage and raise the wheel without rigging floodlights. They took shortcuts that would have driven their NCOIC, non commissioned officer in charge, into spasms of despair and anger. But Warren was a firm believer that an officer told an NCO or airman when to do his job, not how to do it. If there was a problem getting the job done, then he would talk to the NCOIC and let him sort it out. Warren keyed off Hale, and since the flight engineer was satisfied with the way the wheel change was going, stretched out on a jump seat and was asleep in less than two minutes.

A loud clunk and a little bump woke him when the repair team lowered the big hydraulic jacks and dropped the C-130 onto its main gear. The repair team had switched out the damaged wheel in less than forty minutes and were reloading their equipment on the C-123 when an Army fuel browser pulling a trailer drove up. It was an M49 fuel tanker based on the venerable Deuce-and-a-half. "How much JP-4 you need?" the driver called.

"We'll take what you got," Hale told him.

The Trash Haulers

"Got a full load. Twelve hundred gallons plus another 400 in the trailer." The trailer was an unauthorized modification of a Water Buffalo water trailer. The driver and his fellow tankers had found a way to increase their efficiency and, at the same time, protect fuel by moving it out of the dumps, which were stationary and highly vulnerable targets. "Only got a hose though." The M49s did not have a single-point refueling nozzle, which was much more efficient and had to refuel C-130s over the wing with a conventional fuel nozzle. "Need a ladder."

"We ain't got one," Hale said. They waited while the C-123's props spun up and the engines came on line. The small cargo aircraft taxied out.

Flanders had been through the refueling drill many times and crawled through the emergency hatch on top of the flight deck. He scrambled to his feet and walked out on the left wing. "I'm getting too old for this crap," he called.

Hale grinned, ragging on him. "Where's Boyle when you need him?" He tossed the loadmaster a line to haul up the fuel nozzle. Flanders dragged the heavy hose along the left wing, over the fuselage, and onto the right wing, filling the tanks as he went. It was hard work and he was soon sweating. He was filling the last tank when another Deuce pulled up, stopping under the tail.

Boyle hopped off the back. "I'm back," he called. "I got it."

"What's he up to now?" Hale muttered, loud enough for Warren to hear.

177

2000 HOURS

Se Pang River Valley, South Vietnam

A loud scream pierced the dark, echoing over the hillside and waking the gun crew sleeping beside the ZSU-23. The men stirred and tried to ignore it, but the screaming only grew more intense and more agonizing. Finally, the gun captain switched on a flashlight with a shrouded red lens and motioned for two men to follow him into the night. A few minutes later, the screaming stopped.

The gun captain and the two men returned. Visibly shaken, the gun captain headed for the nearby cave that housed the command post to report in. Tran was waiting by the entrance. The young Vietnamese spoke in a low and trembling voice describing how a young woman who was searching for privacy to relieve herself had triggered a booby trap set by the Bru. She had broken a trip wire that released a bamboo stalk bowed horizontally that drove a sharp spike through her abdomen and severed her spine. The gun captain had applied pressure to her carotid arteries until she passed out, and then held it until she stopped breathing. Tran motioned him inside to brief the colonel from Hanoi. "He needs to hear it from you." Tran didn't think it would make an impression on Dinh but he had to try.

Dinh listened impatiently as the young gunner repeated his story. "So you silenced a stupid woman." He didn't ask how and turned on Tran. "And can you explain how the Bru managed to penetrate your perimeter, and what you are going to do about it?"

"We have discussed this before, Colonel. They will be gone by first light and safe in their camp before we can find them."

Dinh paced the floor. "Since you are unable to act, I must. Are my mortar teams in place?"

"The mortar teams report they are in range," Tran answered.

"Are you in radio contact with the teams?"

Tran glanced at the radio operator at the back of the cave. The woman nodded in the affirmative. "We are," Tran said.

Dinh glanced at his watch. "Order them to attack."

Tran spoke quietly to the operator to relay the order and followed Dinh outside to listen. Within moments, the dull thuds of 37mm mortars detonating echoed over the valley. Tran shook his head in disgust. "Without visual targets, the mortar teams are laying down a barrage in the dark hoping for success."

"Then you must go forward and lead them to success." Dinh smiled in triumph. "Now."

The Trash Haulers

Phu Bai, South Vietnam

The two pilots, navigator, and flight engineer gathered around Boyle at the back of the Deuce. Resting on the bed of the truck was a C-130 wheel with a fully inflated and balanced tire. "You said you could change the wheel if you had one," Boyle said, very proud of himself.

"I got to go," the truck driver said. "Do you want it or not?" The private gave off a strong body odor, his jungle fatigues were a disaster, and he needed a shave and haircut.

Warren made the decision. "We want." He looked at the men. "Okay. Let's get it off." It took three of them to lift the wheel and roll it off the truck, letting it bounce on the cracked asphalt. The wheel fell over and was still rolling around on its side when the truck driver darted back into the idling truck, ground the gears and accelerated away, disappearing into the dark.

Hale stood bolt straight, a good four inches taller than the raggedy airman, and stared at him. "Boyle, where in God's name did you find him?"

"I . . . ah . . . well . . . I know some people."

"And I suppose," Hale snapped, "that rat-bag private just happened to know where a C-130 wheel was lying around ready to be traded for something useful."

"That's the way it works" Boyle said. He was obviously confused. Boyle honestly thought everyone knew how the military black market worked where almost anything, including women, weapons, or vehicles, could be traded for drugs and liquor. "You said you wanted one."

"So what did you trade for it?" Hale asked.

"You know. Stuff."

Warren's inner alarm went off. "Where's your AWOL bag?"

Boyle's head jerked and he blinked. "Don't know, must've lost it."

"By any chance, did it have some 'stuff' in it that scumbag might have wanted?" Warren asked.

"I don't know."

The sound of the fuel truck echoed over the men as it drove away. Warren turned in time to see Flanders crawling into the top hatch. Warren pointed at the wheel. "Get it on board. We'll take it back to where it belongs." He headed for the Hercules, more than willing to put the problem of Billy Bob Boyle on a back burner.

Flanders was on the flight deck filling out the maintenance log. "We took on 10,400 pounds of JP-4 for a total of 17,400."

Warren automatically divided the fuel on board by 3300 and calculated they had over five hours endurance. "More than enough to get us back to the barn," he said. He settled into the pilot's seat and waited for his crew to manhandle the wheel on board and tie it down. Bosko was the first to join him. Santos and Hale were right behind.

"We're good to go," Hale said.

It was pure music to Warren. "Time to get the hell out of Dodge." He checked his watch. It was exactly 2015 hours local and now fully dark. It had been one hell of a day and he was feeling it. "Hey, Boz. You want this takeoff?"

The copilot grinned at him. "I though you'd never ask. I'll do it from the right seat. Good practice."

Warren gave himself a mental kick for not letting Bosko fly more.

The Trash Haulers

Over South Vietnam

Warren handled the radios as they climbed into the night sky, heading south for Cam Ranh Bay. "Damn," he muttered. "they're jamming the livin' hell out of the radios."

"The VC at work," Hale replied. Like Bosko and Santos, he had switched off the radio channel to spare his hearing.

"Work the backups," Bosko said, referring to the alternate radio frequencies.

"I'm trying," Warren said. He finally found a clear frequency and tried to transmit. But he was stepped on by priority traffic and two Maydays. They were just trash haulers heading for home plate so he quite trying. Then he heard it. "Boz, Dave, listen up on the VHF. Someone is calling for an emergency med evac." They often transported wounded soldiers between field hospitals, and rigging the C-130 for litters was a routine operation.

The three men listened, trying to sort out the chatter. "Oh, my God," the navigator groaned, finally making sense out of the chatter. "It's Se Pang."

"Why aren't the Dust Offs handling it?" Bosko asked. Helicopters flew the wounded out of combat to battalion aid stations or MASH units, not C-130s. "Has a Herk ever done that?"

"Not that I know of," Warren replied.

Flanders was listening on the intercom. "It's been done. Back in '66. Before I got to Okinawa."

Warren hit the transmit switch. "Da Nang ALCE, say situation at Se Pang."

"Aircraft calling Da Nang, say call sign."

183

"ALCE, Roscoe Two-One, You are coming through broken," Warren answered, barely able to read the airlift command element.

"Roscoe Two-One, are you headed for home plate?" Now, the radio transmissions were coming through more clearly as they flew south.

"That's affirmative, ALCE. Say situation at Se Pang."

"Numerous marines wounded. Dust Off fully tasked and not available."

Warren looked at Bosko, then Hale. "What do you think?"

Flanders answered from the rear. "It's what we do." The NCO had simply cut to the heart of why they were there. It was nothing profound, but a basic truth.

"Go for it," Hale said.

"We're too late for Happy Hour anyway," Bosko added.

"I guess that means no pussy tonight," Santos muttered.

Warren hit the transmit button. "ALCE, Roscoe Two-One will cover tasking into Se Pang."

"Roscoe Two-one, negative. Repeat, negative. Continue to home plate and report in as directed." The frequency was now clear and the radio transmission loud and readable.

Warren shook his head and made the decision. "ACLE you are unreadable. Roscoe Two-One transmitting in the blind. Proceeding direct Se Pang for med evac."

"Roscoe Two-One, proceed to home plate. Repeat, proceed to home plate."

"Too bad I couldn't understand that last transmission," Warren muttered.

"Heading 301 degrees" Santos said. "ETA Khe Sanh 2104 local."

The Trash Haulers

"Sergeant Flanders, start rigging for litters," Warren said.

"On it," Flanders answered.

2100 HOURS

Se Pang River Valley, South Vietnam

Captain Lam knelt in the brush and motioned Tran to follow him. They darted across an open area. "Over here," a voice whispered in the dark. Lam directed the red beam of his flashlight in that direction and led his commander to the mortar team hidden in the undergrowth. Lam crouched down and dowsed his light. He could hear the river flowing in front of them and estimated they were less than 300 meters from the airfield on the far bank.

Tran smelled the men on the mortar team but couldn't see them. He spoke in a quiet voice. "We saw the fires you started. Well done."

"We were lucky," a voice replied. "We heard them and focused on the sound. But they are learning fast and are quiet now."

"How many rounds do you have left?"

"Six," the voice replied.

"Dig in and wait for a target," Tran said. "Do not be afraid to strike in the dark. Once you have fired your last round, retreat to safety."

"We understand," the voice said.

"Excellent," Tran replied. He touched Lam on his forearm. Lam quickly moved out, paralleling the river bank, searching for the next mortar team. He did not use his flashlight this time.

Over South Vietnam

"Over Khe Sanh now," Santos said. "Fly 330. Se Pang on the nose in four." They were four minutes out. Ahead, flashes of light marked the night sky. "Okay, Se Pang ford on the radar." The distinctive Y of the river ford and east-west mountain ridge lighted the radar repeater in front of the pilots. Warren reached up and turned the gain down, making the screen go dark. He needed to preserve his night vision and Santos would keep them clear of high terrain as he directed them to the Special Forces compound.

Bosko was still flying the Hercules from the right seat and Warren keyed the UHF radio. "Se Pang, Roscoe Two-One three minutes out."

Banks, the Green Beret captain, answered. "Roscoe Two-One, hold clear. We are taking incoming mortars, the field is closed. Repeat, the field is closed."

"Lovely," Warren muttered. "Boz, hold south while I sort this out."

"Rog," Bosko replied. He turned hard to the left and entered a race track pattern. He would vary the altitude and pattern, never flying the same heading twice. "Dave, keep us out of trouble." Then, "Lights out." Hale reached up and

The Trash Haulers

turned off their navigation and anti-collision lights. They were running in the dark.

Warren stared into the night, trusting Bosko to fly the aircraft. He relaxed, closed his eyes, and let his mind work the problem. He did a mental pull-back, going for a bird's-eye view of the situation. Suddenly, it hit him. *What the hell! We've got twenty flares on board and Flanders knows how to use them.* He hit the transmit button.

"Se Pang, Roscoe. Say type of incoming."

"Roscoe, Se Pang. We're taking small stuff from the south side of the river. Probably 37mm mortar shovels, maybe a 50mm." The 37mm mortars had a range of 300 meters and the 50mm a range of 800 meters, which meant they were close in.

"Se Pang, say status of Trip A."

"Roscoe," Banks transmitted, "a flight of F-4s hit them after you departed. They got a secondary. Looked impressive from here."

"Copy all," Warren radioed. "I'll try to arrange something." He dialed in a radio frequency he remembered from flying Blind Bat, the night flare mission over the Ho Chi Minh trail. He may have been dog tired, but there was nothing wrong with his memory. He listened for one minute. Nothing. He dialed in a second frequency and listened for another minute. Again, no radio traffic. He dialed in a third frequency, still with the same results. He cycled back to the first frequency to repeat the listening watch. He hit pay dirt.

A flight of two marine A-4s, call sign Condole, was on the frequency trying to establish contact with a FAC on the ground at Khe Sanh. But as so often happened, the coordination between the Army, Marines, and Air Force had broken down and there was no response. "Pity," Santos said, "We've got a target for 'em."

"No way Moonbeam will release them to a trash hauler," Bosko said. Moonbeam was the airborne control and command post that ran the air war at night over Laos and I Corps and controlled all fighters. But Moonbeam was an Air Force unit and the marine A-4s were an independent bunch who barely tolerated being controlled by the Air Force.

"Maybe we won't have to ask," Warren said. "Time to play FAC." He keyed the radio, calling the marine fighters. "Condole, Roscoe Two-One. How copy?"

A gravelly voice answered. "Condole copies you five by."

"We have trade, twenty miles north of your location."

"Negative on the trade, Roscoe. Moombean wants us to hold while they find tasking." Warren caught the perversion of Moonbeam's call sign and that the pilot had said 'tasking' and not 'a target.' He had an opening he could work – if he played it right.

"Condole, we're taking it in the neck here." Warren was betting the pilot leading the flight of two fighters would catch the allusion to leathernecks. Hopefully, the controller on Moonbeam would be too preoccupied to make the connection. He was right on both counts.

"Go cheap suit," was all the marine said. Cheap suit was $29.95, the price of a famous stateside tailor's men's suit. Warren changed the radio frequency to 299.5. It was an unauthorized frequency aircrews used to talk among themselves without Moonbeam's knowledge. Warren checked in. Condole was waiting for him. "Roscoe, Two-One, authenticate Sierra Hotel."

The Trash Haulers

Santos let out a hoot of laughter. He had expected the challenge and response and had already spun his code wheel, setting S opposite H, the initials for shit hot. "Sierra Hotel authenticates Tango," he told Warren. Later on, Santos recorded the incident in his journal but changed the authentication to Foxtrot, making a connection to the *f* word.

"Roscoe Two-One authenticates Tango," Warren transmitted.

"What'cha got?" the marine asked.

"A company of marines is in contact at Se Pang with wounded. We're tying to air evac 'em out but need fire suppression to land."

The marine never hesitated. "I can do that, if I can find 'em."

"I'll kick some flares and light 'em up."

"Sierra hotel!" the marine radioed. "Coming your way."

Warren turned in his seat and looked at the other three men while he spoke. "Sergeant Flanders, can you and Boyle drop some flares by hand out the port parachute door?" On a normal flare mission, the loadmasters placed twelve flares in a dispenser rack mounted across the end of the ramp and literally kicked the flares out the back.

"Piece of cake," Flanders replied. "I'll tether us in. Just fly straight and level while we're doing it." They would be standing in the open door without parachutes.

"How long you need?" Warren asked, wondering how long it would take to uncrate the flares and hook up their harnesses.

"Ready in three," Flanders replied.

Now Warren had to get his crew in sync. "Okay, here's the game plan. The Gomers are on the south side of the

191

river, and I'm guessing within 800 meters of the field. No way we're going to engage a ZSU, but I'm willing to bet that brace of F-4s nailed it." Trash Haulers avoided anti-aircraft artillery like the plague for good reason, but this particular AAA had raised its head and paid the price. But Warren wasn't ready to write it totally off. "We're gonna do a Blind Bat and drop some flares, and see if the Condoles can kick some ass. We'll run in on a westerly heading right up the river valley, 8000 feet, displaced to the left of the river with the air patch on our right. I wanna kick two flares and then circle back to the left to see if we lit anything up. Everyone, keep your eyeballs peeled and try to get my eyes on anything you see that looks like a target. I'll call the Condoles in using the flares as a reference.

"Except for Sergeant Flanders, I know this is a first flare drop for you. I also know that a ZSU may still be out there, but it has to get a visual and we're dark. I'm also betting the Gomers, if they are there, will hear the Condoles and not engage. They know a Blind Bat can bring down holy hell on 'em. There is a chance they might try for a lucky shot once we're past and they're at our deep six. But we'll be jinking like hell and I'll turn out to the south to get the ridge between us for terrain masking. Any questions?" There were none.

"Dave, you've got to find the compound on radar and guide us in, right down the river valley, but keep us to the left of the river. If we can't get a visual on the field, you'll have to make the call."

"What's the command?" Santos asked.

Flanders answered from the rear. "'Ready – ready – kick' works best for me. We're good to go in the rear."

The Trash Haulers

"Boz, I've got it," Warren said, taking back control of the Hercules. He keyed the radio. "Condole, say state and position."

"Flight of two. Two Mark-82s. Playtime eight. Lox sweet. Overhead, no joy." The two A-4s were each carrying two 500-pound bombs, could stay in the area for eight minutes, had good oxygen, and were in the area but did not have the Hercules in sight.

"Condole, Roscoe Two-One is at angels eight. There may be an active ZSU in the area."

"Condole at angels fourteen, looking." The two A-4s were at 14,000 feet, 6000 feet above the Hercules and looking for it.

"Okay, folks," Warren told his crew, "here we go. This is gonna go down fast. Dave, inbound heading."

Santos's face was buried in the radar scope. He played with the receiver gain and antenna tilt, breaking out the ridgeline and distinctive Y in the river. It matched the returns he had shaded in on his chart, and they were two miles southeast of the Se Pang river ford. "Fly 345, expect a hard port turn to 270 in eighty seconds."

Warren turned to the new heading. "Anti-collision light on." Hale reached up and hit the switch turning on the bright strobes located on the top and bottom of the fuselage.

"Condole has you in sight." This over the UHF.

"Strangle anti-collision," Warren said. If the two A-4s could see them, so could any AAA gunners on the ground. Hale turned the beacon off. Warren reached around to his side console and lifted the guard over the toggle switch that opened the air deflector doors. "Air deflectors open," The air deflector panels located on each side of the fuselage just

193

forward of the parachute doors opened thirty degrees, protecting anyone standing in the parachute doors from wind blast. "Port parachute door open," he ordered.

Flanders was ready. "Port parachute door open."

They were almost ready. "Loadmaster," Warren said, "set two flares for parachute, delay twenty-five seconds." Flanders and Boyle quickly set the two dials in the top of each flare and held on to the four-foot lanyard that would arm the flare when dropped. The flare would fall for twenty-five seconds before the parachute would deploy and the flare ignite. It would burn for about three minutes, descending around 1100 feet, lighting up the ground below with two million candle power.

"Turn in ten seconds," Santos said. "Ready – ready – turn. Heading 270."

Warren rolled 45 degrees and turned to the inbound heading. He rolled out and rooted their indicated airspeed on 150 knots. "No joy," Warren said, indicating he could not see anything on the ground.

"No joy," Bosko repeated.

"Come right three degrees," Santos said, still directing the Hercules, his eyes locked on the radar screen.

"Kickers in the door," Warren ordered.

"Kickers ready," Flanders replied.

"No joy," Warren repeated. "Dave, you've got it." Santos would have to call the drop.

And he did. "Ready – ready – ready – KICK ONE!"

"One gone," Flanders said. He quickly stepped out of the door for Boyle to step in for the second drop. But the airman just stood there, frozen with fear. Flanders jerked the

The Trash Haulers

flare out of his hands, almost dropping it, grabbed the lanyard, and stepped onto the open door.

"Ready – ready – KICK TWO!" Santos called.

"Two's gone," Flanders said, quickly stepping out of the door. He pushed Boyle into a jump seat and sat down, holding on. "Secure in the rear," he told the flight deck.

Warren didn't hesitate and tuned sharply to the left as he nosed the aircraft over and pushed the throttles up. A line of tracers reached up from the ground, passing well above and behind the turning Hercules. "Trip A at our deep six," Flanders called. "No threat."

"ZSU in sight," Condole lead radioed.

"Cleared in hot," Warren replied. He rolled out on a heading of 090 in time to see a flashing tail beacon diving at the spot where the ZSU had been firing from. "What the hell?" he wondered. The marine pilot should have turned off his anti-collision light when coming down the wire.

Then, "Check that out, folks." The wind was out of the south, and the two flares were still descending and drifting to the north, lighting the river valley, the Special Forces compound, and runway. "Well done, Dave."

"One's off dry," the lead Condole radioed. The beacon pulled up without releasing its bombs and reached into the night sky, a perfect target of a AAA gunner. On cue, a solid line of tracers reached up from a spot about fifty meters above the valley floor and against the steep face of the karst as the Condole jinked hard to dodge the AAA chasing him down.

195

Se Pang River Valley, South Vietnam

Tran watched the tracers reach up for the escaping jet. He jammed the old walkie-talkie radio he was carrying against his ear and mashed the transmit button. "Cease fire, cease fire," he ordered. But nothing happened and the tracers continued to etch the dark night. It was a mistake, perhaps fatal, to keep firing at the escaping jet just because it was still in range. The gun captain knew better. "I'm coming in," Tran radioed.

There was no answer.

Over Se Pang, South Vietnam

Another voice came over the Hercules' radio they had not heard. "Condole Two's in. Triple A in sight." This time there was no flashing beacon as the second A-4 came down the wire, locked on to the still firing ZSU battery. "Ripple two," the second marine radioed. "Two's off." Two explosions flashed in the night and neatly bracketing the ZSU. It stopped firing.

"Shack," the first marine pilot radioed. The Condoles had suckered in the AAA gunners.

A fireball erupted on the side of the ridge, sending a bright mushroom cloud into the night sky. "Jesus H. Christ," Bosko whispered. "They got a secondary. What in hell would go up like that?"

"I'm guessing an ammo or fuel dump," Warren replied.

The radio squawked. "Roscoe Two-One, Condole. I've got two remaining. Any more trade?"

"Roger, Condole. "I'll lay another string of flares over the south side of the river. You're cleared in hot."

The Trash Haulers

Warren banked the Hercules sharply for another run in. "Okay, folks," he said over the intercom, "one more time. Dave, you've got it."

Santos had it wired. "Come left five. Ready – ready – kick one." He paused. "Ready – ready – kick two."

"Secure in the rear," Flanders said, telling the flight deck the two kickers were strapped in. Warren jinked hard, just in case the AAA was still alive. But it wasn't.

"Condole One is in," the marine radioed. "I have movement on the ground, south side of the river, moving away from the river." A short break. "One's off, bingo fuel, RTB." Two bright flashes walked along the side of the river.

"Roger, Condole," Warren replied. "ready to copy BDA?" BDA was bomb damage assessment.

"Roger that."

"One ZSU battery destroyed. One secondary, suspected ammo or fuel dump. Sorry, no joy on the last run."

"No problem," the marine replied. "I bracketed the fuckers and bodies don't do secondaries."

"Condole," Warren radioed, "great show all around. I'm buying the bar."

"We'll hold you to it," the marine replied. Both men knew it would never happen, but they were a band of brothers. "Good luck on the med evac."

"We'll get 'em out," Warren promised. He glanced over at Bosko who was looking directly at him. The copilot gave a little nod. "Okay, folks. Strap in and let's get this puppy on the ground. Boz, see if you can raise Se Pang." He flew a descending spiral as Bosko made radio contact with the Special Forces compound. The field was secure and they were cleared to land.

Se Pang River Valley, South Vietnam

The young Vietnamese captain rolled over and came to his knees, his head still pounding from the shock of the bomb blast. "Colonel Tran," he called, surprised that he could hear his own voice. There was no answer. He looked around. Flickering tongues of flames set off by the two bombs cast a weird half-light around him. He could barely make out the lump on the ground that was twisting and turning, moaning in pain. It was Tran.

Lam crawled over to his commander and gently rolled him onto his back. Shrapnel from the second bomb had ripped a gapping wound in his abdomen and part of his intestines were hanging out. Lam silently cursed the bad luck that had caught them in the open as he uncapped his canteen and washed the exposed intestines. He gently pushed them back into to place. Fortunately, there wasn't too much blood, but every instinct, all of his experience, warned him it was bad. He rolled up his shirt to used as compress to close the wound before wrapping his equipment belt around Tran's torso, holding the makeshift compress in place. He placed his left hand over the compress, relieved that the bleeding had slowed to a soft ooze. But for how long? He felt around on the ground, finally scooping up Tran's walkie-talkie. He hit the transmit button.

"Calling Lieutenant Colonel Du, calling Lieutenant Colonel Du." There was no answer. He hit the button and transmitted in the blind. "This is Lam. Colonel Tran is down and seriously wounded. I need immediate help."

A man's voice answered. "Where are you?"

The Trash Haulers

Lam looked up, thinking. He glanced at the button compass on his wrist watch. The luminescent numbers glowed faintly in the dark. He was due north of the karst where the command post was located. "Shine a light," he radioed. On cue, a light blinked at him from the hillside. He held his compass up to read the numbers and sighted across it. "I am on a bearing of zero-four-five degrees from your location, at approximately twelve hundred meters."

A woman's voice answered. "We can find you." It was Kim-Ly.

"We need a litter and a medical kit," Lam transmitted.

There was no answer.

Over Se Pang, South Vietnam

Roscoe 21 was passing through 4000 feet when a red road flare ignited on the ground. Six more flares popped in succession, etching a straight line on the ground. "Field in sight," Warren and Bosko chorused.

Warren called for the before landing checklist as they continued to spiral down. He rolled out on a close-in base leg and called for gear down. A loud, and all too familiar, rumbling sound echoed up from the cargo compartment. "Sergeant Flanders, check the gear." He leveled off and pushed the throttles up, stabilizing their airspeed at 120 knots.

"It's the left rear main again," Flanders said. "Flat as a pancake but the forward main looks okay. Right gear checks good. Down and locked."

Warren made the correct decision. "Time to head for the barn." He reached for the throttles.

"Sir," Hale said, "we got a wheel and I can change it. All we gotta do is dig a hole. I'm guessing an hour, tops."

"We'll be in and out before any Dust Off can get here," Bosko said. It was his way of saying "Go for it."

"Turn final and I can breakout the runway," Santos said.

Flanders was with them. "Rigging for litters complete. All secure back here." Then, "And no one gives a shit what Billy Bob thinks."

"Turning final," Warren said. He rolled out on final approach and called for full flaps.

"One mile out," Santos said, concentrating on the radar scope. "Half a mile."

Warren flew with right wing low to touch down on the right landing gear. "Landing lights," Warren said. Hale flicked the switch on the overhead panel and the high-powered lights cut the night in front of them. Santos had them lined up perfectly.

Se Pang, South Vietnam

The Hercules touched down, first on the right main, then more gently on the left. Warren reversed the props, careful not to brake too hard. "Crater on the nose" Bosko called at the same moment Warren saw the shallow hole in the runway. He lifted the throttles out of reverse and pulled back on the yoke, lifting the nose gear up to clear the hole. The main gear on the Hercules straddled the crater as it rumbled down the dirt strip. They stopped with fifty feet to spare.

"Let me be the first to welcome you to the land of no Base Exchange and warm beer," Flanders said. "Door coming open, clear in the rear." He lowered the loading

The Trash Haulers

ramp to level and stood at the edge, directing them as they backed up.

"There's a crater dead center," Warren warned.

The loadmaster was in his element, doing what he did best. "Crater in sight. Come to your right, go straight, we're clear."

Warren braked to a halt two-hundred feet short of the approach end of the runway and turned into the open area that served as a parking ramp. Captain Wes Banks was waiting for them. "Let's go check for damage," Warren said, quickly climbing out of his seat. Hale and Flanders joined him outside as they did a quick walk around, their flashlights scanning the fuselage and wings for battle damage. They finished their inspection at the left main gear door. Other than being flat, the tire looked good. "Look at that," Warren said, sticking his finger in a small bullet hole in the main gear door. "The golden B-B." A lucky shot from a small caliber rifle had punctured the tire.

Banks examined the hole in the gear door. "Probably an AK-47," he said. "What now?"

"We change the wheel," Hale explained. "Luckily, we've got one on board but no jack. We have to dig a hole around the wheel to pull it off. Then we mount the good wheel and taxi out of the hole."

"Have you ever done it?" Banks asked. "Like personally?" Hale shook his head. The Ranger captain thought for a moment. "The Bru are world-class hole diggers," he said. "And they want to say thanks. Just don't get in their way. I'll get them to fill in the crater on the runway. They've done it before." He disappeared into the night to make it happen.

201

Warren followed Santos to the edge of the parking area where they unzipped their flight suits and relieved themselves on the hard packed dirt. "Hell of a day, Captain," Santos allowed. "The Condoles did good and nailed that ZSU."

Warren didn't reply but stared at the darkened ridge to the south, hoping it was true. But an inner voice warned there was a ZSU gunner out there, still waiting for his chance. The war had become very personal.

2200 HOURS

Se Pang, Vietnam

A soft red light bathed the flight deck as Santos and Hale filled out the flight log and maintenance forms. It was a never-ending process and both men were tired. Hale rubbed his eyes and double-checked the gauges on the overhead fuel control panel. The numbers didn't quite add up.

Normally, the gauges were accurate enough, but Hale was old school and never fully trusted any readout, always double-checking and worrying over what might be wrong. The fuel remaining didn't quite match what he calculated they should have. It was only two-hundred pounds low and they were parked on a slope, which might make a difference. He rationalized it away. They had more than enough fuel to fly to any base in Vietnam and land with six or seven thousand pounds to spare. He humphed. Once they changed out the wheel, they were good to go. He closed the log and dropped it into its holder. "Time to help Flash," he said, climbing down from the flight deck.

Warren was sitting on the entrance steps as Flanders, Boyle, and Bosko chipped away at the hard-packed laterite soil with the three folding entrenching shovels Banks had found. The small shovels had a sharp edge, but were intended for digging a foxhole. "It's going more slowly than I expected," Warren admitted.

"It is dark out here," Hale murmured. He could barely see the men working in the dim glow of a flashlight. He thought for a moment. "We better douse the lights on the flight deck to save the battery."

"Good idea," Warren replied. "Hey, Dave, strangle the lights," he called, saving Hale the trouble of climbing back on board. On cue, the red lights went out and Santos climbed down, feeling his way.

"Sum'bitch, it's dark out here," the navigator said.

"Much cooler though," Warren said. Then, "We could sure use some help." They had been waiting for almost an hour.

"I'll go spell 'em," Hale said.

"I'm with you," Santos said.

Warren listened as the two men relieved Bosko and Flanders. "They are the best," Warren murmured to himself.

A soft "Sir" caught his attention. His head jerked to the left, towards the sound. A small dark shadow was standing less than six feet away. A Bru.

"You scared me," the pilot admitted. He could barely make out the shadows standing behind the Montagnard.

"We help," the man said. He walked silently past. The shadows followed, and twelve of the small-framed mountain men filed past. Each was carrying a single tool; a shovel, pick, digging stick, basket, or a water jug. The last in line was Captain Wes Banks.

"That got my attention," Warren said. "I never heard or saw them."

"The Bru own the night," Banks explained. "The VC and North Vietnamese shit a brick having nightmares about them. Have your men stand back. They know what to do."

"Hey, guys," Warren called, "take a break. Let 'em at it." The five Americans stepped back and let the Bru go to work.

The Montagnards started by building a small campfire to see by. "The VC are attracted to lights at night," Banks explained, "but won't go anywhere near a campfire for fear of the Bru. It's a surefire way to get booby trapped."

"What the hell are they doing now?" Bosko wondered. The Bru were lining up to urinate on the hard dirt around the wheel. Finished, they emptied the jugs of water, further softening the laterite. Silently, five men disappeared into the dark to refill the jugs while the others went to work digging.

"Wish we had done that," Flanders said.

Warren thought for a moment. "Captain Banks, how many wounded are we looking at?"

"Fourteen litters and at least thirty walking wounded. Another dozen or so are wounded but can still fight, so they'll come out later."

"How bad are the litter patients?" Warren asked.

"Two or three probably won't make it."

"Sounds like you took a pounding."

"Could have been worse." The Ranger looked into the night. "Close air support made the difference. But they'll be back, probably at first light. Damn, we need a gunship on station."

"Time to make some radio calls," Warren said. He needed to tell Moonbeam that they were NOR, not operationally ready, when they would be OR, operationally ready, and that they were bringing out wounded. "Sergeant Hale, does the battery have enough juice for the radios, or do we need to start the GTC?"

"We got a full charge," Hale answered.

Banks frowned. "Your GTC makes a lot of noise. It might attract some unwanted attention."

"So they are out there," Warren said.

"Oh, yeah," the Ranger admitted. "Best to use battery power."

"I'd prefer to save it for starting the GTC." They needed the Gas Turbine Compressor to start engines.

"Keep it short," Hale said, making the decision.

"Will do," Warren replied. He stood and stretched his right arm, working his aching shoulder. The sniper round was taking a toll. Hale followed him onto the flight deck to power up the radios. Within a minute the UHF radio was on line. Warren went to the common frequency used to contact Moonbeam. Nothing. He cycled through the frequencies they used most often, again without making contact. They were in a fairly deep river valley, and, as the radios were line-of-sight, the mountains were blocking their transmissions. Then he tried an ALCE frequency. Almost immediately a voice answered. "Roscoe Two-One, MAC Fourteen-Twenty copies you five-by." MAC 1420, was a Military Airlift Command transport aircraft.

The Trash Haulers

"Roger MAC Fourteen-Twenty," Warren answered. "Request you relay our status to Moonbeam."

"Go ahead, Roscoe."

"Roscoe Two-One is on the ground at Se Pang, NOR for left aft main gear. Repair in progress, expect to be airborne in one plus thirty with fourteen litter patients and thirty walking wounded. Will transport to Da Nang or Chu Lai unless advised otherwise. Se Pang is hot."

"Copy all," the MAC transport replied. "Standby."

"I wonder where he's from," Warren muttered.

"That droning noise you heard in the background was a recip," Hale said. A recip, or reciprocal, was a conventional piston engine. "I'm guessing a C-124."

Warren laughed. "Old Shakey! Probably left over from the Korean War."

The C-124 Globemaster II built by Douglas was the primary heavy-lifter for the Air Force until the C-141 Starlifter replaced it. Old Shakey was powered by the biggest radial piston engines ever built and flew low and slow. But it could still haul cargo. The radio came alive. "Roscoe Two-One, MAC Fourteen-Twenty. Moonbeam copied all. Second Surgical Hospital at Chu Lai is expecting you."

Warren hit the transmit button. "MAC Fourteen-Twenty, thanks for the help." He turned the radio off.

"I hope they repaired the runway," Hale muttered. "We don't need another wheel change."

Warren climbed out of the pilot's seat. "Time to see how the Bru are doing."

"Roger on the Bru," Hale said, following him off the flight deck.

207

Banks was waiting under the wing with bad news. "They hit rock and can't dig through it."

"Shit-oh-dear," Warren mumbled. He thought for a moment. "We can move the Herk and try another spot."

"Yeah, but where?" Hale asked.

"Why don't we dig the hole first and move the Herk to the hole?" Santos asked.

"You'll have to taxi over the hole to get the rear wheel into it," Banks said. "Doesn't sound good."

"We don't have to taxi over the hole," Warren said. "We can back into it."

Banks nodded. "I'll get the Bru on it. They can dig test holes before going for the whole shebang." He turned to the Bru and spoke in a low voice. Within seconds, they disappeared into the night.

"I don't think we're going to be OR in one plus thirty," Hale said.

"So we wait," Santos added.

"It's not like we have a choice," Warren said. "I'm gonna crash." He made his way into the darkened cargo compartment and stretched out on a jump seat.

Se Pang River Valley, South Vietnam

Kim-Ly moved fast, her flashlight's red beam sweeping the way as she led the two men through the underbrush. She held a U.S. Army field compass in her other hand at eye level, her eyes fixed on the sight wire as she held true to 045 degrees. Lam saw the light when they were fifty meters away. He blinked his flashlight, giving her a red beacon to home on. She skidded to a stop beside him, falling to her knees. She shrugged off her backpack as she caught her

The Trash Haulers

breath. The two men following her lowered the bamboo cage suspended from the two poles between their shoulders to the ground. The North Vietnamese used the cage to transport livestock southward on the trail and hold POWs for the northward journey into captivity.

Lam ran his hand over the bamboo framework, asking an unspoken "Why?"

"We have many wounded," Kim-Ly explained. "It was the only litter available. Where is he?" Lam moved aside so she could see. She scrambled to Tran's side and used her flashlight to scan his wound. Frustrated, she twisted off the red lens to examine him in a better light. She gently removed Lam's equipment belt and shirt that served as a compress to examine the gaping gash in his abdomen. The wound was amazingly clean and she felt a surge of hope. "My pack," she whispered. She looked around, fully aware the Bru were watching. Lam handed her the pack.

Kim-Ly had treated many wounded comrades with similar wounds. Again, she probed the wound, thankful the bleeding had almost stopped. But for how long? She emptied a bottle of antiseptic over the wound and rolled Tran on his side to let it drain. Next, she layered three compresses together and placed them over the wound. Gently, she wrapped a big bandage around his torso. There was nothing more she could do. She sat back on her haunches and ran the trail's grim calculus. She understood the protocol; without a fully equipped surgery, make them comfortable and place them aside to die. She closed her eyes and rocked back and forth. It was an easy decision.

"Please place Colonel Tran in the cage and lock it." She waited, not moving while the three men gently moved Tran

209

into the cage and locked it. Lam handed her the key. She reached through the bars and felt the bandage. It was still dry. "Captain Lam, please lead our two comrades to safety and rejoin your men." Lam acknowledged the order and disappeared into the night, leading the two porters.

She waited. Satisfied the men had enough time to reach safety, Kim-Ly stood and held the light under her chin, illuminating her face.

"I have a prisoner for you," she called in Vietnamese, knowing it was her death sentence. Two small figures emerged from the shadows. One squatted in front of her, his machete laying across the top of his thighs. "This is Colonel Tran Sang Quan, the commander of the Binh Tram in Laos. You know he is an honorable man and not a killer. He knows much and is valuable. Take him to the Americans."

The Bru said nothing and didn't move.

She knelt in front of the man as he came to his feet. "I am his wife. My name is Kim-Ly. I am a lieutenant colonel. I give him to you." She handed the key to the Montagnard, closed her eyes, and bent her head, waiting for the machete. Nothing, no searing pain, no sudden agony. She opened her eyes. She was alone and the bamboo cage was gone. Her flashlight was still on, lying on the ground and aimed to the south, pointing to the karst formation and safety.

2300 HOURS

Se Pang River Valley, South Vietnam

"Sir," the radio operator said, her soft voice echoing in the cave, "Captain Lam will be here within the hour. He reports that Colonel Tran is seriously wounded and Lieutenant Colonel Du is with him. They cannot move Colonel Tran."

Dinh stood and took a deep breath. His will had proven invincible and he had prevailed. He forced himself to remain calm as he searched for the right words. "We have lost a valiant comrade-in-arms. His memory will be enshrined with the heroes of the War." Another thought came to him. "We will honor his sacrifice by attacking the scum who killed him and removing them from our land. The order of the day is attack! Always attack! Forever attack! It is our duty to attack! Transmit the order." He sat down, exhausted.

Se Pang, South Vietnam

Warren glanced at his watch. "Come on," he urged. They had been on the ground almost ninety minutes and he was deeply worried. But there was nothing he could do except wait. He closed his eyes and tried to sleep, but visions of a court-martial played out in his imagination. An inner voice told him that unless he got them safely out of there, he deserved it. Unable to sleep, he stood up and made his way to the crew entrance. Hopefully, the Bru were making progress. He stepped outside in time to see a bright flash half way down the runway, quickly followed by a dull boom. "Incoming!" he shouted, running for cover. A second mortar exploded, moving towards the C-130. His crew were right behind him. They piled into a log and sandbagged bunker just as a deep quiet settled over the runway and nearby compound.

"Hell of a way to wake up," Bosko said.

They crawled out of the bunker and walked back to the C-130. Banks' sergeant was waiting for them. "Should be okay for awhile," the NCO told them.

"How long is 'awhile?'" Warren asked.

"Hard to say. Most likely, that was it for the night." The gravelly-voiced Ranger was a man of few words.

"Why only two rounds?" Santos asked.

"Just harassing fire from a patrol. A 50-PM mortar." The old Soviet-made 50mm mortar weighed twenty-six pounds and fired a grenade-sized round. "Un-aimed barrage. Range, maybe 800 meters. Got to get in pretty close. The Bru are out looking for 'em right now. So they shoot and scoot. I expect we'll take some heavy rounds in the morning when they can get a visual target." A small light flashed on the southern ridge. "Incoming," the sergeant said, his voice amazingly calm. He surprised them with a burst of speed as he ran for the bunker.

The Trash Haulers

The six men followed him, piling on top of each other in the bunker. Boyle was the last in. A much louder boom echoed over them. "So much for the small stuff," Bosko quipped. Again, a hard silence captured them.

"That was an eighty-two, one heavy mutha," the sergeant said. The BM-37, Battalion Mortar, could reach out almost two miles and lobbed a six-pound, 82mm round that could do serious damage. "They're getting serious and ranging on the 50, going for the lucky shot."

"They won't need luck when they can see," Warren added, desperately hoping they would be long gone by first light.

The sergeant stood and stared into the night, looking towards the invisible ridge line. "They might have a spotter in position. Don't show a light." Then he was gone.

"Don't show a light," Bosko groused. Then it hit him. "Starting engines is going to be sporting."

"To say the least," Warren added, at last figuring it out. The VC, or PAVN, he didn't know which, knew they were there, had the range, but needed to visually acquire a target to aim at, and any light would do until morning. He sat on the ground and clasped his hands in front of his knees. His crew joined him, sitting silently, waiting. "Sergeant Hale, you ever do an engine start touchy feely in the dark?" he asked.

"No, sir. Not sure I can. I've got to see the instrument panels."

"How far can you see a red light at night?" Warren wondered.

213

"Far enough for a spotter," Flanders replied. "We can always button up and hang some blankets to blackout the flight deck."

An explosion cut the dark, this time between the runway and the compound. "Still ranging," Santos said.

"And forcing everyone to keep their heads down," Bosko muttered. "It would be nice to have a gunship on station returning the favor."

"Oh, yeah," Warren murmured. He pulled into himself, running 'what if?' scenarios through his mind, trying to plan ahead.

Santos jumped to his feet. "I hear a C-130."

Warren stood and listened, not hearing it at first. Santos did have excellent hearing. Then he heard it, very faintly. He checked the time – 2338 – almost midnight. They had been on the ground four minutes shy of two hours. He listened and pointed to the west. "Over there." The distinctive rumble of four Allison T-56 turboprop engines grew louder. Warren gave a silent prayer, hoping that it was a gunship out of Ubon. Now they could hear the C-130 as it flew by to the south of them. A flare popped in the night, shortly followed by a second, a third, then a fourth. The ridgeline lit up like a stadium at night under full flood lights as the flares drifted down underneath their parachutes. "It's a Blind Bat!" Warren shouted. They ran for the C-130.

They scrambled on board in the dark, scraping their shins and bumping against bulkheads as they felt their way onto the flight deck. Behind them, they could hear Flanders curse in eloquent terms that would make a marine gunny

The Trash Haulers

sergeant take notes as he rummaged around the cargo deck. In less than a minute, he passed up two blankets. He closed the crew entrance hatch before scampering up the crew ladder. He squeezed between Warren and the left side control panel. "Boyle," Flanders ordered, "squeeze your scrawny ass next to the Lieutenant." The airman did as ordered and stood beside Bosko. "Make like a scarecrow," Flanders said, "and hold up a blanket to cover the windscreens." The two men spread their arms across the cockpit and held the blankets up, effectively creating blackout curtains.

Hale reached for the overhead panel and switched on the instrument lights and electrical bus to power up the radios. Warren hit the transmit button. "Blind Bat, Roscoe Two-One. How copy?"

Hardy's distinctive voice answered. "Blind Bat Zero-One copies you five-by. Well, here's another fine mess you've gotten us into, Ollie."

"Now he's a fuckin' comedian," Bosko groused, not appreciating the play on the famous Laurel and Hardy routine. But he was thankful the flare ship was overhead.

"Roscoe Two-One," Hardy transmitted, now all business. "I've got a flight of four inbound and will be working the area. I would appreciate a sit rep on what it looks like from the ground. I'll work south of your position and keep you dark."

"Will do," Warren replied. "Going radio out to save the battery."

"Blind Bat Zero-One copies. Monitor Guard on your PR-90." The PR-90 was the survival radio they each carried

215

in the survival vest. By using Guard, the emergency radio channel, they could stay in contact with the flare ship.

"The Colonel does have a clue," Santos said.

"The man is full of surprises," Warren allowed. "I'm guessing Moonbeam relayed our call and dropped the ball in his court. They gotta be up to their collective asses in alligators. I wonder how he scraped up a crew."

Hale switched off the power and the men climbed off the flight deck to watch the show from outside. Three minutes later, another string of flares illuminated the night, and they heard the distinctive roar of an F-4 screaming down the wire on a bomb run. Six explosions rippled across the side of the ridge. "Holy shit," Bosko breathed. "It's the fuckin' Fourth of July on steroids."

They started to cheer wildly when a second string of bombs walked across the ridge. "Now who's fuckin' head is down?" Boyle shouted, jumping up and down.

Warren felt a tug at his left elbow, startling him. A Bru was standing there. "Sir, the hole is okay."

"Thank you," Warren replied, his spirits soaring. It was the moment he had been waiting for. "Okay, here's the game plan. We're gonna start two and three and taxi on two. Sergeant Flanders, I want you out in front with a Bru. He guides you, you guide us. Use a hand to shield your flashlight and aim it at our nose gear, not the cockpit, otherwise, might get a reflection off the glass. I'll follow your light, and you back us into the hole. Dave, I want you outside by the left main on the intercom extension to guide us into the exact spot. It's gonna be tricky in the dark. Boyle, I want you doing the scarecrow blanket thing beside me during engine start and taxi. Dave, you do the same beside Boz

The Trash Haulers

during engine start. Then head for the rear while I taxi the Herk. Boz, you take over from Dave and hold the blankets to keep the flight deck blacked out, but give me a crack to look out and follow Sergeant Flanders. Any questions?"

There weren't any. "Okay. Let's do it." They ran for the Hercules and were taxiing three minutes later. They had moved less than a hundred feet, curving to their left, when Flanders blinked his flashlight to stop. He made a sweeping motion to the right and Warren slowly backed the Hercules in that direction.

"Slow, slow," Santos said over the intercom, as he walked beside the left main gear. The roar of number three engine was deafening but he ignored it. "Stop!" Warren hit the brakes. "We're there," Santos said.

"Shut 'em down," Warren said. Hale quickly shut the engines down, and the two men cocked the Hercules for a quick start. Without a word, Hale ran for the rear, stumbling in the dark.

"We're gonna need some light," Santos said.

"Get Boyle and whoever to do the scarecrow thing," Warren replied. He scrambled out the crew entrance and called into the pitch black. "Please tell Captain Banks to bring the wounded."

A Bru answered in a low voice, only a few feet away. "Yes, sir."

"No wonder the VC shit a brick," Warren muttered. He checked his watch, thankful that he could at least read it in the dark. It was exactly midnight.

217

2400 HOURS

Se Pang River Valley, South Vietnam

"Major Cao," Dinh shouted, his voice echoing over the cave. "What is our status?"

The young-looking major was huddled with three soldiers, listening to their reports. "In a moment, sir. The last reports are just coming in." He broke away and sent the men back to their posts. Cao studied his clipboard, searching desperately for a way to tell Dinh what he did not want to hear. An idea came to him. It was all too simple and he would tell Dinh the truth, starting with the good news.

"Sir, we are in radio contact with Group. However, our status report must be encrypted for transmission."

"Do not send it until I have reviewed it in detail," Dinh ordered. He liked being in total command of the regiment.

"Yes, sir. We have suffered heavy casualties with 223 wounded and eighty-seven killed. Our mortar teams in place on the river report nine rounds remaining, but we should be able to resupply them by morning. The Sergey was damaged in the last attack but should be in commission shortly.

However, the gun captain and an aimer were killed and we have no one to replace them."

"It is a matter of motivation, Cao. Do you understand that? Motivation! When can I attack?"

"Even with mortars, we must move our comrades across the river and into position to bring their weapons to bear."

"Make it happen," Dinh ordered. "And let me see the status report." Cao handed him the clipboard. Dinh reduced the number of wounded and killed by half. He scratched out the damage to the ZSU-23, but left the number of mortar rounds remaining unchanged. He handed Cao the clipboard. "Send it. Now."

"Immediately, sir," Cao replied. He added it to the other message that would also be transmitted.

Se Pang, South Vietnam

A string of flares popped in the night, closer to the runway but still on the far side of the river. A dim, but very eerie light illuminated the Hercules, and Warren could see well enough to make out the four men clustered around the wheel well. Boyle was standing over them, a blanket spread between his outstretched arms, shielding the light from a flashlight dangling from around his neck as best he could. His face glistened with sweat. The old wheel was laying on the ground and they were rolling the new wheel into position. "Damn," Warren muttered. If he could see them, so could any nearby spotter.

He keyed his survival radio. "Blind Bat, Roscoe on Guard. Be advised the flares are drifting towards us. We're getting too much light over the runway."

The Trash Haulers

Hardy answered. "Roger that, Roscoe. There are troops in the open coming your way. A flight of two is inbound."

"I really needed to know that," Warren muttered to himself. The unmistakable sound of twin radial engines echoed over the Hercules. Unable to switch to the Blind Bat frequency, he watched in fascination as the dark shadow of an aircraft flew under the flares and two canisters separated from under the wings. The aircraft pulled off, its engines screaming at full throttle as the two canisters tumbled into the ground. A river of flame washed over the ground, chasing the departing aircraft. Napalm.

Then he heard a second aircraft roll in. But it didn't need flares to light a target. This time, Warren could make out the distinctive shape of an A-26 as it came in low on a strafing pass. The six .50 caliber machine guns in its nose erupted in smoke and flames as a barrage of tracers ripped the night. It was an A-26 out of Nakhon Phanom making a strafing run. The 56th Air Commando Wing had also gotten the message. The World War II vintage A-26 light tactical bomber was a proven tank killer on the Ho Chi Minh trail, able to loiter for extended periods of time over a target and carried an awesome bomb load.

The first A-26 rolled in for a second pass, a strafing run, and sent a stream of death and destruction into the men caught in the open. For some reason, the guns sounded sharper, more crisp on this run. The aircraft pulled off and he caught a brief glance of the aircraft's plan form as it banked and climbed. The flames set by the napalm set down and darkness claimed the river valley. He could still see a few small fires on the far side of the river flickering in the night as the sound of the A-26s receded. Hardy wanted to know

221

how the attack looked from the ground, but nothing could describe the hell he had just witnessed, even from his distance. He keyed his PR-90 radio. "Blind Bat, that was one awesome show. Ordnance on target. Looks like crispy critter time from here. Is anything still moving?"

"Roscoe, standby."

A few seconds later, another string of flares illuminated the night as Blind Bat flew down the valley. Suddenly, a solid red line reached up from the side of the ridge, chasing after the flare ship – tracers. "Break right! Triple A six o'clock!" Warren shouted over the radio just as the C-130 jinked sharply to the right. One of the flare kickers in the rear of the Blind Bat had seen the tracers at the same moment and called for the break. The gunner missed, not able to visually track the C-130 as it moved away and took evasive maneuvers in the dark.

Hardy's voice came over the radio, amazingly cool. "Roger on trip A. Turning downwind to see what we've got." Warren grunted, giving Hardy high marks, certain that he would fly a racetrack pattern on the far side of the ridge line with the gunner on the north side and unable to bring the deadly cannon to bear. "Roscoe, no movement at this time. Suggest you get the hell out of Dodge soonest."

"Why did I know that?" Warren muttered. "Copy all," he replied. He ran back to the C-130, almost bumping into the number three prop. Up close, he could barely make out two men standing over the discarded wheel. "Say status," he asked.

Hale answered. "She's good to go, Captain." Fatigue edged every word, but there was triumph. They had changed out the wheel in less than thirty minutes.

The Trash Haulers

"Bring on the marines," Flanders said, a disembodied voice in the dark. His voice carried a hard resolve mixed with jubilation.

Warren gave a silent thanks for being teamed with his crew. He couldn't ask for better. He keyed his radio. "Blind Bat, Roscoe is OR. Waiting for evacs."

"Copy you are OR at this time," Hardy answered.

The sound of the C-130 grew louder. "What's he doing now?" Bosko asked.

"I think he's coming in for another flare run," Warren replied.

They all moved slowly forward, standing by the nose of their Herk. "I can't believe he's going to challenge that ZSU," Santos said.

A hard silence held them as they waited. A flare popped, shortly followed by three more. Warren mentally ran the geometry and figured it out. "Shit hot!" The four men stared at him, not understanding. "He's using terrain masking. Blind Bat is south of the ridgeline. The wind is out of the south and the flares are drifting across the ridgeline and towards us. The ZSU is on the northern side of the ridge, facing us. It's on a pretty steep face and the ZSU can't traverse around to the south. The best they can do is shoot straight up. If they want to hose Hardy down, they'll have to drag it up to the crest of the ridge. That will take some doing."

The flares drifted across the ridgeline and towards the river, slowly casting a growing light over the river valley. It was enough to see by. A line of Bru emerged out of the dark carrying canvas stretchers. They filed silently by the Americans, heading for the tail of the Hercules. Flanders was the first to react. "We've gotta turn on the overheads to load 'em," he said, referring to the cargo compartment lights.

"Do it," was all Warren could say. Flanders ran to the back of the aircraft. Warren stood silently, not moving, as the litters moved past. The marines were bloodied and bandaged, their uniforms cut away. At least three of them were missing limbs and two were badly burned. "Go help Flanders," he said. Bosko, Santos, and Hale bolted up the crew entrance to help secure the litters onto the stanchions Flanders had rigged. Boyle didn't move. "Go!" Warren ordered. Boyle hesitated for a moment, weaving slightly back and forth, before following them.

The walking wounded were next, almost ghostly, vague and indistinct in the flickering half-light. Ghosts or not, they were his responsibility.

And there was a ZSU gunner out there waiting for him.

Warren climbed through the crew entrance and closed the hatch behind him, hoping to help seal the light in. He walked back into the dimly lit cargo compartment. The smell of disinfectant in close quarters hung heavy in the air. Bosko was helping a marine fasten the jump seat's seat belt without moving the bloody stump of his left arm. It amazed him that the marine had walked to the aircraft on his own power. Then he saw Pender. She was at the aft end of the litters that were stacked along the center line of the Hercules, talking to the man lying on the last stretcher. Warren made his way aft. He stepped on a discarded compress bandage and slipped, leaving a streak of blood across the deck. Hale was right behind him, throwing paper mats on the wet flooring.

The Trash Haulers

Warren stood behind the doctor for a moment as she spoke to the heavily bandaged man. Her hair was pulled back in a tight ponytail, the sleeves of her flight suit rolled up and she smelled of sweat and disinfectant. There was another scent that he couldn't place, earthy and strong. "How's it going, Captain," he said. She turned and looked at him. Her face was etched with fatigue and hurt. "Are you okay?" he asked.

"I'm okay," she replied.

But he knew. Her pain was the anguish of a person who cared, perhaps too much, for those in her care.

She managed a little smile. "Captain Warren, let me introduce Warrant Officer Wilson Tanner. That was his helicopter you saw at the end of the runway."

"Dust Off?" Warren asked. Tanner nodded. "I hope the Doc is taking good care of you." It was all he could think of to say.

"She is," Tanner said. "Wouldn't even let me walk here on my own steam."

Pender shook her head. "Walk here? Mr. Tanner, I just amputated your right foot and you are in shock."

"Okay, so you wouldn't even let me hobble here."

She reached out and touched his cheek. "I've got to check on the others. I'll be back." She was gone.

"Sorry about the leg," Warren said, knowing he would never fly again. Maybe, he thought, that's a good thing. He tried not to look at the blood-soaked bandage wrapped around Tanner's torso.

"I'll be okay. She's a good doc. Saved a lot of people."

"I know," Warren said.

225

Tanner reached out and grabbed Warren's arm. His face was streaked with sweat and his grip clammy. "The bastards got my crew," he said, his voice filled with anguish.

Warren understood all too well, but there was nothing he could say. Then, "Time to get the hell out of Dodge." He looked around for Flanders to find out how much longer he needed to finish loading. The loadmaster was standing at the bottom of the ramp talking to Pender. "How we doing?" he asked.

"We're good to go," Flanders answered.

"Tanner is hurting pretty bad," Warren told Pender.

She looked at him, her eyes full of worry. "I gave him my last shot of morphine before I amputated his foot. It's wearing off."

"Will he make it?"

"If we can get him to a field hospital. It's not so much his leg but the wound to his abdomen. The shock alone would kill most men."

"What the hell is that?" Flanders growled, interrupting them. He pointed behind the two officers. They looked in the same direction. Four Bru were standing there, in pairs, with two long poles between them resting on their shoulders. Hanging from the poles was a bamboo cage. A heavily bandaged man dripping blood was lying in the bottom of the cage.

Warren tried to focus, sensing something was different. Pender saw it first. "Those aren't our type of bandages," she said. "Too yellow."

"They're North Vietnamese," Banks said, stepping out of the dark. "The Bru brought him in. As best I can make

The Trash Haulers

out, a woman gave him to the Bru. Based on what the Bru said, I think she was a lieutenant colonel in the PAVN."

"Why would she do that?" Warren wondered.

Pender was reaching inside the cage, examining the man's wounds. "To save his life. Get him on board so I can work on him."

Banks motioned for the Bru to carry the cage up the ramp. But Flanders wasn't having any of it. "Not the cage. Not on my aircraft."

"He's a fuckin' Commie," Boyle said. Warren whirled around, surprised to see the airman standing so close. "He's the goddamn enemy," Boyle snarled. His words were high-pitched and cracking, almost incoherent. "We ought'a leave him behind."

"He's a POW," Warren said, "protected by the Geneva Conventions."

"Fuck the Geneva Convention," Boyle said. "Let him bleed to death."

"No way he's a threat," Warren said. "Open the cage. Get him out." No one moved. "Now," he said, his voice full of command. He spun around and headed for the flight deck. "Flanders, button us up. Engine start ASAP."

A startled Flanders looked at his back. "The Captain wants to kick some ass," he said, not in the least bit upset. "Okay, get the lead out, Boyle." They quickly cut the bamboo cage apart and gently laid the Vietnamese on the deck. Pender bent over him, carefully unwrapping the bandage. Flanders never hesitated and dragged the cage off the ramp, giving it a final kick. "No fuckin' slave cages on my aircraft."

227

Flanders grabbed the long intercom extension cord and ran down the ramp. "Boyle, button us up and turn out the lights. Raise the ramp to the horizontal." He didn't wait for an answer and ran around to the front of the Hercules, ready to start engines and marshal the aircraft onto the runway in the dark. He plugged the cord in and stepped clear of the props as GTC spun up. "Three's clear," he said, giving the flight deck clearance to start engines. Within moments, the engine was on line and he ran to the left wheel well to button up the GTC panel. It was a well-rehearsed drill and the other engines rapidly spun up in sequence.

"Ready to taxi," Warren said. Now he had to trust the loadmaster to guide them to the runway. Flanders was close enough to see the soft red lights illuminating the flight deck, but everywhere else was pitch black.

"Sir," a soft voice said behind Flanders. "I show you." Flanders turned and saw a Bru standing a few feet away. The Montagnard turned and walked slowly towards the runway.

"Come left slowly," Flanders said, following the mountain man. "Go straight. Turn right. Go straight. You're almost to the runway. Hard right, keep it coming, you are on the runway. Go straight. Stop. You're slightly left of the centerline." He turned to thank the Montagnard, but he was gone.

"We need to back up," Warren said. The entrance to the parking ramp was about two-hundred feet from the end of the runway. "We're gonna need all the runway we can get."

Flanders whipped the long intercom cord unplugging it and ran for the aft of the Hercules, careful to swing wide around the propellers. He skidded to a stop just before bumping into the fuselage. He scrambled onto the ramp, now

The Trash Haulers

able to see enough to plug into the intercom. "Clear in the rear," he said.

As if by magic, the Bru was back, standing by the ramp. "Sir, I show." He walked slowly backwards, angling to the centerline of the runway. Flanders spoke into the intercom and the Hercules slowly backed down the runway. The Bru held up his hands, and Flanders relayed the command to stop. They were positioned perfectly, the main gear at the very end of the runway with their tail over the rough dirt and low vegetation. The Bru stood at attention and gave the loadmaster the best salute he could manage. Flanders returned the salute, but the man was gone.

Flanders raised the ramp to the closed position. But left the cargo door up, against the underside of the fuselage. He felt his way forward and strapped into a jump seat next to Boyle. "Good to go in the rear," he said.

Warren squinted into the night, but his world was confined to the soft red sphere of light illuminating the flight deck. He keyed the radio. "Blind Bat Zero-One. Roscoe Two-One ready to roll."

Hardy answered. "Roscoe, hold. I've got a flight of two, three minutes out. Roll on my command."

"What the hell," Bosko said. "We're a sitting duck here. Let's go."

"We hold," Warren said. "They're gonna laydown some cover for us." They listened as a flight of two F-4s checked in on Blind Bat's frequency. On cue, a string of flares popped over the south side of the ridgeline and started drifting towards them. It seemed an eternity before the north slope of the ridge was illuminated. Hardy cleared the first F-4 in for the attack. Twenty-five seconds later a string of three Mk-82 bombs walked across the north slope.

"Roscoe, GO!" Hardy said. "Turn out to the right."

Warren stepped on the brakes and firewalled the throttles. "Landing lights on," he said, his voice loud and strained. Hale reached up and flicked the lights on just as Warren released the brakes. The runway stretched out on front of them.

The C-130 moved forward, accelerating faster than before in the cooler night air. Bosko called the airspeed. Then, "Rotate!"

But Warren held the nose down, using every inch of runway. At the last possible moment he hauled back on the yoke, lifting them sharply into the night. "Landing lights off, gear up." He jinked to the right and then back to the left as they climbed and the gear came up. No sooner had the gear clunked into the locks than he started to inch the flaps up, gaining all the airspeed he could coax out of engines. He was flying blind, relying on his instruments. "Dave, keep us out of the rocks." They had always turned out to the left, flying over the south side of the river valley and the lower ridgeline. By turning out to the north, and into higher terrain, Hardy hoped to surprise any AAA gunner who might have survived the bombing.

"Clear in the rear," Flanders called. The loadmaster had stood up immediately after takeoff and was looking out the open cargo door and over the raised ramp, clearing their six o'clock.

Santos buried his head in the radar scope. "High terrain ahead, come left. Roll out. Clear on this heading."

The Trash Haulers

"Break left!" Flanders called from the rear. "Triple A!" Warren jinked left, then left again as they climbed, now able to see a line of tracers reaching out for them from the far side of the river. The solid line of tracers waved back in forth in the night as the gunner tried to chase the C-130 down. Flanders' call had saved them.

"Hot damn!" Flanders shouted, still looking out the back. "They just laid a string of six Mark-82s over the fucker!" Hardy had coordinated the covering attack for their takeoff and called in the second F-4 before the ZSU started to fire, allowing the pilot to place the pipper in his bombsight over the muzzle flash. The Phantom nailed it. "Nothing but hot hair and smokin' eyeballs down there now." He calmed and added a more restrained, "Clear in the rear."

"We're clear all terrain," Santos said. "Heading 125 degrees." He checked his watch. It was 0045 hours, local time. "Chu Lai at 0112." He double-checked his work. "Correction on the ETA. Make it twenty-two past the hour."

"Rear door closed," Warren said. "Give the folks some light back there so they can take care of things." The lights came on as they climbed into the night.

Warren keyed the radio. "Blind Bat Zero-One. Roscoe Two-One is clear and proceeding to Chu Lai."

"Copy all," Hardy replied. Then, "Roscoe, well done."

231

0100 HOURS

Over South Vietnam

Bosko dialed in the airborne command post's radio frequency and tried to check in. But it was chaos and he couldn't break into the stream of transmissions. He cycled through three backup frequencies before finally capturing the controller's attention and telling Moonbeam they were airborne. The answer was chilling. "Roscoe Two-One, Moonbeam. Be advised Chu Lai is down due to rockets, mortars, and intruders. Expect a diversion."

"I would think so," Santos said over the intercom. He noted the time on his flight log. It was exactly 0100 hours, and they had been airborne fifteen minutes.

"Roscoe Two-One copies," Bosko answered. "Standing by this freq." He shook his head. "Jesus H. Christ, we can't catch a break."

Santos ran possible alternates through his mental calculus. "Expect a divert into Qui Nhon. The Army's got a field hospital there." He was already working on a new heading and estimated en route time.

"The 85th Evac is at Qui Nhon," Warren added. "They could also send us into Da Nang. The Air Force hospital there could take us." He thought for a moment. "Dave, let's go feet wet and hold over the South China Sea."

"Roger that," Santos said. "Fly 060 degrees and we'll coast out in two minutes. Once feet wet, we can head south and hold near Da Nang."

Bosko turned the autopilot to the new heading. "How far off the coast do you want to hold?"

"Ten nautical miles will keep us clear," Warren answered.

"Altitude?" Bosko asked.

"Sixteen thou should do it," Warren replied. "We need to check for pressurization." It was time to find out if they had patched all the holes in the fuselage or if they still had unseen battle damage. "Try to hold three thousand feet cabin altitude." Hale reached for the overhead air conditioning control panel and set the cabin pressure controller as they leveled off at 16,000 feet. "Sergeant Flanders," Warren asked, "How's the heat back there."

"We could stand a little more," the loadmaster replied.

Hale turned the temperature rheostat up, his eyes rooted on the pressure controller. "Cabin pressure holding," he finally said.

"You can turn the heat down," Flanders said. Getting the temperature right on the cargo deck always took some adjusting.

"Hey," Bosko said, "we finally got a break, for what it's worth."

Silence ruled the flight deck as they headed south towards Da Nang. Warren glanced at Bosko whose chin was

The Trash Haulers

slumped down on his chest. He was asleep. He checked Santos and Hale, not surprised that both were asleep. He tuned in the Da Nang TACAN for the bearing and distance to the air base. He entered a racetrack holding pattern east of the air base on the 090 degree radial at ten nautical miles, well over the South China Sea. He felt a soft touch on his left shoulder and turned to see Pender standing behind him. She leaned next to his ear so as not to wake the sleeping men. He felt the warmth of her face next to his. "How long before we land?" she asked.

"Not sure. Problems. Chu Lai is under attack and down. We're waiting for a divert. How's it going in the rear?"

"We need to get them to a field hospital. Tanner is coming out from under the morphine and in pain, I've got four critical who also need morphine, and I don't think the North Vietnamese is going to make it unless we get him into surgery very soon."

"I'll work on it," Warren promised. He motioned for her to put on a headset. She did and he keyed the radio. "Pan-pan, pan-pan, pan-pan." The call was second only to a Mayday and used to clear the frequency and declare they needed to land for the safety of someone on board. It worked. "Moonbeam, Roscoe Two-One requests immediate clearance to nearest field hospital. We have wounded on board requiring immediate attention."

"Standby," Moonbeam answered.

Warren pressed it. If Moonbeam wouldn't make a decision, he would. "Say status of Da Nang."

"Da Nang runway is closed for craters. Base currently under rocket attack."

"Say status of Qui Nhon."

235

"Radio contact lost. Base last reported taking heavy mortar fire."

"Fuck!" Warren roared, waking the sleeping men. He hit the transmit button. "Moonbeam, I repeat, Roscoe Two-One has six critical wounded on board who need immediate medical attention. Get us on the ground."

The controller's voice changed. "Roscoe, I'm working it. Checking on Saigon. It's the only option I've got." Tan Son Nhut Air Base at Saigon was an hour and twenty minutes flying time away, but the Army's 17th Field Hospital was a long ambulance ride from the air base. The controller was back. "Tan Son Nhut is open but status of ground transportation extremely questionable. Recommend Clark." Clark Air Base was in the Philippines, 720 nautical miles away across the South China Sea.

"We need something closer than that," Warren replied.

"Roscoe, it's chaos on the ground here. Every hospital in-country is maxed out and calling for help. Clark is wide open and the hospital can take your wounded."

Warren turned in his seat and looked at Pender. "I think we better go to Clark."

"It's two hours thirty minutes flying time," Santos said. "But the hospital is only minutes away, and they'll get first priority."

Pender shook her head in despair. "I'm going to lose them. Can we land somewhere and get some morphine?"

Warren's chin jerked up. He cursed himself for being a cretin. It was an easy decision. "Moonbeam, Roscoe Two-One is headed for Clark at this time. Will file a flight plan en route."

The Trash Haulers

"Moonbeam copies all," the controller replied. "And God speed."

"Track outbound 092 degrees on the Da Nang TACAN," Santos said. "ETA Clark 0345 hours. We should get a tailwind above twenty grand."

Warren pushed the throttles up and started to climb. "Let's try flight level two-one-zero." Flight level 210 was twenty-one thousand feet on a standard altimeter setting of 29.92 inches of mercury. He turned to Pender who was staring at him. "We'll keep it as low as we can to hold cabin pressurization below 3000 feet."

"It might help, but I doubt it." Her voice was heavy with reproach and despair. She turned to go.

Warren reached out and held her wrist. "Wait." He ripped the first aid kit out of his survival vest and tore it open. He handed her a small tube that held a morphine injection. "We've got five more." Bosko, Hale, and Santos did the same and handed her the small tubes. They all dropped their heavy survival vests to the deck, relieved to finally be free of the burden.

Pender leaned forward and kissed Warren on the cheek. She rushed off the flight deck. Bosko grinned at Warren. "A little fraternizing there, Captain? What would the good Colonel Hardy say?"

"Especially after all that skinny-dipping," Santos added.

"Civilians," Warren moaned. "You can put 'em in a uniform, dress 'em up, but you can't take 'em out."

"Seriously, Captain," Hale said, "you need to pursue that one. Think about it."

Warren did.

Over the South China Sea

Warren pulled the throttles back, leveled off at 21,000 feet, and the crew went through a well-practiced routine. Lacking a high frequency long-range radio, Bosko established contact with a MAC flight that had an HF, and it relayed their flight plan to Manila Air Traffic Control. Santos plotted a level off fix using the bearing and distance off the Da Nang TACAN. He would plot another fix in twenty minutes while still in range. Just to be on the safe side, he constructed a fuel graph to monitor their consumption and asked Hale for a fuel reading.

"We're right at 10,200 pounds," Hale replied. "Seems a little low."

Santos plotted the fuel reading on his graph. "Not a problem. That gives us two hundred pounds extra."

"Does that include reserve?" Warren asked.

"Yep," Santos replied. "Twenty minutes. So what's the problem?"

"Not sure," Hale replied. "I figure we should have maybe five hundred pounds extra. We may have a fuel leak."

"Or we got a guzzler," Bosko said.

"Or bum gauges," Santos added.

"Stay on top of it," Warren said. "We can always divert into Cubi Point if we have to." Cubi Point was the huge U.S. Naval base on Subic Bay on the western side of Luzon, the largest island in the Philippines, and thirty miles short of Clark. He pulled himself out of his seat. "Gonna go see how they're doing in the back."

The Trash Haulers

Three sets of eyes followed him as he climbed down to the main deck. "And to say 'hello' to a captain," Santos said. They all nodded in agreement.

Warren pushed through the canvas curtain separating the flight deck from the cargo compartment. He froze. It had been bad enough when he first saw the wounded marines arrive in the vague and uncertain shadows of night. But he was now in the harsh glow of full reality and was standing at the edge of hell. It was his aircraft and he was warehousing the wreckage of war. Every man was bloodied and bandaged and the smell was horrific in the confined space; a stench of disinfectant, blood, dirt, feces, urine, sweat, and charred flesh. And standing in the middle of it all was Lynne Pender. He made his way past a moaning Marine, careful not to step in a pool of blood.

Pender was bent over the North Vietnamese prisoner, stitching up the gash in his abdomen. She never looked up. "He's critical and needs a shot of morphine." He could hear the resignation in her voice.

"You said there were five that needed morphine. We've got six survival vests, which means six shots."

"I only got one more from Sergeant Flanders. Boyle ignored me."

Warren whirled around, searching for the airman. He was stretched out on the ramp asleep, still wearing his survival vest. "Boyle, get your ass over here." The airman sat up, confused. "I said, get over here!" Warren shouted, his voice carrying over the drone of the engines.

Flanders joined them. He had flown with Warren for over a year and never heard him so angry. "Let me handle it, sir. What do you need doing?"

Warren forced himself to calm down. He could protect Flanders if the sergeant beat the living hell out of Boyle, which he hoped would happen. "Captain Pender needs the morphine out of Boyle's survival vest."

Now Flanders was angry. "I told the bastard to give her . . ." his voice trailed off. Then, much more calmly, "Boyle, give me your first aid kit."

Boyle heard the menace in his tone and never hesitated. He handed the small kit over and pulled back. He watched as Flanders ripped it apart and handed the plastic tube to Warren, who handed it to Pender. Boyle made the obvious connection. "You gonna give it to the slopehead?"

"Captain Pender is a doctor and will use it as she sees fit," Flanders answered. He jammed the first aid kit into Boyle's gut. Hard. "Take care of this."

Boyle staggered back, gasping for breath, his eyes filled with hate. "You never got dumped in a pile of shit."

"Nothing you didn't fuckin' deserve, asshole."

"Captain Warren," Boyle protested, "he can't talk to me like that."

"Like what," Warren said. He joined Pender who was still working on the North Vietnamese. He studied the man's face, now in full light, as she administered the injection. "I'll be damned. That's Colonel Tran."

"Colonel who?" Pender asked.

"Colonel Tran Sang Quan, the commander of the logistical regiment in Laos. I saw his photo at the briefing at NKP. According to what I heard, he's one of their best commanders. We got something here." He made his way forward to the flight deck.

The Trash Haulers

Boyle sat on a jump seat and hunched forward, his elbows resting on his knees, his hands clasped tightly together, his face drenched in sweat, and his eyes riveted on Warren's back.

The marine sitting next to Boyle snorted. "You think you got a problem? That fuckin' Commie killed eight of my buddies, and the doctor is a fuckin' bitch." Boyle glanced at the marine's name tag – Denlow.

"Billy Bob Boyle," he said, shaking the marine's hand.

Warren slipped into the left seat and pulled on his headset. He glanced at the TACAN readout – seventy-three nautical miles from Da Nang. That seemed low and he had expected them to be further down track, closer to ninety nautical miles. *We've been climbing, and I'm dead tired.* "Boz, can you raise Moonbeam on the VHF?" Bosko dialed in the frequency and made the call. Moonbeam answered immediately. "Moonbeam," Warren transmitted, "be advised we have a North Vietnamese POW on board who matches the description of Colonel Tran Sang Quan. I believe Tran to be an extremely high-value prisoner. Please have Security Police meet the aircraft at Clark."

Moonbeam gave the standard answer. "Roscoe Two-One, standby."

"Sum'bitch," Santos muttered. "Is 'standby' the only word they know?"

Another voice came over the radio. "Roscoe Two-One, mission commander. If correct, you have an extremely high-value POW. Say his current condition."

241

"Tran is badly wounded, survival doubtful. The doctor on board has stabilized his bleeding at the present time."

"Roscoe, advise the doctor to keep Tran alive at all costs. Repeat, at all costs."

"What the fuck," Bosko said. "Does that mean at the expense of our guys?"

Warren hit the transmit button. "Moonbeam, does 'at all costs' mean at the expense of our wounded."

"Roscoe, I repeat. Keep the prisoner alive at all costs."

"Moonbeam, Roscoe Two-One copies all." Warren ripped off his headset and threw it in his lap. "What the hell?"

A hard silence captured the men. Santos finally spoke. "Captain Warren, my father often butted heads with the embassy's CIA station chief over intelligence. There is always a price to be paid, and not necessarily in money, for getting good intelligence."

"And what exactly does that mean?" Warren asked. But he knew the answer.

"Hold on for a second," Santos replied. "I need to get a fix." Bosko read the radial they were on and the distance from the TACAN station on the DME, or distance measuring equipment. Santos quickly plotted it on his chart and measured the distance they had travelled since leveling off. They had flown thirty-five miles in ten minutes. "We got a problem," Santos said.

"That's par for the course," Warren muttered. "What now?"

"Our ground speed is 210 knots. It should be around 280 to 290. We got at least a seventy-knot headwind." He

The Trash Haulers

didn't have to explain what that meant – they didn't have enough fuel.

Warren worked through a mental fog of fatigue. "Get another fix in ten minutes. The TACAN will still be locked on."

"I don't think so," Bosko said. The TACAN had broken lock and the mileage counter and bearing needle were spinning. "We just lost the TACAN." He recycled the frequency and waited to hear the identifier. Nothing. "No signal," Bosko announced. "It's off the air. A mortar or rocket hit, maybe."

"Sum'bitch," Santos moaned. "We cannot catch a break. Some one really pissed off the gods." He shifted into high gear and went to work. "Sergeant Hale, can you rig the step for the sextant." The sextant mount was mounted on the overhead immediately behind the flight engineer, too high even for Santos to reach without a step stool.

"Can do," Hale replied. "I can rig the sextant, if you want." The Kollsmann D-1 Sextant had a short periscopic barrel that extended the sextant lens through the top of the fuselage and eliminated the need for a bubble astrodome. It was a delicate and sophisticated instrument that took special care.

Santos was bent over a form scratching in numbers, pre-computing a three-star celestial shot. "Appreciate that. Take a look and see if we got an overcast."

"Will do," Hale answered. He looked through the eyepiece. "Clear as a bell," he said.

"How good is your celestial?" Warren asked. Navigators only used celestial navigation for long overwater legs, which they seldom flew.

243

"If no turbulence, good to a half mile," Santos answered. While not as accurate as a TACAN fix, it was close enough. Two minutes later, he jumped onto the step and started shooting the first star. It took him eight minutes to accurately determine the elevation of three stars and plot the three lines of position on a chart, forming a tight triangle. He measured the distance flown between the two fixes. "Fuck me in the heart!" he roared. He took a deep breath. "We still got a sixty-knot headwind."

"Recheck your numbers," Warren said.

0200 HOURS

Over the South China Sea

Santos double-checked his work and plotted the numbers on the fuel graph. He passed it to the pilots and the flight engineer. "We can make Clark if we do a long-range descent," Santos told them. A long-range descent traded altitude for airspeed and fuel.

"But we'll land with no reserve," Bosko added.

"That's cutting it too close," Warren replied. "Figure we do a long-range descent with a straight-in approach and landing into Cubi Point. How much fuel will that gain us?"

Again, Santos ran the numbers and plotted them on the fuel graph. He passed it forward. "That should gain us maybe 1500 pounds, assuming we don't have a fuel leak."

"If we do have a leak," Hale said, "it's showing up as high fuel consumption, which you've factored in."

It all came down on Warren. He had to weigh the tradeoffs balancing safety against time in order to get his precious cargo on the ground where they could be cared for as quickly as possible. He was dealing with too many unknowns; the aircraft had taken battle damage and had high fuel consumption. Hell, he though, I've taken battle damage and I'm still flying. It wasn't a rational comparison, but for some reason, it increased his faith in the Hercules. He made a decision and kicked the can down the road. "For now, press ahead for Clark. Boz, contact Moonbeam and see if there's a field we can divert to for fuel and pick up some medical help. Dave, get another fix in twenty minutes and let's see what's happening with the ground speed."

Bosko worked the radios while Santos updated their DR position and pre-computed a second three-star celestial fix. After repeated radio calls, Bosko finally got through. The situation was still bad, and only Tan Son Nhut and Cam Ranh Bay were open. Then, "Roscoe Two-One, Moonbeam. Be advised Tan Son Nhut is down for mortars and Cam Ranh's main runway is closed." The controller on Moonbeam lost it. "Roscoe, I'm trying, for God's sake, I am. But a jet just pranged at Cam Ranh. Really bad news everywhere. We're headed to hell in a hand basket."

Another voice came on frequency. "Roscoe Two-One, Moonbeam. Disregard all. Proceed on course for now. Will advise if situation changes."

"Copy all," Bosko replied, breaking contact. "We'll be out of radio range before that happens," he muttered to himself.

Santos finished pre-computing the celestial fix and kicked back in his seat. He took a drink of water and closed his eyes for a moment. *Why the high headwind? It doesn't make sense.* His eye's snapped open. Their ground speed had increased ten knots between fixes. Were they flying out of whatever pressure system they were caught in? He

The Trash Haulers

scanned his instruments, looking for any clue. He glanced at the outside temperature gauge. "Sum'bitch!" he roared.

Warren, Bosko, and Hale twisted in their seats as one, looking at the navigator. "What's up?" Warren asked.

Santos pointed at the temperature gauge like a man possessed. "It's too fuckin' warm! The outside air temp is zero, it should be around minus twenty or twenty-five Celsius."

Bosko was confused. "So?"

"We're caught under an inversion layer. I'm guessing a warmer high pressure system has overrun a cooler low pressure system and reinforced the winds aloft."

"So what do we do about it?" Bosko asked.

"We climb out of it," Santos said.

"Altitude?" Warren asked, reaching for the autopilot altitude control.

"Try flight level two-five-zero," Santos said. They needed to stay as low as possible to maintain a low cabin pressurization. The navigator stood, his eyes fixed on the temperature gauge as they climbed. He suppressed a chuckle when the temperature took a sharp drop. "Yes!" he said, pumping his fist in triumph. "Minus thirty-one degrees."

Warren leveled off at 25,000 feet. Santos waited for their airspeed to stabilize and leaped onto the step to shoot a second celestial fix. He finished the shot and quickly sat down to resolve the readings and plot them on his chart. He stepped on the intercom switch under his right foot, trying to sound as cool as possible. "Groundspeed 260. And that was during a climb. I'll get another fix in twenty minutes, but I'm guessing we're out of it."

"Well done," Warren said. "How we doing on fuel."

Richard Herman

Again, Santos and Hale went through the drill, and Santos plotted the results on the fuel graph. "We're okay for Clark, but we'll cut the reserve in half."

Warren felt the heavy weight that had been bearing down on him start to yield. "That's why they call it reserve fuel," he said.

"Clark at 0400," Santos said, announcing their new ETA.

Warren glanced at his watch. It was exactly 0232. "We finally caught a break," he announced. He reached for his water bottle and took a long pull. He felt unbelievably weary and his right shoulder ached. "Boz, I'm gonna catch a little shut-eye."

"I got it," Bosko replied. He glanced at his aircraft commander. Warren was sound asleep.

"The Captain deserves the Air Force Cross," Hale said. The Air Force Cross was the Air Force's second highest award for valor, exceeded only by the Medal of Honor.

Santos grunted an affirmative but kept working on a pre-comp for a third celestial fix. He stood up and stretched. "A high roller will have to write the recommendation."

"That would be Hardy," Bosko said. "Do you think he'll do it."

"Twenty-four hours ago," Santos replied, "I'd have said 'fat chance.' But now?" He thought for a moment. "Yeah, he would. I'll ask him."

Se Pang River Valley, South Vietnam

The soldier escorting Kim-Ly and Captain Lam gave the smoldering ZSU-23 a wide birth, worried that a high-explosive round might cook off. They all covered their noses

The Trash Haulers

at the smell of burning flesh. Small fires still burning in the underbrush gave off enough light to reveal the cave entrance. Kim-Ly spoke to the guard posted outside and handed him a note. They didn't have to wait long for a young woman to escort them inside.

The woman immediately recognized Kim-Ly and, with tears in her eyes, motioned them into the cave. They were careful to step over the human wreckage lying on the floor, and Kim-Ly counted twenty-three wounded near the entrance alone. They found the alcove where Dinh was holding court and stood quietly against the side wall, waiting to be recognized. Major Cao saw them and whispered a warning in Dinh's ear. Lam was holding his AK-47 across his chest.

"You do not bring weapons into my command post," Dinh said. Cao drew his semi-automatic and held it at the ready against his chest, the butt resting in the palm of his left hand. Lam ejected the magazine without clearing the chamber and lowered the assault rife, its muzzle pointed down. He tossed the magazine to Cao who quickly holstered his pistol. The two men exchanged studied looks. "I do understand why you forgot," Dinh said, willing to drop the point. There was no doubt that he was in control. "Your report."

"We are destroyed," Lam said.

"Nonsense," Dinh snorted.

"You may go outside and see for yourself," Lam said. His voice was flat, without emotion. "The Sergey and crew destroyed. The observation teams above us destroyed. All our mortar teams destroyed. My entire company killed or wounded. Over three hundred of the cadre killed or wounded."

"And may I ask how this happened?" Dinh said, his voice sharp and on the edge of panic.

Kim-Ly answered. "We were caught in the open by the Air Pirates and could not hide from their bombs."

"Nonsense!" Dinh roared, coming to his feet. He sat down, needing time to think. Cao handed him a note, giving him the break he needed. Dinh glanced at the note and looked up, genuinely shocked. "Who gave you this?" Cao pointed at Kim-Ly. "This is treason!" Dinh shouted.

Kim-Ly nodded in agreement. "I gave my husband to the Bru so he might live." She smiled. "I was surprised that they did not kill me."

"A mistake that must be rectified," Dinh said. He thought for a moment. "The comrades must be told why they failed. They must know of your dereliction of duty that caused so many of them to be sacrificed." He liked the sound of his words. "Because of your treason, we have no choice but to fall back and regroup in the Binh Tram. There, you will be executed by hanging before the assembled cadre." The more he envisioned the scene, the better he felt. "Captain Lam, you will carry out the execution." He turned to Cao. "And you will give the order."

"I cannot give that order," Cao said.

Dinh's eyes widened as Lam swung his AK-47 up and squeezed the trigger. A single shot rang out, driving everyone to the ground except Kim-Ly and Lam.

Cao was the first to react. He struggled to his knees and crawled over to the prostrate colonel. Dinh's mouth was moving but no words came out. The single 7.62mm round had struck him in the chest, ripping his right lung out. Cao moved his right forefinger in front of Dinh's eyes. Satisfied

The Trash Haulers

that he was still conscious, Cao stood up, his hands spread wide in peace. "We have lost a valiant comrade-in-arms. His memory will be enshrined with the heroes of the War." He looked down, smiling. "We will honor your sacrifice by burying you with our fallen comrades in an unmarked grave."

Cao reached into his shirt pocket and handed Kim-Ly a folded piece of paper. "I received this message ten minutes ago. You are promoted to colonel and will assume command upon receipt of this message. May I inform General Dong that you are in command?"

0300 HOURS

Over the South China Sea

Warren was dreaming. A sharp voice was shouting in his ear and an invisible hand was pushing him off a cliff. "Captain, wake up." He struggled through a heavy fog, fighting his way to consciousness. A knife-like pain shot across his right shoulder blade, jolting him into semi-consciousness. Bosko was holding onto to his right forearm and leaning into him. It amused Warren that he could read the copilot's watch. The second hand was passing 0259. He was awake.

"We got a problem," Bosko said.

Warren forced the fog of sleep away. He automatically checked the time; it was six minutes past the hour. His eyes swept over the instrument and engine panels. They were flying straight and level at 25,000 feet, indicated airspeed 190 knots, and the engine instruments all in the green. *Must be a fuel problem.* "Whatcha got, Boz?"

"We can't raise anyone on the cargo deck," Bosko said. "That's not like Flanders. He's always on headset."

Warren glanced up at the pressure controller. The cabin altitude was holding steady at 4000 feet, which was better than expected. "It's been a hell of day," he said. "He might be asleep."

"That's what I thought," Bosko said. "But if he crashed, he'd have told us and Boyle would be on headset. It's probably nothing, but considering what's going on back there, I thought it best to check with you."

Warren stifled a sigh. Bosko was just being a good copilot and given the fatigue they were all dealing with, it was best to take everything slow and deliberate. But it was much ado about nothing. Or was it? *Pay attention to basics first.* "Dave, how we doing on groundspeed and fuel?"

"I got a fix ten minutes ago. We're okay. Ground speed 300 knots, ten knot tailwind. ETA Clark on the hour with seven minutes fuel reserve."

Warren shifted that problem to a back burner and concentrated on the situation in the cargo compartment. If they had been hauling Vietnamese, he would have assumed VC had infiltrated the passengers and treated it as a hijacking. He would have ordered the crew to don their oxygen masks and then depressurize the aircraft. At their altitude, everyone would be unconscious from hypoxia in less than a minute. Then he would have put Santos on a walk-around oxygen bottle and sent him back to check – navigators being the most expendable. But they weren't hauling Vietnamese. "Okay, let's go take a peek and see what's going on back there."

"I got it," Santos said. He stood up, understanding how it worked.

The Trash Haulers

"Take a walk-around bottle in case of fumes," Warren said. Santos plugged his oxygen mask into the portable bottle. "And get on headset," Warren added, telling him the obvious. Santos eased himself down the ladder onto the cargo deck.

They waited. "Dave, you on headset?" Warren asked. Nothing. Again, they waited. "Dave, you up?"

Nothing. "What the . . ." Bosko grumbled.

"Sergeant Hale, could we have an intercom problem with the cargo deck?" Warren asked.

The flight engineer shrugged. "It's possible, but I never heard of it happening."

"Maybe smoke and fumes knocked everyone out." Bosko offered.

"That's what I'm thinking," Hale said, "but why haven't we been affected?"

"What the hell," Warren muttered. He shifted mental gears and went into a deep defensive crouch. Something was definitely wrong, but whatever it was, it didn't appear to be a safety of flight item. At least not yet. Hard experience had taught him not to ignore it. So who to send next and possibly into harm's way? He only needed one pilot and the flight engineer to land the Hercules, so the choice was obvious. Or was it? He had a minor wound and Bosko was in better shape, more rested and alert. He made the decision. "Boz, you got the stick. I'll check on the back."

He grabbed the boom mike on his headset and pulled it back, followed by a cutting motion with his right hand, the signal to go cold mike and not speak over the intercom. Bosko and Hale understood and pushed their boom mikes back. Warren reached for his survival vest lying on the deck

255

and unsnapped the Smith & Wesson revolver. He balanced it in right hand, wondering if he should holster the weapon and just wear the survival vest.

"Hide it in your boot," Hale said, careful not to transmit over the intercom.

Warren quickly unzipped the right cuff of his flight suit and pulled the quick release zipper on the tongue of his boot half way down. He shoved the revolver into the top of his boot, surprised at how snug it fit. "I'm out of ideas but if you hear shots or shouting, dump pressurization."

"Why not right now?" Hale asked, thinking anti-hijacking tactics.

"I don't think we're dealing with a hijacking," Warren replied, "and I'm not sure what depressurization would do to the wounded. I'm guessing fumes of some sort, so get on oxygen."

"Got it, sir," Bosko said, reaching for his oxygen mask. Hale did the same as Warren climbed down from the flight deck.

Warren pushed through the heavy canvas fire curtains that opened onto the cargo deck. He half expected to be hit with heavy fumes, but the cargo compartment was quiet and bathed in a dim light. He paused, letting his eyes adjust to the low light. He looked around for the intercom extension cord and a headset. He couldn't find it. At the aft end of the compartment, he could clearly see Pender bent over the last litter – Tran. He made his way aft, checking on the marines as he moved down the compartment. All seemed quiet, but where were Santos and Flanders? He reached the first of the litters that were stacked three high down the center of the compartment. Again, all was quiet. He moved down the

The Trash Haulers

right side of the compartment, not able to fully see the wounded marines on the other side of the litters. But from what he could see, everything was normal. Pender looked up, her face etched with worry.

"Mark," she said, shaking her head and pointing towards him. He felt a sharp jab in his back.

"Don't move." It was Boyle.

"What the hell?" Warren said. He started to turn around only to have three short, very hard punches pound at his back, driving him to his knees.

"I said, don't fuckin' move, Cap'n, or are you just fuckin' stupid." It wasn't a question.

Warren turned his head slightly towards the voice. Boyle was standing over him holding a Smith & Wesson and wearing a headset. He had overheard everything they had said on the flight deck. The airman slowly cocked the revolver and aimed at Warren's forehead. "I was beginning to think you'd never show up."

"What's going on, Boyle?"

The airman's face twisted into a deadly rage. "It's fuckin' Sergeant Hale or fuckin' Sergeant Flanders, but it's Boyle, just fuckin' Boyle." Beads of sweat cascaded down his cheeks and neck. The top of his T-shirt and flight suit were drenched.

An inner voice warned Warren not to move. "Are you okay?"

"I'm fuckin' fine, which your good buddy over there ain't gonna be." He pointed the revolver at Tran. His words were slurred as he rocked back and forth.

"Man, you got a fever. At least let the doc check your temperature and give you some aspirin."

257

"That ain't gonna happen, Cap'n Asshole. You must think I'm fuckin' stupid or somethin'. That bitch ain't gonna slip me a mickey." He glared at Warren in triumph. "You got that, Cap'n Asshole?"

"Are you going to shoot me?"

Boyle looked at him, his eyes full of contempt. "I ain't that stupid. I need you to land the plane."

"I can do that. We land at . . ." he slowly looked at his watch, checking the time. "Touchdown in forty-five minutes at Clark."

"We ain't going to Clark." Again, that look of triumph. "We're going to Hainan."

Warren couldn't believe what he was hearing. Hainan was a large island in the South China Sea located 150 nautical miles north of Da Nang. It was also part of the People's Republic of China's southernmost territory, Guangdong Province. "We don't have enough gas to get there."

"You're fuckin' A lying, Cap'n Asshole."

"Check with Santos, he's the navigator."

Boyle rocked back and forth. "I'll do that."

"Where is he?" Warren asked. "Is he okay?" Boyle waved his revolver over the litters, towards the left side of the aircraft. Warren stood up to get a better view. Santos and Flanders were seated side-by-side in a jump seat, their wrists tied in front of them. A marine was standing over them, also holding a revolver.

"Why Hainan?" Warren asked. He needed time to work the problem.

"We're fuckin' A defecting, me and Denlow there." He jerked his head toward the marine standing over Flanders and

The Trash Haulers

Santos. "Remember him? He's the guy that stood up to you two assholes after you dunked me in shit. If I got a fever, it's because of you assholes."

Warren was now certain that Boyle was irrational from a high fever. Given incubation times, Boyle had probably picked up a virus days before, and not because of the latrine incident at Chu Lai. But that was beyond Boyle and Warren needed time to think. *Keep him talking*. He nodded in understanding. "Private Denlow is a good man. We know that."

Boyle was caught off guard. "It was his idea to go to Hainan. We can trade the C-130 and every fuckin' asshole on board for political asylum."

"If they don't shoot us down first," Warren said.

Boyle grinned wickedly. "You won't let that happen, right?"

Warren slumped his shoulders, a sign of surrender. But the pieces were coming together. He did a mental count, locating every weapon on board. He hoped Boyle and Denlow hadn't bothered. "Okay, but tell me one thing, why defect? Why do you need political asylum?"

Boyle sneered. "Because me and Denlow are gonna dump that fuckin' Commie bastard overboard."

Warren knew enough. "We got to depressurize the aircraft to do that. That means we have to descend first. We don't have enough fuel to climb back up."

"Jesus Christ, you must think we're dumb or somethin' stupid. We thought of that. You descend over water coming into land, and we lower the ramp. That's when we jettison the bastard."

Warren nodded. "What about all the wounded?"

259

"The Chinese will take care of 'em and trade 'em with the good old U-S-of-A." He snorted. "Fuckin' politicians."

"Okay, that all makes sense. I think I can make it happen."

"Damn right you can make it happen, Cap'n Asshole." He flipped the finger at Pender. "Or she goes out with the fuckin' Commie."

Warren shifted gears. "Can you check my back? I can feel blood. You may have opened my wound." He turned around facing Pender, and gave her a questioning look. She nodded, indicating she had heard everything. He felt Boyle's fingers probing his wound.

"Yeah, it's bleeding."

"Can the doc check it out?" He was careful to avoid using any rank.

A long silence answered him. Then, "Yeah. But don't try anything stupid." Boyle motioned for Pender to join them. She did. "Check out Cap'n Asshole here and make sure he's not bleeding. Don't do anything stupid."

Warren turned to face Boyle and felt her fingers on his back. "Ouch!" He half turned towards her and looked at her feet. "That hurts. You'll need a fire extinguisher to kill the pain."

"Now you know how it feels," Boyle said. He laughed.

"On Denlow," Warren whispered, still looking at Pender. She gave a little nod.

"He needs a fresh bandage," Pender said.

"Get one," Boyle ordered, now confident that he was in full command. She hurried to the rear of the Hercules. She was almost at the fire extinguisher just aft of the right parachute door when Warren abruptly sat down on the deck.

The Trash Haulers

"I think I'm gonna puke," Warren said, bending over and holding his head between his knees. He sensed Boyle leaning over him. He looked up and around Boyle's knees. Pender was moving around the back of Tran's litter and headed for Santos and Flanders. Her left hand was down and at her side, holding the fire extinguisher.

"Private Denlow," she called. "Please hand me the first aid kit on the wall above Sergeant Flanders head." She stopped six feet short.

Denlow turned to the sound of her voice. "Don't move, bitch."

She froze as the marine reached for the first aid kit. He ripped it off the fuselage and turned to toss it to her, only to meet a stream of fire retardant in his face. At the same moment, Flanders came out of his seat and threw his shoulder into Denlow, driving him against the litters in the center of the aircraft. Denlow shrieked a profanity and raised his revolver to pistol whip Flanders. A hand reached up from the litter and grabbed Denlow's arm, pulling him back. It was Tanner. Denlow kicked Flanders back as he twisted free. He smashed the revolver into the side of Tanner's face.

Pender rushed forward, swinging the fire extinguisher like a club. "Not my wounded!" She bashed Denlow on his right temple, dropping him like a rock.

Boyle was slow to react before he pushed Warren to the floor. He gave the pilot a vicious kick in the ribs. He turned towards Pender and raised his revolver but couldn't get a clear shot because of the litters between them. He moved forward as Warren rolled on the floor and drew the revolver

261

out of his boot. Boyle now had a clear shot at Pender and raised his Smith & Wesson.

"Boyle!" Warren shouted. "Behind you, fuck face!"

Boyle whirled around as Warren fired. The bullet tore into his right hip and spun him around. Warren fired a second time, striking him in the back of the same hip. Boyle fell to the floor, shrieking in pain, as his revolver skidded across the deck. Warren didn't hesitate and scrambled to his feet as a loud hissing sound echoed over the cargo compartment. Hale had heard the shots and hit the depressurization switch.

Warren ran for the flight deck, hoping he had enough time of useful consciousness to make it. He stumbled through the fire curtains and grabbed the ladder leading to the flight deck. But he couldn't go any further. "We're okay!" he shouted before passing out.

Warren jerked, coming awake. He was belly down, sprawled out on the cargo deck behind the crew entrance door. Flanders was bent over his back, bandaging his wound. "Sorry, Captain. I had to cut your flight suit away. You're good to go." Warren rolled over and Flanders helped him sit up.

"We okay?" Warren asked.

"All under control," Flanders told him.

"Captain Pender?"

"She's working on Boyle as we speak," Flanders said. "You really did a number on him. Blew his right hip to shit. The doc is saving his worthless ass." He let out a very contented guffaw. "She's sewing him up, no anesthetic. He's squealing like a stuck pig."

"Denlow?"

"Pretty bad shape. Might lose an eye."

"From the fire retardant?" Warren asked.

"Nope." Again, the deep chuckle. "Captain Pender bashed the shit out of him with the fire extinguisher and shattered his left eye socket. Popped his eyeball out. She shoved it back in and bandaged him up. He can't see a thing, and I hogged tied him up good." He helped Warren to his feet. "The Captain is one hell of a lady."

Flanders helped Warren up the ladder to the flight deck. He moved forward and sat in the pilot's seat. He pulled on his headset and turned to Bosko. The copilot brought him up to date. "Cubi Point TACAN is locked on and we're in contact with Manila ATC. ETA Clark two minutes past the hour."

"Fuel," Warren said.

Santos answered. "It's tight but okay."

"We definitely got a fuel leak," Hale said. "No reserve. We don't want to go around."

Warren understood. "That's cutting it pretty close."

"We got company," Santos said. Lynne Pender was climbing up the ladder. Without a word, Hale handed her a headset.

"How's it going back there?" Warren asked.

"Not good," she answered, her voice tired and strained. "Two marines are critical, Tanner is unconscious, and I haven't totally stopped Boyle's bleeding. And his fever is touching 106."

"So he's delirious," Bosko said.

"Definitely," she answered.

"A good defense for when they court-martial his sorry ass," Santos said.

"We need to land as soon as possible," she told them. "Make it as smooth as you can." It wasn't a request.

"Are they that bad?" Warren asked.

"I'm afraid so." Then she disappeared, returning to her patients.

Warren took a deep breath. "I really needed to hear that." He keyed the radio. "Manila, Roscoe Two-One has wounded on board that require immediate medical attention. Request priority handling. Also, have Security Police meet aircraft on landing."

Manila never hesitated. "Roscoe Two-One is cleared direct Clark. Descend at your discretion, I will clear all traffic." Bosko retarded the throttles and they headed down.

"Boz," Warren said over the intercom, "I'm bushed and hurtin'. You've got the landing, if you want."

"I thought you'd never ask," Bosko said.

"Makes sense to me," Santos said. "The good Captain Warren never made a soft landing in his life." The tension was broken.

Over the Philippines

Bosko maintained a high airspeed as they descended, and leveled off at 5000 feet as they coasted in over Subic Bay. The weather was VFR and the huge Navy base at Cubi Point was lit up like a Christmas tree, welcoming them to the Philippines. Bosko turned to a more easterly heading as they flew past the southern slope of Mount Pinatubo, an inactive volcano. As soon as the Clark TACAN clicked on, and he

The Trash Haulers

was certain they were clear of the high terrain, he turned northward and racked the throttles aft, starting the descent. "Dave, keep us out of the rocks," he said. It never hurt to have a backup.

"Clear of all terrain," Santos said. "Clark on the nose at thirteen."

Bosko glanced at the TACAN readout. Thirteen nautical miles to go. Ahead, he saw the runway approach lights cutting a path over darkened terrain and the lights of the air base further on, off to the left. Manila ATC cleared them to Clark Approach as he reread the approach plate. "Roscoe Two-One, you are cleared for a straight-in approach. Contact Clark tower." Warren dialed in the new frequency and made the call.

"Roscoe Two-One," Clark tower radioed, "you are cleared to land runway Zero-Two-Left. Wind light and variable, visibility twenty plus." Then, "Welcome to Clark, Roscoe."

"Sounds like the world is watching," Santos said.

Bosko laughed. "Boz, don't blow it now," he told himself. He called for the before landing checklist and started the flaps down.

"Gear down," Warren said. For a moment, the tension was back as the main gear cranked down. This time, it sounded normal.

"Three in the green," Bosko called.

"Gear scans clean," Flanders said from the back.

"Flaps one-hundred percent," Bosko said, slowing to landing speed. Over ten thousand feet of lighted runway stretched out in front of them. He eased the Hercules down.

And he greased it.

Clark Air Base, the Philippines

"Are we down yet?" Flanders asked from the rear.

"Reversing inboards," Bosko said. He touched the brakes, slowed, and lifted the throttles out of reverse, gently slowing them to taxi speed as they reached the turnoff to the main parking ramp. They turned off to the left. Ahead, the brightly-lit ramp was packed with waiting vehicles. A follow-me truck, its yellow light flashing, joined from their left, leading them into the chocks.

"Captain Warren," Bosko said. "Tell 'em we're here."

Warren didn't hesitate. He reached for the throttles and played a tune. Dah-da, dah-da-da-da-da-da. It was the Colonel Bogie March announcing Roscoe 21 had arrived.

0400 HOURS

Clark Air Base, the Philippines

The follow-me truck stopped and a heavyset man jumped out holding lighted wands. He motioned them forward and then crossed the wands over his head, the signal to halt. Another airman plugged in a power cord from an auxiliary power unit as the heavyset man came to attention and threw them a perfect salute. "I'll be damned," Bosko said. "Check out the stripes on his sleeve. First time I've ever been marshaled into parking by a chief master sergeant." The chief dropped his salute and climbed back into the truck as ambulances and vehicles converged on the rear of Hercules.

"Shut 'em down," Bosko said. They could feel the rush of footsteps on the cargo deck as they shut down the engines. Santos closed out his flight log at 0402 hours, 1 February 1968. "Sergeant Hale, say fuel remaining."

"Six hundred pounds," Hale answered. They had ninety-two gallons of fuel in the tanks. "Yep, we got a fuel leak somewhere."

Warren pulled himself out of his seat as the props spun down. "Let's go see how they're doing." The three men followed him down to the cargo compartment. Except for Flanders standing at the base of the loading ramp, the cargo compartment was deserted. Behind Flanders, the last of the taillights and flashing beacons were pulling away, disappearing into the night. The stadium lights rimming the parking ramp started to click off, surrounding them in semi-darkness. They were alone. "Well, I guess we had our two minutes of fame," Warren said. Flanders joined them in the brightly lit cargo compartment and handed Warren a clean flight suit. "Thank you, but where . . . ."

"It's the one you were wearing at Chu Lai," Flanders replied. "It was easy to mend, so I washed it out while we were waiting on the ground at Phu Bai. I threw it on the radio rack to dry." He half gestured at Warren's shoulder. "Sorry about cutting that one up."

"No problem," Warren said. "Let's call for crew transport and head for billeting." He looked around the cargo deck. The floor was littered with bloodied bandages, parts of uniforms that had been cut away, scattered boots, and discarded equipment belts and suspenders. He was standing on paper mats soaked in blood and urine. Fortunately, the stench was yielding to a gentle night breeze. "I'll tell transient maintenance to clean it up."

Hale's chin came up. "No, sir. She's our bird and deserves better than that. It won't take long to do it right."

"What's another thirty minutes?" Flanders added. "Call the crash crew for a pumper and we'll hose her out."

"Sounds like a plan," Bosko said. He went forward to make the radio call.

The Trash Haulers

"That was some off load," Santos said.

"I never saw anything like it," Flanders said. "I think every doctor, nurse, corpsman, and ambulance within fifty miles was here. Even the wing king, a brigadier general no less, was here rootin' and urging them on. Five minutes max."

"What happened to Captain Pender?" Warren asked.

"The last I saw," Flanders replied, "she was surrounded by six doctors, a dozen nurses, and four Security Cops." He laughed. "For a moment, I thought she was going to spit at Boyle and Denlow when the cops read them their rights."

"What about Tanner and Tran?"

Flanders shrugged. "They were alive when they carried them off."

Bosko was back. "A pumper is on the way. They want us to taxi over to the hazardous cargo area next to the drain culverts." Without a word, they filed back to their duty stations to start engines. Within minutes they were taxing on the inboards. A pumper truck was waiting for them at the far end of the parking ramp. They shut the engines down and set the parking brakes.

Flanders had raised the rear door and lowered the loading ramp to the level position. Every hatch was open and he was pulling a two-inch diameter black fire hose through the crew entrance. Warren stepped over the hose and down the steps. Bosko, Santos and Hale followed him out and around to the rear of the aircraft. A flood of water was cascading off the end of the loading ramp, a bloody waterfall carrying the wastage of war. Slowly, the water turned clean. Flanders walked to the end of the ramp and hosed the concrete down, washing the debris into the storm drains.

269

"Hey," Flanders called, "I got two brooms and could use a little help."

Warren extended his left hand and Flanders pulled him onto the ramp. Bosko, Santos, and Hale were right behind him. "Sorry, Captain," Bosko said. "Not with your shoulder." He gently pushed Warren into a jump seat. Santos and Hale swept the remaining water out the back while Flanders directed a stream at the hardest spots that would not yield.

"I think we got it," Flanders said, satisfied with the results. Within moments, the pumper was gone and the brooms stored. Warren changed into the clean flight suit and joined his crew who were sitting on the aft edge of the loading ramp, their feet dangling over the concrete. The cool breeze drifted over them and the Hercules smelled fresh and clean.

"I'll call for crew transport," Bosko said, heading for the flight deck.

"I suppose the CABOOM bar is closed," Santos said. The Clark Air Base Officers Open Mess was infamous for carousing and drinking.

"I don't know about you," Flanders said, "but I've got to hit the sack. It has been one hell of day."

"Indeed," Santos said. "Hard to top it."

"Probably can't," Flanders allowed. "Time to retire." Years later, he would joke to his friends that he peaked on January 31, 1968. They would rag him about "being a has been," and he would mutter "better than being a never was."

Bosko was back. "Crew transport is on the way."

"What about you, Captain Santos?" Flanders asked. "Got any plans?"

The Trash Haulers

Santos though for a moment. "I think I'll stick around for awhile. Maybe go to Squadron Officers School. Sergeant Hale, you got anything planned?"

"Ah, I'm a lifer," the flight engineer replied. "I'll probably go back to school after I retire." The school was a seminary. "What the heck, I'll only be thirty-eight."

Bosko joined in. "The airlines are hiring and looking good. My DOS is thirty-one August." DOS was date of separation. He thought for a moment. "I always wanted to fly flare missions. I wonder if Blind Bat Zero-One needs a copilot."

"You could do worse than Hardy," Warren said. "You got time. Ask and find out."

"I think I'll give it a go," Bosko said. "What about you, Captain?"

"I'm thinking about getting out," Warren said. "There's a new type of electronic calculator called a microcomputer, and a friend wants to start a business."

"I never heard of a microcomputer," Santos said. "Here's crew transport."

The panel van rattled to a stop and Lynne Pender jumped off. She ambled across the short space separating them, a six-pack of frosty San Miguel beer in each hand. She handed one six-pack to Flanders and one to Warren. "They made it," was all she said. She turned and pulled herself onto the edge of the ramp, sitting beside Warren, their shoulders barely touching. Without a word, Warren used his survival knife to uncap the beers and passed them out. Bosko raised his bottle in a silent toast and they all sipped, slowly at first and then with gusto.

271

"I spoke to Tran," she said. "He thanked me for saving his life."

"Did you?" Warren asked.

"Probably. But he is very strong willed and that makes a big difference. He was in worse shape than the two marines who went critical. He said to tell you that he will make it right. I'm not sure what he meant."

Warren worked through the fatigue that was demanding its due. "What did he actually say?"

"He speaks English with a heavy French accent, but I'm fairly sure his exact words were 'Tell the Captain I will make it right.'"

"That could be a threat."

"I don't think so."

"And Tanner?" Warren asked, wondering about the helicopter pilot.

"I had to amputate his foot when they brought him in at Se Pang. When I told him, all he said was 'Go for it, Doc.'" She laughed, low and full of warmth. "I think we made a date."

"That's one way to encourage a guy," Warren said.

"That was the idea." She stuck out her lower lip. "I hope he doesn't remember."

Warren laughed. "I know I would. What about Boyle?"

"He'll live."

Warren touched her hand. He searched for the words to tell her that she was incredibly brave, but nothing seemed appropriate. He finally managed a "You are something else."

She gave him a look he would remember forever. "You're no slouch yourself."

The Trash Haulers

The pilot gave a little shrug. "Just doing what I get paid for."

"And what do you just get paid for?"

Warren managed the sardonic grin required of all trash haulers. He gestured at Flanders, the loadmaster. "To get him to where he can do his job."

Steven Bosko couldn't help overhearing. "Wrong, Captain. We're a team that hauls cargo. That's *our* job. And, by the way, you are damn good at it." They fell silent as the cool breeze washed over them and the faint chirping of an insect played a soft background refrain in the early morning dark.

"This is one good beer," Flanders murmured. Years later, they would all claim it was the best beer they ever had, and Mark Warren would place a bottle of San Miguel in the loadmaster's coffin as Lynne Pender Warren held his hand, her eyes full of tears. The Reverend Michael Hale would deliver the eulogy and Major General David Santos, on bended knee, would present a folded flag to Glen Flanders's family.

Santos cracked open a second beer and took a long drink, his body aching with fatigue. "Sum'bitch, that was one long haul today."

"It's what we do," Hale said.

"We're trash haulers," Bosko added.

"Oh, yeah," Warren said.

THE END

L'ENVOI

Approach Vietnam from the east with the sun low and at your back as it breaks the horizon. Fly high enough above the South China Sea so the ships remain in miniature, but never forget that much of the world's shipping plies these waters. As the sun rises, the sea gives up its dark grays and turns a vibrant blue, reflecting the sky above. At first, the coastline appears as a blur on the western horizon, without definition, but that is the mirage. The reality is always striking as the sea shallows and turns an emerald green, the harbinger of what lies ahead. The coastline takes definition as the craggy shoreline and white sandy beaches come into sight.

Fly low enough to see the fishing boats that litter the coastal waters like dainty insects. The fishermen still wear the *nón lá*, the conical leaf hat, and work the same net traps as their ancestors did so many years ago, and, like their ancestors, they still keep faith with their culture and traditions that have endured years of pain and sacrifice. Occasionally, an ancient fisherman will look up at the faint sound of jet engines, searching the sky for the contrails that still scar his memories.

Immediately behind the shore, a jungle-green carpet adds to the majesty of the ancient land locked in the annual rhythms of the monsoon, neither welcoming nor warning an intruder. Far to the south, the land is low and flat where the Mekong opens to the sea, but stretching over four-hundred miles to the north are the highlands of Vietnam, marked by the limestone mountain ridges called karsts, river valleys, and the ever-present jungle that reluctantly yields to open areas filled with cutting razor grass.

The same narrow roads still twist through the land following the coast, rivers and valleys, linking villages, towns, and cities. Names roar out of the past – Saigon, Cam Ranh Bay, Da Nang, Chu Lai, Phu Bai – each with its burden of painful memories. Forty miles north of the ancient capital of Hue, Highway Nine works its way inland from the coast, past the city of Dong Ha and into the highlands, reaching for the border with Laos. It follows a river and the east-west valleys, finally reaching the sleepy town of Khe Sanh with its memorials to a fruitless, bitter battle fought almost fifty years ago.

But it is on the ground where the full impact of Vietnam strikes the unwary. From Khe Sanh, drive northward on the road now called the Ho Chi Minh Highway, out of the river valley and into the mountains. The road is narrow and twisted but now paved and not the rutted track of fifty years ago. The jungle is overwhelming, cut by jagged karsts, defying time and man as the road snakes upward, repeatedly cresting a ridge before falling into the next valley. Vista piles on vista and the indescribable beauty of the mountains beguiles the casual tourist, for it is a harsh terrain, cruel and unforgiving, and its inhabitants strain to carve an existence from the earth, somehow surviving.

Not far from the killing grounds of Khe Sanh, twenty miles as the crow flies but double that by road, and only a few miles south of the seventeenth parallel and the old Demilitarized Zone that separated North and South Vietnam, the highway crests a ridge and plunges into a valley where a bridge crosses the Se Pang river. The village has been rebuilt, and the old Special Forces compound is now only a level field. The outline of the red-dirt runway is still etched in the earth on the north side of the river, and at the eastern end, closest to the village, a small shrine hides in the shade. In a generation, it will be gone, swallowed by the vegetation, climate, and time, and the land will again claim its sovereignty, humbling the proud with a mute lesson – this was no place to fight a war.

AUTHOR'S NOTE

While this is a work of fiction, much of it is based on fact and personal experience. The passage of time has dulled many memories and changed perceptions about the war in Vietnam, all of which shaped this story. Writing *The Trash Haulers* has been a long haul extending over two decades, and without the encouragement and help of Sheila Kathleen Herman, my wife, and Eric Herman, my son, along with the wisdom and guidance of William P. Wood, my former publisher, I would have never typed 'The End'. I cannot thank them enough. Also, a heartfelt thanks to Judy Person who labors to find and correct my many attacks on the written word.

The magnificent Lockheed Martin C-130 has been in production longer than any other aircraft in aviation history and is still the workhorse of tactical airlift, the movement of personnel and material in the forward area of combat. C-130 operations as depicted in *The Trash Haulers* are based on my memory and experiences, along with many war stories and recollections from old friends and associates. I deliberately simplified the complexities of flying the Hercules and used generic numbers, especially for fuel consumption and airspeeds, for the sake of telling a story. Throughout the story, I emphasized the use of checklists. While a poor storytelling technique, checklist discipline is critical to safe operations, especially at the end of a long crew duty day. For my mistakes, and for those purists who I have offended, I apologize.

Without doubt, the overwhelming image of the war is of the Bell UH-1 "Huey" helicopter, which was instrumental in changing the way the United States goes to war. I have only flown in the Huey three times and owe Ken Fritz and Joel Dozhier a special thanks for introducing me to the Huey and the reality of helicopter operations. Also, I must thank the many members of the Vietnam Helicopter Pilots Association who shared many of their experiences and vignettes of Vietnam.

As always, any mistakes or omissions are mine alone.

Printed in Great Britain
by Amazon